Crystal Creek

KELLY COLLINS

BOOK NOOK PRESS

Chapter One

"OH, HELL NO!" The words burst out before I can stop them as I hold the bride's bouquet at arm's length like it might explode. My heart is still hammering from the most mortifying five minutes of my entire professionally-embarrassing life.

Seriously, who shows up in a floatplane—piloted by a man who clearly moonlights as a stand-up comedian—only to crash-land into someone else's wedding? *Me. That's who.*

Teetering off that deathtrap wearing heels completely unsuitable for anything but a red carpet, I vaguely register a crowd I naively assume might, just might, be a tiny welcome committee for yours truly—TV's Hottest Rising Star, according to *People* magazine about five years ago. Then, boom. Wedding. Not for me. Obviously.

And then the questions. "Are you my driver?" I ask the handsome, scowling one who looks like he wrestles bears for fun—the groom, as it turns out. Wrong guy. Then the other handsome, scowling one—Finn, my agent calls him, the one I am supposed to meet— immediately points out I am "two days late."

"I had a medical procedure," I say, only for Finn to dead-pan, "You mean Botox and a facial?" How does he know? My agent, of course. The same agent who had to beg for this last-chance gig in the Alaskan wilderness to "rehabilitate my image" after the champagne flute incident. So much for a dignified, mysterious arrival.

And then, the ultimate indignity, strutting down that rickety dock like it's a runway, only for my heel—my Louboutin heel—to get swallowed by a rogue board. Finn wrenches my foot out, then tugs the shoe free, snapping the heel clean off in the process. "You won't be needing those here," he says, before kicking the evidence into the water like it's common trash. The horror.

Before I can collect what's left of my pride, someone ushers me off the dock and into a chair at the back of the ceremony like I'm the class delinquent being seated in detention. Then, the bride—a woodland goddess type, naturally—has to go and toss her wildflowers straight at me.

My face burns. I can feel it—a sudden, prickling awareness as the festive sound of the crowd dies down. *Oh, no. They're all looking.* The blissful newlyweds are momentarily forgotten. Every single pair of eyes swivels to fixate on me. I can only imagine what they see, the disastrous state I'm in, instantly branding me the ridiculous, out-of-place outsider. My stomach twists. Confused and deeply embarrassed, I scan desperately for an escape route, but the sea of curious faces offers none.

"You can put that down, you know," rumbles a deep voice beside me. It belongs to the tall, irritated man from the dock —Finn, the lodge owner I'll be staying with. "It's not actually a grenade."

"Could have fooled me," I mutter, still holding the arrangement of wildflowers as far from my body as possible.

"Where am I supposed to put it? I am not prepared for wedding attendance today."

Finn lets out a sigh, a long, drawn-out sound that seems to carry the weight of every inconvenient tourist he's ever dealt with. The slight, almost imperceptible tightening around his eyes doesn't bode well either.

"Bring it with you to the community center," he begins, and the tone he uses—so deliberately level, so painstakingly patient—is a dead giveaway. Oh, I am definitely testing the limits of his legendary Alaskan fortitude, or whatever they call it up here. "They've got tables set up for the reception. Then find somewhere to sit. The celebration's starting, and I have best man duties to attend to."

"Wait, you can't leave me here," I say, still clutching the bouquet like it might bite. "I don't know anyone, I'm down to one functional shoe, and I'm pretty sure half these people think I crashed the wedding on purpose."

"You made an entrance," Finn points out, his expression a mix of disbelief and annoyance. "Two days late."

"That wasn't my fault," I begin, but the skeptical tilt of his head stops me cold. That look—as if maintaining my appearance is some frivolous crime, not the cornerstone of my entire career. *Please.* I've invested more in this face, these cheekbones, than he's probably seen in a lifetime. I didn't fly across the continent for an image-rehab gig to be silently condemned by a man in flannel.

"Reception's in the community center," he tosses over his shoulder, already turning away. "Food's good. Try not to cause another scene."

I take a tentative step away from the dock, following the crowd as they head up a small incline—presumably toward this community center Finn mentioned—but my damaged Louboutin creates a lopsided gait. With each uneven step, I sink into the soft ground, nearly toppling me face-first into a puddle. I'm forced to tiptoe on the foot with the missing heel, each step a wobbly disaster that only increases my humiliation.

As I limp along, I pass a group of middle-aged women clustered near an old picnic table. They lower their voices as I approach, but not enough. "That's what twelve thousand dollars of plastic surgery gets you?" one woman says under her breath with a snort. "My sister in Juneau could've done better for the price of a fishing license."

"Shh! She'll hear you," another whispers, not nearly quietly enough.

"Look at her trying to walk. She's like a foal on stilts," says a third, followed by muffled laughter.

I freeze, heat rushing to my face despite the chill in the air. For a terrifying second, I'm twelve again—the poor Appalachian girl in hand-me-downs, mocked by classmates. The memory, one I spent years and thousands of dollars burying under couture labels and the poise I'd painstakingly built, knocks the air from my lungs. Shoulders back. Chin up. I summon the ice-queen persona that's served me well on Hollywood sets. But inside, my stomach twists with the familiar shame. The fear that no matter how perfect I look, how flawless the smokescreen, people can still somehow see the girl who once bathed in a creek because the water had been shut off again.

"Steady there, Hollywood." A strong hand catches my elbow, steadying me.

I glance up to find an older woman smiling at me. Her face is lined with decades of Alaskan living, but her eyes are kind. "Those fancy shoes aren't built for Alaskan terrain."

"So I'm discovering," I say, trying to recover both my balance and my dignity. "Thank you, Ms...?"

"Call me May," she says, her grip steady as she steers me toward solid ground. "Like the month. I own the diner in town."

"Lena," I offer, though her expression makes it clear she already knows.

"I know who you are," May confirms with a wink. "Every teenage boy in Port Promise has your poster on their wall. That vampire show made quite an impression."

"Oh," I say, feeling my cheeks heat. "That was a long time ago. Let's say the fanbase wasn't exactly there for my nuanced performance."

May snorts. "They're teenage boys. Their taste runs to pretty faces and revealing outfits. But they'll lose their minds when they hear you're in town." She looks down at my footwear disaster. "Though I might leave out the part where you're stumbling around like a newborn moose."

Despite myself, I laugh. There's something refreshingly direct about May that cuts through the exhaustion and humiliation. "Come on," she says, motioning toward the path. "Let's get you to the reception before you break an ankle. I'll ask Finn to check if Timber has some spare shoes in the community center. She keeps a pair there for rainy days when she's teaching."

"Teaching?" I ask, carefully navigating the uneven ground, still hyper-aware of the attention following me.

"The community center doubles as our school," May explains. "Timber teaches the kids. Not that we have many—only about seven total from kindergarten through high school. That's Port Promise for you."

Inside the community center, long tables are laden with food that smells surprisingly appetizing, and an older man with a beat-up guitar is tuning it up in the corner. I finally spot a gift table and gratefully deposit the bouquet among the wrapped presents. A weight lifts from my shoulders. As I turn away, I catch my reflection in a window. My Hollywood armor is cracked—mascara smudged beneath one eye, hair disheveled by the Alaskan wind, leather dress comically formal among flannel and denim. For a second, I see beyond the expensive styling to the terrified woman beneath, the one who aches to belong but knows, deep down, she never truly will.

May guides me to a table in the corner, mercifully away from the bulk of the crowd, and disappears momentarily. When she returns, it's with a plate piled high with unfamiliar foods and a glass of amber liquid. "Eat," she commands. "It's a long time until breakfast, and from what I hear, Finn's cooking is questionable at best." Her gaze drops to my feet— one shoe intact, the other nothing but straps attached to the base where the heel used to be. "I asked him to check with Timber about those spare shoes I mentioned. He should be back soon."

I eye the plate May's brought me uncertainly. "That's wild-caught salmon with dill," May explains, noting my hesitation. "Wild rice pilaf with local cranberries, and that's venison sausage from a deer Finn got last season. All Alaskan fare. Go on, try it." I've never been a fish person—the smell, the texture, all of it has always turned my stomach. But I'm hungry enough to at least try a bite. I brace myself, but the salmon is delicate and smoky, a world away from the heavy fish dishes I've endured at Hollywood charity dinners where chefs try too hard to impress. I take another bite, then another, suddenly ravenous.

"I see you found your appetite," comes Finn's voice as he appears beside our table, holding a pair of rubber boots. "May suggested you might need something more suitable. These are my sister-in-law, Timber's—the bride."

I stare at the boots with undisguised disgust. They're practical, sturdy, and possibly the ugliest things I've ever been asked to put on my feet. "I can't wear those."

Finn gives me a dubious expression. "Would you rather keep stumbling around until the reception ends? We'll be heading to the lodge on the Polaris afterward, and trust me, you don't want to climb onto a four-wheeler with one usable shoe."

The memory of him having to pull my foot from the dock earlier makes my face flush. With a deep sigh of surrender, I take the boots. "Fine. But if anyone takes a picture of me in these, I will sue for defamation of character."

Finn's mouth twitches in what might be the beginning of a reluctant smile. "Your secret's safe with us. Now eat up. Reception goes for at least another three hours, and I'd like to enjoy my brother's wedding without babysitting duties. We'll head to the lodge when things wrap up here."

"I'm not asking you to babysit me," I snap, my patience finally fraying. "I can entertain myself."

Three more hours? My feet are already killing me, I'm exhausted from traveling, and now I'm expected to hang around a stranger's wedding until midnight. A headache is brewing behind my eyes, but what choice do I have? I'm literally stranded here.

"Don't mind Finn," May says as he walks away. "He's got a chip on his shoulder when it comes to outsiders, especially the celebrity kind."

"What's his problem?" I ask, taking a cautious sip of the homebrew, which burns pleasantly down my throat.

"About eight years ago, some reality TV fishing crew came up here, made a mess of things, nearly got themselves killed, and then tried to sue Finn when he rescued them," May explains. "They didn't have a legal leg to stand on, but it left him with a healthy distrust of cameras and the people who follow them."

"I'm not here to cause trouble," I say defensively. "This is a job for me. A few weeks at a scenic lodge, some staged videos for social media and a wilderness special, then back to real life."

May regards me over her glass. "Honey, everyone who

comes to Alaska says they're passing through. This place often changes plans and people."

As the evening progresses, I gradually relax, the homebrew helping to loosen the knot of tension between my shoulders. I even laugh at the locals' stories, especially when they involve Finn's apparent tendency to rescue tourists from their poor decisions. "Remember when he had to save that family who tried to kayak to the glacier without life jackets during a storm warning?" someone recalls, setting off a round of laughter. "Or the hikers who decided bear spray was optional?" adds another.

At the mention of bears, a chill prickles my skin. "Are there really bears around here?"

The table falls silent, and then everyone bursts into renewed laughter.

"Oh. honey," May says, patting my hand. "Bears are practically our neighbors. Then there are the wolves who think they're the local welcoming committee, deer that'll empty your garden faster than tourists clear out the general store before a storm, and if you're exceptionally lucky—or unlucky, depending on how you view it—you might catch sight of a lynx. They're like oversized barn cats with murder mittens."

Eventually, the crowd thins as the night wears on. Finn makes his way back to my table, where May has been keeping me company with stories about Port Promise that alternate between fascinating and terrifying. "The reception's winding down," Finn says. "We should get you to the lodge. It's been a long day."

May rises from her seat and gives me a warm expression. "It was lovely meeting you, Lena. Come by the diner tomorrow for breakfast. My sourdough pancakes will change your life."

"I'd like that," I say, surprised to find I actually mean it.

"Thank you for everything tonight. You made this accidental wedding crash much less mortifying than it could have been."

May laughs and pats my arm. "That's what we do here in Port Promise. Care for each other—even the fancy Hollywood types who catch our bouquets." She turns to Finn, her expression shifting to stern. "You take good care of her, you hear? Don't go showing her your Alaskan hospitality by driving through every mud puddle on the way."

Finn raises an eyebrow. "Would I do that?"

"In a heartbeat," May says, but there's affection in her voice. She gives me a quick hug. "Remember, diner tomorrow. Don't let this grump make you think all Alaskans are as charming as he is."

"I'll be there," I promise.

With last goodbyes exchanged, I follow Finn out of the community center, carefully navigating in my borrowed boots. The night air grows chillier, and I wrap my arms around myself, wishing I'd brought a jacket more appropriate than my flimsy designer wrap. Finn catches my shiver. Without a word, he shrugs out of his flannel overshirt and hands it to me, leaving himself in a simple black t-shirt that does nothing to hide the impressive muscles of his arms and chest.

"I'm fine," I protest weakly.

"You're shivering," he counters. "Take it. I'm used to the cold."

Too tired to argue, I slip the shirt on over my dress. It's warm from his body and smells like pine and something uniquely masculine that I refuse to acknowledge as pleasant.

"Your luggage is already loaded in the trailer," Finn says, leading me to where a rugged four-wheeler is parked at the edge of the property. "It's about a thirty-minute ride."

As he helps me climb onto the back seat of the Polaris, I gather my courage to ask, "So, what exactly should I expect at your place? My agent was vague on the details."

Finn gives me a sideways assessment, his expression unreadable in the darkness. "From what I understand, you'll be staying at my lodge while they take some publicity photos and videos of you pretending to enjoy nature. The production company booked it for the rest of the summer."

I nod, relieved. This is exactly what I signed up for—a comfortable stay at a scenic retreat with occasional forays outside. Nothing too strenuous or authentic. Just enough to convince my fans I've gone "back to nature" and rehabilitate my image.

"Sounds perfect," I say, settling onto the seat. "The place has all the amenities, right? Wi-Fi, hot water, decent cell reception?"

Something that might be humor flickers across Finn's face as he swings his leg over the front seat. "We have hot water. Most days." Before I can demand clarification on that unsettling answer, he starts the engine.

The ride up is an adventure in itself. My luggage follows behind us in a small trailer, bouncing precariously with every rut and bump in the rugged trail. I cling to the seat, grateful for the borrowed boots as we splash through puddles and navigate around fallen branches. The engine's roar makes conversation impossible, leaving me to my thoughts as the Alaskan wilderness rushes past, dark and shadowed in the moonlight.

As we round a last bend in the trail, a sprawling log structure nestled among towering pines comes into view, warm light spilling from its windows. Finn cuts the engine of the Polaris, and the abrupt silence is almost startling after the constant roar. "Welcome to Crystal Creek Retreat," he says, a clear note of pride in his voice. "Home for the duration of your stay."

The building is impressive, a perfect blend of rugged charm and modern comfort. "It's beautiful," I say honestly, momentarily forgetting my exhaustion.

Finn appears surprised by my sincerity, but nods in acknowledgment. "Built it myself, with all my brothers' help. Took nearly two years. Named it after the creek that runs behind the retreat."

As we dismount from the Polaris, I spot several smaller structures scattered around the main building, barely visible in the moonlight. "What are those used for?" I ask, gesturing toward the shadows.

"Seven of them, used for guests," Finn says, unloading my luggage from the trailer. "The retreat has common areas— dining room, great room, kitchen. Guests stay in the cabins for privacy."

"I'll be in one of those?" I ask, trying to mask my disappointment. I'd been picturing myself in a cozy room inside the main building, not isolated in a separate cabin.

"Cabin Three is yours," Finn confirms, hefting two of my suitcases. "We call it Stargazer's Retreat. It's got a great view of the night sky from the bedroom skylights."

"How far is it from the main lodge?" I ask, already picturing the long, dark walks between buildings.

"About fifty yards," he says. "Cabin One is closer, but it's being renovated right now."

Fifty yards seems like a mile as I peer nervously at the dark woods surrounding us. "I've already heard about the local wildlife from May. Is there any chance of those bears or wolves deciding my cabin seems like a good place to visit tonight?"

Finn actually laughs at this. "Just use common sense. Don't leave food outside. Make noise if you're walking around after dark. You're in their home, not the other way around."

That's not exactly the reassurance I hoped for.

"Don't worry," he adds, perhaps seeing the real fear on my face. "The path to your cabin is well-lit, and I've never had a guest eaten by wildlife yet."

"Yet," I mutter under my breath as Finn unlocks the cabin door. "Very comforting."

Finn flips on the lights, revealing a cozy but decidedly basic interior. A river rock fireplace dominates one wall of the main room, with a worn leather couch and armchair arranged in front of it. The kitchen area is little more than a corner with a small refrigerator, a two-burner stove, and minimal counter space. A round wooden table with four mismatched chairs sits between the living and kitchen areas. The walls are decorated with what appear to be local landscape photographs and, alarmingly, the mounted head of some antlered creature I don't want to identify.

This is a far cry from the luxury accommodations my agent promised. Where's the high-speed internet workstation? The jetted tub? The king-sized bed with premium linens?

Finn drops my suitcases unceremoniously inside the bedroom door, then gives me a perfunctory tour. "Bathroom's through there," he says, gesturing to another door. "Hot water's limited, so keep your showers short. The kitchen's stocked with basics."

I look around, searching for any sign of modern amenities. "Is there Wi-Fi?"

"Sometimes," Finn says with a shrug. "Signal's spotty out here. Cell reception too."

Great. I'm stranded in the wilderness with unreliable communication to the outside world. My agent is going to hear about this, assuming I can get enough bars to make a call.

"I'll leave you to get settled," Finn says, already heading for the door. "I'm over in the lodge if you need anything." He pauses, hand on the doorknob. "Breakfast is served between six and eight, up at the big hall."

I blink. "In the morning?"

A hint of amusement touches his mouth. "That's when breakfast usually is."

I swallow my horror—mostly—and simply nod, pretending the concept of willingly being vertical before eight in the morning isn't fundamentally offensive.

Before I can protest or ask any of the dozen questions forming in my mind, he's gone, the door closing with a decisive click that echoes in the now-silent cabin.

I stand in the middle of the room, feeling abandoned.

A quick inspection of the bedroom reveals a full-sized bed —not the king I'm used to, but at least it appears comfortable. The bathroom is functional but spartan, with a shower stall that's going to make shaving my legs a contortionist's challenge.

After unpacking enough for the night, I realize I'm hungry. Again. Apparently, stress burns through snacks at an alarming rate, because despite all the food at the reception, my stomach is staging a full-blown protest.

As I settle onto the couch with a cup of tea and some crackers with peanut butter, I'm struck by the absurdity of my situation. Twenty-four hours ago, I was in a luxury spa, panic-packing after indulging in treatments I was convinced I needed before facing Alaska. Now I'm sitting in a remote cabin, wearing borrowed boots after crashing a wedding, surviving on crackers, and worrying about becoming bear food. Somewhere in the distance, a wolf howls—a long, mournful sound —and I nearly drop my tea.

I came to Alaska to save my career, but judging by how things are going, I might have to survive it first.

Chapter Two

FINN

I CHECK the breakfast casserole that has been baking for the last thirty minutes, the aroma of eggs and cheese filling the kitchen. I'm not known for my culinary skills, but I'm getting better. At least the food's edible these days, a definite improvement from when I first opened.

Dawn breaks outside, with the first light hitting the mountains and pushing back the darkness. This is my favorite time at Crystal Creek—before guests get up, before the weight of the day's responsibilities settles on my shoulders, when I can pretend I'm the only one here. I move through the kitchen with efficiency, slicing fresh sourdough bread for toast, arranging berries in a blue ceramic bowl my mother gave me years ago. The coffee bubbles and hisses in the ancient percolator that I refuse to replace despite my youngest brother Nash's insistence that I "join the current century." This old percolator still makes decent coffee. No need for fancy junk.

Unlike the overnight Hollywood celebrities who show up in my Alaskan paradise wearing leather dresses and designer heels. The memory of Lena Kensington teetering on the dock yesterday, one shoe stuck in the planks, has irritation and amusement wrestling in my gut. I've encountered her type before—city people who arrive in Alaska expecting postcard adventures, then complain when reality fails to match their Instagram-worthy expectations. But I need her money. Or more specifically, the production company's money. My attention shifts to the stack of invoices, pinned beneath a smooth river stone on the desk in the corner.

Atop the pile sits yesterday's mail—a crisp white envelope stamped with the Alaskan First Bank logo. I already know what it says. I read it last night, tearing it open even though the outcome was inevitable. The words, sharp and final, still echo in my head: Payment of $42,500 required within 60 days to avoid legal action.

Sixty days. The number hangs there in my head, sharp and unwelcome. Two years ago, an avalanche nearly demolished Cabin One and severely damaged the main lodge while I was visiting a friend on the mainland. I returned to devastation—broken windows, collapsed roof sections, and the worst of it: a massive pine tree had fallen through the great room, destroying furniture and leaving the place exposed to the elements. Insurance covered some of the damage, but the business loan I took out to fully rebuild and upgrade the property seemed manageable at the time. I made payments faithfully every month, sometimes cutting it close, but never missing a deadline. Then this past winter, an unexpected series of storms knocked out our power for weeks, burst pipes, and added new damage. The emergency repairs devoured my reserve funds, forcing me to miss several payments on the original loan. Now the debt's a relentless pressure, grinding me down month after month. This Hollywood production is supposed to be my salvation. They've blocked out the lodge for the entire summer, and the pay-out from that extended booking is the only thing that'll clear my debts. For now, knowing that money is coming is the only thing standing between me and potential ruin.

I pull the casserole from the oven and set it on the counter. It smells good. At least I got that right. For all the complications of hosting this film crew, at least I can ensure they're well-fed. My mother taught me that before she passed—food is how Alaskans show hospitality, even to guests who might not deserve it.

The thought of my family, all rooted in Port Promise, brings a bittersweet smile to my lips. Dad's only been back in town for about a year, after leaving town following Mom's passing. Now he pitches in wherever he's needed. Each of us Hollister siblings has found our place in this town. Nash runs his hunting guide service from Misty Meadows, stubbornly protective of the wilderness he knows so well. The twins, Rhys and Reid, handle different aspects of our waterfront businesses—Rhys managing the dock and store at Birch Bay while Reid charms tourists with deep-sea fishing adventures from Lantern Bay. Then there's Kane, running his fishing boat with a newfound cheerfulness since marrying Timber. Their wedding yesterday seems surreal—my perpetually scowling brother transformed by love. My sister Eliza lights up Serenity Cove, focused on motherhood since her baby arrived. I guess that leaves me as the resident Hollister grump here at Crystal Creek, trying to make this lodge work when hospitality never came as naturally to me as it did to the others.

None of them know how bad things have gotten with the lodge. I've kept the financial troubles to myself, determined to fix the problem without burdening them. They all have their responsibilities, their own struggles. *And their successes*, a voice in my head reminds me. The voice that sometimes wonders if I'm the only Hollister who can't make a go of things on my own. If I lose Crystal Creek, I'll be losing more than a business. This place holds too many memories. My mother helped design the great room, handpicking the river rock for the fireplace and choosing the wood for the beams. The blue ceramic bowls are from her collection, and the river stone paperweight she gathered from the creek still adorns my desk—a small, polished piece of home that keeps me grounded even on the hardest days. She's everywhere in this place. In the creak of the floorboards. The smell of lemon and cedar. The way the wind hits the window just right. Losing the lodge would be like losing her all over again.

I finish setting the table. The quiet wraps around me—not heavy, but familiar. Eight place settings. One for me. One for Lena Kensington. Six for the crew that rolled in two days ago with more gear than sense. The lodge can accommodate up to twenty guests when fully booked, but these days, I'm lucky to fill half the cabins during peak season.

I hear voices heading this way. So much for the quiet. The door opens, revealing the production team—all appearing too alert for six-thirty in the morning. The producer, a slim man with wire-rimmed glasses named Elliott, leads the group. "Good morning!" he calls out with forced cheerfulness. "Something smells incredible."

"Breakfast casserole," I say, gesturing to the table. "Help yourselves. Coffee's hot."

The crew descends on the food with the focused intensity of people who know they have a long day ahead. They load plates with thick squares of breakfast casserole—eggs, potatoes, and gooey cheese baked together—alongside sourdough toast, chattering about shot lists and lighting conditions.

I stay out of their way, refilling coffee mugs when needed, but otherwise maintaining my distance.

It's nearly seven when the door opens again, and Lena

steps into the lodge. I expect Hollywood glamour—the full makeup, styled hair, and an impractical outfit similar to what she arrived in yesterday. Instead, the woman who shuffles toward the coffee pot is surprisingly normal. Her face is bare, dark circles visible beneath her eyes, and her hair is pulled into a messy bun atop her head. She wears gray sweatpants and an oversized sweatshirt that hangs off one shoulder, revealing a slim collarbone. Her feet are swallowed by fluffy pink slippers, their soles already pincushions for pine needles.

Our eyes meet across the room, and I catch the moment she realizes I'm watching her. Her chin lifts, a flash of defiance crossing her face. "Morning," she mutters, making a beeline for the coffee.

"Sleep well?" I ask, unable to keep a hint of amusement from my voice.

"About as well as anyone could with wolves howling all night," she replies, pouring coffee into a mug emblazoned with a moose silhouette. "Is there a latte machine?"

I blink. "A what?"

"A latte machine. Espresso?" She gestures vaguely with her hands. "Steamed milk?"

I point to the refrigerator. "Milk's in there. It's cold, not steamed."

She regards me like I've suggested she drink from the creek. "You're kidding, right? This is a resort."

"This is Alaska," I correct, handing her a pitcher of milk. "We have coffee. We have milk. Combine them however you like."

Lena eyes the pitcher with resignation, then pours a generous amount into her coffee. "I suppose this passes for a latte in the wilderness."

"It passes for coffee with milk," I reply. "The wilderness doesn't care what you call it."

"Fair point." She loads a plate with food and joins the

production team at the long wooden table, sliding into an empty chair beside Elliott. I busy myself with cleanup, keeping one ear on their conversation.

"So, we'll start with some establishing shots around the lodge today," Elliott says, gesturing with his fork. "Get Lena all contemplative by the creek, perhaps chop a little wood—"

I nearly choke on my coffee.

"—nothing too strenuous, of course, just making sure it reads authentic," Elliott continues, oblivious to my reaction. "Then tomorrow we'll head out to the location."

"Location?" Lena asks, her fork pausing halfway to her mouth. "I thought this was the location."

Elliott scans the table, then clears his throat. "Slight change of plans. The network executives reviewed our preliminary filming plan and decided it wasn't … rustic enough."

A heavy silence falls over the table.

"What does that mean?" Lena asks, her voice dropping to a dangerous tone.

"They want real wilderness immersion," Elliott explains, adjusting his glasses nervously. "We're going to relocate to the Painted Peaks area for most of the shoot. We'll set up camp there."

"Camp?" Lena repeats, her fork clattering against her plate. "What do you mean, camp?"

"You know," Elliott says, gesturing vaguely with his hands. "Tents, campfire, that sort of thing."

"I don't camp," Lena states flatly. "I've never even glamped."

"The scenery is absolutely stunning," Elliott rushes on, desperation coating his words. "Waterfalls, alpine meadows, incredible wildlife opportunities—"

"Wildlife?" Lena's voice rises an octave. "You mean bears?"

I watch the color drain from her face. Pale as birch bark in winter. No doubt she's been fed a line about what this job entails.

"Elliot," she says with a forced calm that barely masks the tremor in her voice, "I agreed to stay at a lodge with actual amenities while capturing some nature videos and photos. Not to sleep on the ground in bear country." She picks up her phone and stares at the screen. Her eyes widen, and she slowly lowers it like it might bite her. "No service? Are you kidding me?"

"Service is spotty," I say, unable to help myself. "Best reception is on the east deck, facing the mountain."

She shoots me a glare that could freeze the creek solid, then turns back to Elliott. "What kind of project is this, exactly?"

Elliott winces, like this is the part he hoped to avoid. "It's a survival documentary," he says with forced enthusiasm. "*Stars in the Wild*. Think *Survivor* meets *Naked and Afraid*. Only PG. Mostly."

"So, I'm the unwitting star of a reality show?" Her eyes narrow.

"A high-end, prestige docuseries," he says, like that somehow makes it better. "With an emphasis on emotional resilience."

She lets out a strangled sound. "You mean I'm supposed to fumble around the forest while America observes me sweating through bug bites and breakdowns?"

Elliott opens his mouth—probably gearing up to call it "empowering" or some equally delusional nonsense—but she's already turning away, lifting her phone over her head and pacing toward the door. "I'm calling my agent. I don't care if I have to hike to a cell tower—I'm getting out of this wilderness nightmare."

She stalks out, pink slippers and all, the door banging shut behind her.

Elliott waits until she's gone before turning to me with a pained expression. "This is where you come in, Mr. Hollister."

"Me?" I set down the dishtowel I've been holding. "I'm simply providing lodging for your production."

"Actually," Elliott says, pulling a document from his bag and sliding it across the table, "according to the contract you signed, you're also obligated to provide guiding services for the duration of filming."

I look at him. "I don't remember agreeing to that."

"Page eleven, section C, subsection four," Elliott says, his tone apologetic as he points to a paragraph of minuscule text. "Crystal Creek Retreat will provide wilderness guiding services as needed for production requirements."

My stomach sinks as I reread the dense legal language. I remember skimming this section, assuming it meant basic information about hiking trails or fishing spots—not leading a full wilderness expedition. I glance at Elliott, whose too-casual posture suddenly seems suspicious.

"Wait—there's a guide component?" I ask.

Elliott nods, clearly trying to sound breezy. "Yeah. But don't worry—you'll get an additional stipend for that."

My breath catches. Their payment for a guide—unexpected but very much needed—would cover a good quarter of what I need to keep the loan sharks at bay. Saying no isn't an option. Not now.

"We need someone who knows the Painted Peaks area," Elliott continues, his voice taking on a pleading quality. "The safety of our star and crew is paramount. A travel agent in Anchorage recommended you specifically when we were planning this expedition."

I bite back a curse. That would be Linda Parker, the persistent travel agent who's always trying to book her mainland clients with local guides. This has her fingerprints all over it.

"How long?" I ask, already mentally calculating what this

will mean for the lodge. I'll have to call Nash and Eliza to see if they can check on the place periodically.

"Maximum three weeks," Elliott replies. "We'll need to depart tomorrow."

"Tomorrow?" I repeat, incredulous. "That's not nearly enough time to prepare for a three-week backcountry expedition."

Elliott's expression turns desperate. "We're on an extremely tight production schedule. The network has already announced the special will air in September."

If I weren't looking down the barrel of financial ruin, I would refuse outright. But the extra money might be enough to help me catch up on the debt that's been hanging over me.

The door swings open before I can respond, Lena storming back in with her cell phone clutched in her hand like a weapon. Her face has paled to the color of winter frost, eyes wide with horror. Her voice is tight with disbelief. "Paragraph twelve specifically states I must take part in 'immersive wilderness experiences' as determined by the production team. My agent says I signed it."

Elliott's expression transforms from worry to poorly concealed relief. "Exactly. The network executives believe strongly that a realistic wilderness experience is key to the narrative of your transformation from Hollywood party girl to nature enthusiast."

"Transformation?" Lena echoes, her voice rising. "I'm not here for some spiritual journey through the woods. This was supposed to fix the Martinez disaster, not create a new one!"

"This will be much more effective for that purpose," Elliott assures her. "Think of the audience response—Lena Kensington, roughing it in Alaska, finding her real self away from Hollywood's pressures."

She slumps into her chair, defeated. "You told me the survival stuff was for show—staged for the cameras, with safety crews hovering off-screen." Her voice cracks. "You said I'd be communing with nature. That there'd be trailers. Catering trucks."

The raw despair in her voice cuts through my simmering anger at Elliott. "Bait and switch," I mutter, the words tumbling out before I fully think them through. A strange, unwelcome sense of kinship washes over me—two damn fools caught in the same professionally negligent trap. "I didn't read my contract properly either."

Her head snaps up. Her eyes, though narrowed with suspicion, show a trace of desperate hope that she isn't the only one thoroughly conned. "What do you mean?"

I fight the urge to shove the contract in Elliott's smirking face and instead tap the offending document on the table. "This little masterpiece of legalese," I say, my voice flat with the effort of keeping it even. "Seems I've also agreed to be your personal wilderness guide for the next three weeks. I thought I was renting out the damn lodge." As the words leave my mouth, I watch her process them. For one hard second, the sharp edges of her Hollywood persona soften, her suspicion giving way to a horrified understanding that mirrors my churning gut. We aren't a jaded Alaskan and a pampered actress. We're two people who've been played, plain and simple. The thought, this brief, uncomfortable alignment with *her*, of all people, is as galling as the looming bank payment.

"You're coming?" A quick flicker of relief crosses her face —raw and plain to see—before her walls snap back into place, suspicion tightening her features.

That brief expression, as if my forced companionship in this farce is somehow a *good* thing, is enough to stamp out this unwelcome shred of camaraderie I feel.

"Apparently," I say, my tone deliberately dry, any hint of

shared misfortune quickly burying itself under a fresh layer of resentment for this entire circus.

"So, problem solved," Elliott says, his voice brightening. "Finn will ensure everything runs smoothly. He's got all the skills to keep us safe and comfortable."

"I doubt that very much," Lena mutters, though some of the fight seems to leave her. She looks down at her barely touched breakfast, then pushes the plate away. "Can I at least get a decent cup of coffee before we're banished to the wilderness?"

"May's Café in town has the best coffee in Port Promise," I say. "And her sourdough pancakes are legendary."

Something shifts in Lena's expression. "May ... the woman from the wedding? She mentioned her pancakes."

I nod, recognizing an opportunity to escape this uncomfortable conversation. "We could head into town now. You'll need proper gear, and the consignment shop has decent outdoor clothing."

"Consignment," she says. "As in worn by strangers. And touched by their ... germs. On fabrics of questionable origin. Is this even sanitary? This wouldn't pass muster on a low-budget set."

"As in practical and affordable," I correct. "Unless you brought hiking boots and waterproof clothing?"

A challenge sparks in her eyes. "Actually, I brought boots."

"Let me guess," I say, unable to suppress a chuckle. "With heels?"

Her silence is answer enough.

"Thought so." I grab my keys from the hook by the door. "Let's go now. May stops serving pancakes at ten."

"But we haven't finished breakfast," Elliott protests.

"You all enjoy the casserole," I say, nodding toward the production crew, who are still eating. "We'll be back in a few hours with proper gear for this expedition you've planned."

Lena pushes up from her chair like she's heading for a firing squad.

"I need to change first," she says, glancing down at her casual attire.

"Ten minutes," I call after her as she heads toward the door. "I'll bring the Polaris around."

The sound of her frustrated sigh is oddly satisfying. Whatever these next three weeks hold, one thing is certain—Lena Kensington is about to experience a very different Alaska than the one she signed up for. To be honest, a small, petty part of me is anticipating witnessing Hollywood's princess face the reality of wilderness living. The woman who showed up in a leather dress to Alaska deserves a little humbling.

As I watch her hurry from the lodge, the full weight of the situation settles over me. Her shoulders droop with defeat, her movements heavy with reluctance. Three weeks in the back-country with a spoiled actress who can't handle regular coffee, a film crew hungry for drama, and wilderness that refuses to accommodate Hollywood expectations. The pristine silence of my mornings will turn to chaos of complaints about mosquitoes and lack of cell service. My structured routines will unravel as I balance guiding responsibilities with their unrealistic demands.

I turn back toward the kitchen, eyes landing on the contract still open on the table.

The microscopic text blurs together, but the message comes through loud and clear—Elliott manipulated us both. The contract lies there, deceptively harmless, its fine print binding me to a disaster in the making. But the bank notice on my desk carries more weight. I could walk away—tell Elliott to find another guide, spare myself three weeks of drama in the backcountry. But Crystal Creek isn't simply some business venture. Losing this place? Can't happen. Too many memories. Dad teaching me the creek sounds. The way the sun hits

KELLY COLLINS

my peaks first thing. This place keeps me grounded when things move too fast.

I fold the contract and tuck it into my pocket. The choice isn't a choice at all.

Give me a hungry grizzly over a pampered celebrity any day. At least the bear would be honest about wanting to eat me alive.

Chapter Three

LENA

I STAND in front of the cabin's cloudy mirror, assessing my reflection. After rifling through three suitcases of designer clothes, I've cobbled together what passes for "outdoor attire" in my wardrobe: cream cashmere joggers that I justified buying because they were "investment loungewear" at $900, a silk-blend turtleneck, and designer ankle boots with gold hardware accents and a subtle wedge heel.

"This is casual," I assure my reflection, running fingers through my hair. God, what I wouldn't give for my stylist right now. The humidity here is staging a full-on rebellion against my flat iron, leaving my usually sleek strands to erupt in frizz at the ends. "Appropriate for a small Alaskan town."

My skincare routine has taken twenty minutes—moisturizer, primer, tinted sunscreen, concealer, cream blush, brow gel, and mascara. The bare minimum to seem "natural" while covering up the evidence of last night's restless sleep, interrupted by what I'm convinced was a wolf lurking outside my window.

A honk sends me scrambling for my handbag. I step outside to find Finn waiting on the Polaris. His expression shifts from impatience to an amused glint as he takes in the effort I've put into looking effortless. "What?" I say, picking my way down the path.

"Nothing," he says. "Nice boots."

"They're designer," I say defensively, lifting one foot. "Limited edition."

"And completely useless for what we're about to do."

"They're fine for a photo shoot at a lodge, which is what I was expecting when I came here," I reply, climbing onto the passenger seat with as much dignity as possible.

The ride into town is a good thirty minutes. Finn handles the uneven ground with ease, the Polaris bouncing over roots and rocks that have me instinctively wrapping my arms around his waist. His body is solid beneath my fingers—all hard muscles radiating heat through his jacket. Each bump shoves me against his back, and my stomach does this ridiculous little lurch I refuse to acknowledge.

"Hold on tighter through this next section," Finn calls over his shoulder, his voice vibrating through his back. "It gets rough."

I tighten my grip, my fingers splaying across the firm plane of his abdomen. I tell myself it's practical, but I can't deny the awareness that is sparking at the contact. The man thinks I'm a pampered princess who can't handle Alaska. I shouldn't be noticing how perfectly my hands fit against his stomach or how his back tenses against my chest with each turn of the vehicle.

Port Promise comes into view—a haphazard collection of old buildings huddled around a grey harbor, fishing boats looking like discarded toys on the water.

"First stop," Finn announces as he pulls up in front of a building with a hand-painted sign reading "Second Chance Consignment."

"Where exactly are we going for proper gear?" I ask, trying

to ignore the lingering warmth on my palms. "I know you said consignment, but isn't there an REI around here? Or perhaps a North Face store?"

Finn makes a sound that might be a choked laugh. "The closest REI is about 300 miles from here. We're going to Second Chance."

"That's the place you mentioned?" I ask, eyeing the storefront with hesitation.

Finn nods. "Don't worry, they wash everything."

A thin woman with salt-and-pepper hair lifts her head from behind the counter as we enter. Her eyes widen when they land on me.

"Well, I'll be. You must be the Hollywood girl staying at Finn's place. May told me you caught the bouquet. I hear you're heading into the mountains."

My cheeks warm. "Word travels fast."

"Town of less than two hundred people," Finn says, already rifling through a rack of jackets. "News moves quicker than salmon during spawning season." He steps up to the counter, voice low. "She'll need boots, layers, thermals—the whole kit."

The woman extends a hand marked by time and labor. "Agnes Wilcox. Welcome to Second Chance."

While Agnes pulls items from various shelves, Finn disappears into a back corner of the shop. He returns with a stack of alarmingly practical clothing—bulky hiking boots with thick treads, wool socks rough enough to exfoliate skin, and what appears to be long underwear with a button-up flap in the back.

"What is that?" I ask, pointing at the peculiar garment.

"Thermal underwear," he replies, adding it to the growing pile. "With a convenient back flap for bathroom breaks in the wilderness."

"You can't be serious."

29

"Deadly serious." His expression doesn't waver. "Unless you want to strip down completely every time nature calls. In thirty-degree weather. With mosquitoes the size of hummingbirds."

I stare at the offending garment, sheer horror clawing its way up my throat. "It has a *butt flap*."

"You'll thank me later," he says, turning back to the shelves.

"Highly doubtful," I mutter, but don't remove it from the pile.

Agnes ushers me toward a cramped dressing room at the back of the store. "Try these on, dear. We need to make sure everything fits before you head into those mountains."

The tiny space has a flimsy curtain instead of a door and smells of mothballs. Agnes hands me a stack of clothing—faded flannel shirts, thermal layers in various thicknesses, and pants with more pockets than I can count. "Start with these," she instructs, pulling the curtain closed.

I shed my expensive clothes and reach for the first item—a pair of thick cargo pants in a muddy olive color. The fabric is rough against my skin, nothing like the soft cashmere I've been wearing. As I pull them on, the sensation triggers something unexpected.

The smell of the small space, the scratchy fabric, the sound of distant voices beyond the curtain—I'm not in an Alaskan consignment shop anymore. I'm ten years old, in a church donation center, my mother digging through bins of castoffs while I try on clothes in a makeshift changing area, the smell of dust and old fabric thick in my nostrils.

"It'll fit fine, baby. You'll grow into it." My mother's voice echoes in my memory, her tired expression as she holds up pants three sizes too big, secured with safety pins because we can't afford a belt. Shame burns hot. I can still hear them—the snickers, the pointing—when my too-big jeans, the ones with the rip Momma patched with a different color denim, showed up on Sarah Miller two weeks after I'd outgrown them.

My chest seizes. The dressing room walls press in, crushing the air from my lungs. I can't breathe, can't escape the memories flooding back—hunger, the power shut off, nights in the car when the rent ran out. I clutch at my throat, vision tunneling. Panic slams in a suffocating wave.

"Everything alright in there?" Agnes calls through the curtain.

I force myself to take a deep breath. Then another. "Fine," I manage, my voice strangled. "Just ... these pants are too big."

"I've got other sizes," she replies cheerfully. "Let me know what works."

I press my palms against my eyes, willing away the memories. This isn't then. I'm not that girl anymore. I'm Lena Kensington, actress. The girl who escaped. The woman who never has to wear hand-me-downs again. When my chest stops heaving, I finally look at myself in the mirror—smudged, streaked, and honest.

My face has paled, eyes too bright with unshed tears. I blink them away furiously. No one here will witness that vulnerability—especially not Finn Hollister, who already thinks I'm some spoiled princess.

Anger replaces the fear—anger at this whole mess, anger at myself, anger at the stain of poverty I can't wash off. My jaw aches from how hard I'm clenching it, but it's better than the damn tears. Anger is easier. Safer. I yank on the remaining clothes with savage efficiency, ignoring how they scratch against my skin. Each item reinforces my determination. I will endure this. I will excel at it. And when I return to Hollywood, my career resurrected, I will burn every piece of this clothing.

When I emerge from the dressing room, my expression is

locked in cool indifference. Finn raises his head from the counter, his eyebrows rising slightly at my transformation.

"What?" I snap, daring him to comment.

"Nothing," he says, regarding me with unexpected intensity. "Those actually fit you well."

Agnes circles me, tugging at sleeves and checking pant lengths with professional assessment. "Not bad. You've got a good frame for outdoor wear."

I want to laugh at the absurdity of the compliment. After years of stylists praising my body for appearing good in couture, I'm now being complimented on how I fill out cargo pants.

Finn disappears midway through, leaving me to Agnes's tender mercies. An hour later, a substantial pile of clothing and equipment sits on the counter. The mirror reflects a woman I barely recognize—dressed in cargo pants, a thermal Henley, and a burgundy flannel shirt. The woman in the mirror isn't Hollywood's Lena Kensington. She looks like she could've grown up here.

I turn away from the reflection, unsettled. "Ring it all up," I say finally, pulling out my credit card. "Whatever you think I'll need. I'll expense it to the production later."

As we exit the shop, I notice Finn across the street, standing outside a timeworn building with a sign reading May's Café. "My brother Nash is meeting us at May's," he announces. "He's bringing the camping gear."

The rich smells from the diner cut through my misery. May emerges from behind the counter, her face lighting up. "Well, if it isn't our reluctant bouquet-catcher and our resident grump! I was thinking you weren't coming."

"Wouldn't miss your pancakes," I reply, surprised by how pleased I am to be here.

A burst of laughter from the corner booth catches my attention. A man who can only be Finn's brother waves us over—the family resemblance is unmistakable, though where Finn is all controlled strength and stoic reserve, Nash Hollister is all easy smiles and charm.

"If it isn't our Hollywood guest," he says as we approach his booth. "Out shopping for your survival starter pack?"

"Nash," Finn warns, but his brother ignores him, extending a hand to me. "Nash Hollister, wilderness expert and the good-looking brother," he introduces himself with a wink. "Hear you're going to Painted Peaks."

"Not by choice," I say, shaking his hand.

Nash laughs. "Few people go into those mountains by choice, Hollywood. That's what makes it an adventure." His casual use of May's nickname for me makes me wonder how many people have been discussing my arrival.

"I've got all the gear you requested loaded on my ATV's trailer outside," Nash says, turning to Finn. "Several tents, portable stove, water filters, bear canisters—the works."

"Bear canisters?" I ask, my voice rising.

"For food storage," Nash explains, amusement in his eyes. "Unless you want hungry midnight visitors with claws and teeth."

"You're not going anywhere until you've had a proper breakfast," May says, cutting in with firm authority. "Sit. All of you." Without missing a beat, she herds us into Nash's booth. Before I can even consider a menu, May has vanished into the kitchen.

"So," Nash says, leaning forward. "How's the lodge treating you so far?"

"It's ... rustic."

Nash snorts. "Translation—my brother builds things to last, not to impress. Not a believer in updates or modern conveniences, our Finn."

"The lodge is perfectly functional," Finn defends, though he doesn't deny the accusation.

"Remember when you tried to install that satellite internet system yourself?" Nash continues, eyes gleaming. "Half the town lost power."

"That was a grounding issue," Finn mutters, his ears reddening.

"My point," Nash says, turning back to me, "is that my brother here is great at many things—building, fishing, scowling at tourists—but technology isn't one of them."

"I'm more concerned about the bears May mentioned."

"Bears are the least of your worries," Nash replies. "It's the mosquitoes you've got to be wary of. They're so big up in the Peaks they've been known to carry off small children."

I narrow my eyes, unsure if he's joking.

"Don't worry, Hollywood. Finn knows those mountains almost as well as I do. You're in excellent hands." He grins and stretches.

The back door opens, and a bearded man enters, nodding in their direction before taking a seat at the counter. Finn and Nash exchange a signal.

"I should talk to Lars about the trail conditions," Finn says, sliding out of the booth. "He was up in the Peaks last week scouting."

Nash rises too. "Need to ask him about the game movement he noticed up there."

As the brothers approach the man at the counter, May emerges with three plates of golden pancakes. She sets them on our table, notices the empty seats, and clicks her tongue. "Men," she mutters, sliding into the booth across from me. "Always business before pancakes." She pushes a plate toward me. "Eat up before they get cold. Best enjoyed with real maple syrup and a side of truth."

I raise an eyebrow as I drizzle syrup over the stack. "A side of truth?"

May's shrewd eyes fix on me. "Why are you here, Lena

Kensington? And don't give me that PR rehabilitation nonsense."

I take my first bite of pancake. The flavor bursts on my tongue—tangy, buttery perfection. "These are incredible," I admit.

"Mmm," May hums with satisfaction. "My sourdough starter is over a hundred years old," she says with pride. "But we're not talking about my pancakes." She leans forward, elbows on the table. "What brings a Hollywood actress all the way to Port Promise? And don't tell me it's for a TV special."

My fork pauses midway to my second bite. "My agent arranged this whole thing after I had a public meltdown on set."

"And of all places, you agreed to Alaska?" May asks, one eyebrow raised.

I set down my fork. "I threw a champagne flute at my director. It made national news. My agent says this nature special will help people view me as more than 'that crazy actress who lost it.'"

"And you believed him?" May asks, not unkindly.

"What choice do I have?" The words come out more bitterly than I intend. "My career was finally getting back on track after years of being typecast as the sexy vampire girl, and I threw it all away in one moment of anger."

May regards me, then nods as if confirming something. "This wilderness adventure might patch over your public image for a while, but it won't solve anything real."

"And what's that supposed to mean?" I say, crossing my arms.

"Only you know the answer to that question," May says, rising from the booth as Finn and Nash return. "But I'll tell you this—the mountains have a way of clearing your head. Might be what you need."

Before I can respond, she turns to the men. "Your

pancakes are getting cold, boys. Lars can wait five minutes while you eat what I slaved over a hot griddle to make."

Nash beams, sliding back into his side of the booth and immediately drenching his pancakes in syrup. "May's sourdough waits for no man."

Finn sits beside his brother, eyes shifting between May and me. "Everything alright?"

"Yep, fine," I reply too quickly, focusing on my plate as May walks away. "May was sharing some local wisdom."

The brothers eat with the efficiency of men accustomed to refueling rather than dining. Nash fills the silence with details about the equipment he's brought—items with names I don't recognize, but that sound alarmingly specialized for wilderness survival.

"We'll need to do a gear check tonight," Finn says between bites.

"I've packed everything you'll need," Nash replies. "Including a satellite phone, first aid kit, and a set of tents. One of them's my best—barely used it last season."

"Satellite phone?" I perk up. "So, we will have communication?"

"For emergencies," Finn clarifies. "Not for checking your Instagram followers."

I glare at him. "I wasn't asking for social media purposes. I'd like some connection to the outside world in case something goes wrong."

"Like what?" Nash asks.

"I don't know. Bear attacks? Falling off a cliff? Hypothermia? Whatever disasters May's been warning me about since I arrived."

Finn and Nash share a brief, knowing look.

"The Painted Peaks aren't Disneyland," Finn says. "But they're not a death trap either. Follow instructions, stay on the trails, and you'll be fine."

"That's not reassuring," I say.

"It's not meant to be," Finn says. "It's realistic. The wilderness deserves respect, not fear."

Something in his tone quiets my comeback. Instead, I nod. "Fair enough."

Surprise flickers across Finn's face, quickly replaced by what might be approval.

May returns with a paper bag that smells of cinnamon and hands it to Finn. "Muffins for the road. And don't you dare try to pay me, Finnegan Hollister."

"Thanks, May."

"You boys go load up that gear," she instructs. "I need another minute with Lena."

Nash slides from the booth, sending me a sympathetic expression. "May's 'minutes' are legendary. Good luck, Hollywood."

As the brothers head outside, May reclaims the seat across from me. Her expression softens as she takes in my face. "City folk come here for the scenery," she says, wiping a spot on the table with her thumb. "But Alaska has a way of changing people. Makes them perceive things differently."

"I'm only here for a few weeks," I remind her.

May's lips curve. "A lot can happen in a short time, especially with Finn as your guide." She pats my hand. "He seems all rough edges, but there's no one better to have on your side in those mountains."

"We're not exactly getting along," I admit.

"The best partnerships rarely start that way." She rises from the booth. "The boys are waiting. I'll have fresh pie when you get back—you can tell me how it all went."

I watch her walk away, realizing what she's implying. As if I would ever fall for someone like Finn Hollister. The man is infuriating, judgmental, and lives in the absolute middle of nowhere by choice. The last thing I need is another stubborn man who thinks he knows what's best for me. I've had enough of those in Hollywood to last a lifetime.

Outside, Finn and Nash are loading equipment from Nash's ATV trailer onto the one behind the Polaris. Both men move with the ease of those accustomed to physical labor.

"Ready to head back?" Finn calls. "We need to finish packing and check your new gear."

I nod, climbing onto the Polaris.

Before starting the engine, Finn turns to me. "This isn't what I signed up for," I say, my frustration bubbling over. "I thought I agreed to stay at a lodge with running water and electricity, not camp in a bear-infested wilderness for three weeks."

Finn's jaw tightens, his hands gripping the steering wheel. "You think I'm thrilled about playing tour guide to a film crew? This wasn't in my plans either."

"Then why are we doing this?"

He's quiet for a moment. "Because I need the money. A bad storm nearly bankrupted the lodge." There's a reluctance in his admission that tells me it costs him something to share.

I sink deeper into my seat. "My agent says this is my last chance to salvage my career."

"We're both trapped," Finn says. "Neither of us want this, but we both need something from it."

"Exactly."

"Exactly." He slows the vehicle as we approach a rough patch of road. "Listen, I don't know what happened in Hollywood, and I don't care. But out here? The mountains don't care about your IMDB page, and the bears don't care about designer labels."

"Is this supposed to be a pep talk? Because it's terrible."

He smiles. "What I'm saying is we're stuck with each other for three weeks. We can either make each other miserable, or we can choke down our complaints and get through it."

"Fine," I huff. "I'll try not to remind you how absurd this whole situation is if you try not to raise your eyebrows every time I don't know something about wilderness survival."

"Deal," he says, looking down at my new hiking boots. "At least you've got proper footwear now."

I can't help the small laugh that escapes me. "Don't remind me. I buried my beautiful designer boots in Agnes's shopping bag. They're completely impractical, but I refuse to leave them behind."

His expression softens slightly. "Speaking of practical items, you got thermal underwear, right? The one with the—"

"The butt flap," I finish, as heat rises to my cheeks. "Yes, against my better judgment."

"Trust me, when you're in a tiny tent in freezing temperatures, you'll thank me for that recommendation."

I sigh. "Add it to the growing list of indignities I'll apparently be thanking you for later."

"I'm keeping track," he says, and I can't tell if he's joking.

As we continue toward the lodge, dread settles in my stomach. This isn't an adventure. It's a nightmare dressed as a career opportunity. And unlike the roles I've played before, there's no script to tell me how this one will end.

Chapter Four

FINN

FOUR IN THE MORNING, and the darkness presses against the lodge windows. I move through the kitchen, packing trail food with efficiency. Dried meat, nuts, fruit leather, granola. Things that won't spoil, are lightweight and packed with energy. The percolator gurgles on the stove, filling the kitchen with the smell of fresh coffee. I pour a cup for myself, then pause before reaching for a second mug. I warm some milk and add it to the cup, the way she likes it. Don't know why I bother. Perhaps because eight miles of listening to complaints about black coffee would make the hike seem twice as long.

Elliott knocks at 4:15, his travel mug in hand. He and the crew are already on the porch, packs ready, checking camera equipment by headlamp light. These aren't first-timers—they know what they're doing.

"Everyone set?" Elliott asks.

I assess the group. "Where's Lena?"

The silence tells me everything I need to know. I grab the extra coffee. "I'll check on her."

The night air bites through my jacket as I cross to her

cabin. Light peeks from behind her curtains. Good. At least she's awake. I knock. Wait. Knock harder.

"One minute!" Her voice sounds frantic.

Three minutes later, the door opens. She stands there fully dressed in hiking gear, hair pulled back, eyes wide. "Is it time already?" She blinks at me, openly shocked. "I thought you said five o'clock."

"Departure at five. Prep at four." I hand her the coffee. "Made this for you. Added some warmed milk."

Surprise flickers across her face, then her shoulders lose some of their stiffness. "Thanks." She takes a sip, closing her eyes briefly. "I needed this."

"Pack check in fifteen minutes."

She steps back, letting me have a view inside the cabin. Three bags sit on her bed, along with piles of clothing and equipment. "I wasn't sure what to bring, so I pulled everything out."

"That's why we're doing a pack check." I nod toward the main building. "Finish that coffee, then we can sort through this."

She takes another long sip. "I've barely slept."

"The trail will wake you up." I turn back toward the lodge, trusting she'll follow. "First day's always the hardest."

In the lodge kitchen, Elliott is reviewing the day's shooting plan with his team. They sit around the table with their coffee, examining maps and shot lists. Professional. Prepared. Lena observes from the doorway, her coffee mug clutched between both hands. "What's the plan?" she asks.

"Eight miles today. Five uphill to reach the basin, then three across to our first campsite. Roughly eight hours of hiking, accounting for breaks and filming."

Her eyes widen. "That long?"

"Could be six if we keep a good pace."

"And how far is this place? Total, I mean."

41

"Nineteen miles from here to the peaks." I lay out a map on the kitchen table. "We'll take three days to get there, camping twice along the way."

She stares at the map, brow furrowing at the cluster of topographical lines. "Those are ... mountains?"

"Those are our route."

Elliott joins us, setting down his coffee. "Everything on schedule?"

"I'm finalizing Lena's gear," I say. "Then we can move out."

Back in her cabin, I help sort through what she'll need. All those clothes we bought at Second Chance are now spread across her bed. "Let's start with clothes," I say, picking up the items I helped her select the day before. "Two base layers, one mid-layer, one outer shell. Two pairs of pants, three pairs of socks." She nods, observing as I arrange the items.

"Now sleeping gear, cooking equipment, safety supplies..." I stop as I unzip a side pocket of her pack. "Seems like there's more in here." I pull out a small makeup bag, then several bottles labeled "serum." Tubes of creams and lotions follow, a whole counter's worth.

Lena snatches one bottle from my hand. "I need those."

"You need all of them?"

"Yes. My skin dries out. The sun, the wind—"

"Sunscreen will protect you from the sun. A good hat will handle the wind."

She clutches the products to her chest. "These are necessary." Her face is clear and perfect, even at this ungodly hour. I sigh. "Pick three. The smallest ones."

"Five."

"Four. Including the tinted sunscreen." I hold up a tube. "This at least serves a practical purpose."

She considers, then quickly selects a few. "These four. They're vital."

I don't argue, only make room in her pack. Eight ounces isn't worth the battle. "The rest stays here."

The relief on her face tells me I've made the right call. I sigh. "Besides, Elliott's got Carlos—his Director of Photography—filming most of your solo camp life scenes. I suppose you'll want to look the part."

The sky has lightened when we finally hit the trail, almost an hour behind schedule. The path begins behind the lodge, winding through pine forest before climbing toward the Painted Peaks. Headlamps carve tunnels of light through pre-dawn darkness. Lena walks behind me, her footsteps uneven on the rough ground. The crew spreads out between us, filming equipment bouncing on their backs alongside personal gear.

"First water break at the ridge overlook," I call back. "About two miles up."

The group falls into rhythm, the only sounds our breathing and the crunch of boots on the trail. Lena keeps pace better than I expect, though I can hear her breathing grow labored on the steeper sections. She'll feel this tomorrow, but she's not complaining yet.

When dawn hits the peaks, we stop to film. Elliott positions Lena against the sunrise, her silhouette sharp against the dark mountains and the brightening sky.

"How are you feeling about the journey ahead?" Elliott asks from behind the camera.

The change is remarkable. Lena straightens her posture, her expression shifting to calm determination. "The mountains have their own schedule, their own wisdom. I'm learning to move on their time, not mine."

The words sound good. The emotion behind them? Pure fiction. The moment the cameras lower, she slumps against a tree, massaging her shoulder where the pack straps dig in.

Figured that pack was a mistake. She wouldn't listen. "How much do these things weigh?" she asks.

"Yours? About twenty-five pounds."

"Could've fooled me. Seems like fifty."

"Wait until day three. It'll seem like ten."

She appears skeptical. "Is that how it works? It gets lighter?"

"No. You get stronger."

The trail side blueberries distract her from the discomfort, at least for a while. At our first water break, I show her which plants are safe to eat. "These are edible," I say, plucking a handful of berries. "Small but sweet."

She examines the bushes, head tilted. "Blueberries, obviously. *Vaccinium uliginosum.*" The Latin name surprises me. She catches my expression and quickly adds, "I think that's what they're called. I read a nature book once."

"You read a book on arctic berry plants?"

She avoids eye contact as she pops a berry into her mouth. "I like to be prepared."

Something isn't adding up. Most people who can identify plants by their scientific names don't also pack four different face creams for a camping trip.

By mile four, her pack adjustments can't hide her discomfort. The cheerful hiker who appears for the cameras vanishes the moment filming stops, replaced by a woman who looks like she is questioning every decision that led her to this moment.

"How much farther?" she asks during our second break.

"To lunch? Another mile. To camp? Four beyond that."

She groans, leaning back against a boulder. "I can't believe this is still the *first* day. I need food. Real food. Not trail mix."

"There's jerky in your side pocket."

"I need more than dried meat."

I consider our location, checking the sun's position.

"There's a stream up ahead. Good lunch spot. Might even catch some trout if you're interested in learning."

Her nose scrunches slightly. "I don't eat fish." Right. Another princess-ism.

"Right. Forgot about that. Then it's jerky for you."

"Great," she mutters. "More dried meat."

The stream spot is one of my favorites—a small clearing where the water pools into a deep, clear basin before continuing down the mountain. Perfect for refilling water bottles and cooling sore feet. We drop packs, and the relief on Lena's face is almost comical.

"Thirty minutes," I tell the group. "Rest, eat, drink. Then we push on to camp."

While the crew sprawls in patches of shade, I pull out my collapsible fishing rod. "Whether or not you eat it, fishing is a useful skill to learn," I say to Lena. "Survival basics."

She observes as I assemble the rod, her interest seeming sincere despite her aversion to fish. "You're going to catch something? Here?"

"These pools are full of small trout. Perfect for teaching."

Elliott perks up. "We should film this. Lena's first fishing lesson."

The cameras appear, and with them, Lena's performance. She listens intently as I explain casting basics, asking perfectly timed questions, her mistakes clumsy enough to be charming for the lens. The cameras capture it all—her surprise when she feels a nibble, her triumphant beam when we land a small trout.

"I did it!" Her exclamation is clearly for the cameras, the six-inch fish dangling from her line.

"Perfect eating size," I say, showing her how to remove the hook. "Want to try cleaning it? Even if you don't eat it, the crew might appreciate fresh protein."

The cameras keep rolling as her expression falters slightly. "Clean it? As in ... gut it?" There's the reaction I expected.

"Prepare it for cooking."

Her attempt is messy but determined. Her face pales considerably by the time she finishes, but the job is done.

"Not bad," I say, impressed by her determination. "Natural talent."

She arches a brow. "I'm a quick study."

While Lena is cleaning her catch, I land a few more trout. Between the fish and our packed provisions, we have plenty for everyone's lunch. The trout cooks quickly over our small camp stove. Lena passes on the fish, sticking with her trail mix and jerky, but she seems pleased with her contribution to the meal.

With the break finished, we pack up and continue toward our campsite. The afternoon stretches into a grueling climb, the sun beating down as we switchback up a rocky slope. Lena falls silent, her focus narrowing to placing one foot in front of the other.

At a steep section, I drop back to walk beside her. "Use your trekking poles. They'll take some weight off your knees."

She adjusts her grip on the poles, mimicking my stance. "I don't know how much more of this I can take."

"You've already done the hard part," I say. "Only two more miles to go—we'll be there before sunset."

She groans softly but keeps walking.

I point to a distant ridge. "See that line of trees? That's our campsite. Running water, level ground, good views."

She squints toward the horizon. "It appears impossibly far."

"It always does. Until you get there."

Something in my tone draws her eyes to mine for the first time in hours. "Do you actually enjoy this? Or do you tolerate pain better than normal humans?"

46

The question is blunt enough to surprise a laugh out of me. "Both, perhaps."

"Seriously. What's the appeal of walking uphill for hours with heavy packs?"

I consider her question. "The views. You see things up here nobody else does. It's quiet. You can actually see the stars clearly."

"That's very poetic for a mountain man."

"Mountains inspire poetry in most people."

She falls silent after that, apparently thinking about what I've said. We continue climbing, and I notice her using the trekking poles more effectively, finding a rhythm that eases her strain.

We reach the campsite as the sun begins its descent. The spot is perfect—a flat clearing surrounded by ancient pines, with a small stream running along one edge. From here, the view hits you hard. The valley we spent all day climbing from is a green smear far below.

"We're here," I announce, dropping my pack at a prime tent location. "Home for the night."

Lena practically collapses onto a fallen log, her expression a mix of exhaustion and relief. "We made it."

"You did well," I say, meaning it. "Eight miles on your first day is impressive."

She lifts her head, surprise crossing her face at the compliment. "I didn't have much choice."

"You always have a choice. You could have quit. Most people would have."

She considers this, then shrugs. "Well, I'm an actress. I'm used to pushing through discomfort for the sake of a production."

"This isn't acting," I say, unpacking my tent. "This is actual hardship."

Elliott approaches before she can respond. "We should get

camp set-up shots while we still have good light. Lena, can you help Finn with the tents?"

Lena's attempt to set up her tent with the cameras rolling involved missed stakes, collapsed poles, and increasingly creative cursing under her breath. I intervene when it becomes clear she might actually damage the equipment. "Like this," I demonstrate, slotting poles together. "It's a system. Each piece has a purpose."

She tries to follow my lead, her frustration mounting with each failed attempt. For once, the cameras capture something real. When she finally gets the tent standing—with significant help from me—her expression of accomplishment is real.

"Not bad for your first time," I say, securing the final stake.

"You did most of the work," she admits.

"Next time, you will."

With tents established, I organize the cooking area while teaching Lena basic campcraft. Her city instincts work against her at every turn—reaching for water without filtering it, stowing food in her tent, wandering off without telling anyone where she's going.

"Bears?" she repeats when I explain proper food storage. "Like, actual bears might come into our camp?"

"They might. That's why we hang food away from the sleeping area." She observes with growing concern as I demonstrate the proper technique for creating a bear hang, tossing a rope over a high branch. She asks what happens if a bear ignores the precautions.

"Make noise. Appear big. Stand your ground. They usually avoid people." She still looks terrified.

As darkness falls, we gather around the camp stove for a simple meal of dehydrated stew. The crew shares stories of other shoots in remote locations, their voices carrying in the stillness of the mountain evening. Lena says little, observing the sky as stars appear one by one.

"Amazing, isn't it?" I say, following her line of sight. "No light pollution up here."

"I've never witnessed so many stars," she admits. "In LA, you're lucky to find a dozen."

"Wait until the moon sets. It gets even better."

She pulls her jacket tighter against the evening chill. "How cold does it get at night?"

"This time of year? Low forties, perhaps high thirties."

"That's freezing."

"That's summer in the mountains. Your sleeping bag is rated for much colder. You'll be fine."

As the others drift toward their tents, I spot Lena by the cooking area, eyes fixed on the darkness beyond our camp. "Everything okay?" I ask.

She startles slightly. "Just taking it all in." I don't believe her for a second. "The bathroom is that way," I say, pointing to a designated spot at the edge of camp. "Take a headlamp. Make noise. You'll be fine."

Relief crosses her face. "Thanks."

When she returns from her bathroom visit, I expect her to head straight to her tent. Instead, she stops near mine, hesitating.

"Something else?"

"What happens if I need to ... you know ... during the night?"

"Same rules apply. Be smart about it." She nods but still doesn't move. "Lena. You climbed a mountain today. You can handle going to the bathroom in the dark."

"Right. Of course." She squares her shoulders. "Goodnight, then."

"Goodnight." I observe her duck into her tent, zipping it

49

securely behind her. Then I check the bear hang one last time before retiring to my shelter.

Sleep comes easily after the day's exertion, but in the middle of the night, a sound pulls me from deep rest. Shuffling, then a zipper. Then soft footsteps padding across our campsite. I peek out from my tent. By moonlight, I can make out Lena's silhouette as she creeps toward a flat boulder at the edge of camp. She sits down, pulls something from her pocket, and tilts her face toward the moon's faint light. It takes me a second, but yes—she's applying face cream. Maybe she's reading instructions. Or maybe the moonlight is part of the magic. Who knows.

But something about the ritual gives me pause. The careful application, the methodical movements. Not vanity. It had to be about control, some small piece of her old routine.

As she finishes and makes her way back to her tent, I lie awake thinking about the woman behind the performance. The one who knows scientific names of berries but packs a satin pillowcase. Who complains about every hardship but refuses to quit. Who applies cream by moonlight when she thinks no one is observing.

There is more to Lena Kensington than I've given her credit for. I'm just not sure what it is yet.

Chapter Five

LENA

A SHARP TWINGE in my heel wakes me before dawn. My eyes open to darkness, the unfamiliar weight of my sleeping bag heavy across my body. For a disorienting moment, I forget where I am. Then it hits me—the thin sleeping pad, the Alaskan wilderness hundreds of miles from civilization, and my feet already screaming about another day of hiking.

I've never heard such sounds at daybreak. The forest stirs with life—birds call in patterns I can't name. Small creatures rustle through underbrush, wind whispers through pine needles. No traffic noise. No phones chiming with notifications. No assistants knocking with coffee and schedule updates. The profound quiet is alien, almost unnervingly so, though a tiny part of me whispers it might also be peaceful.

Movement outside tells me the crew is awake. A pot clangs against metal, voices whisper, boots crunch on dirt. I force myself to sit up, every joint protesting. This is day two. Only a lifetime of wilderness torture to go.

I crawl out of my sleeping bag and pull on yesterday's clothes, hating how worn they are. Dressing in the cramped tent is like performing contortions in a phone booth, but I manage. I brush my tangled hair and secure it in a ponytail, then dig through my small bag of allowed toiletries for tinted sunscreen. Without a mirror, I apply by feel, hoping I didn't smear it on like a toddler with finger paint.

When I emerge from my tent, the camp is bustling with activity. The crew huddles around a small stove where water boils for coffee. Elliott reviews notes with the camera operators.

And Finn watches from a nearby rock, already dressed. His face gives nothing away, but the way he looks at me makes me wonder if he heard anything last night.

"Morning," I say, attempting cheerful but sounding groggy.

He nods, then holds out a steaming mug of coffee. "Black. Strong enough to wake the dead."

I cross the campsite for the cup. It hits me again—*how does he always know what I need before I do?* "Thanks."

"Sleep, okay?" he asks.

"Like a rock," I say, sipping the strong coffee. "A very uncomfortable, cold rock with pine roots jabbing my spine all night."

"It was a toasty fifty degrees."

"Like I said. Cold."

His mouth almost curves into amusement. "We break camp in thirty. Need to cover ground before the afternoon heat."

The thought of putting my boots back on and shouldering that pack makes me want to retreat to my tent. Instead, I nod, drinking my coffee and trying to convince my body it wants to move today.

"Your night cream routine work out okay?" Finn says, not meeting my eyes.

I nearly choke on my coffee. "You saw that?"

He shrugs. "Hard to miss someone wandering around camp at two in the morning."

Heat creeps up my neck. "Force of habit."

"Must be some powerful stuff to be worth hauling up a mountain."

I can't tell if he's mocking me. "My skin is my livelihood."

He looks up, taking his time as his attention settles on my face. "Seems to work."

Before I can respond, Elliott calls everyone together for a pre-departure briefing. I set my half-finished coffee aside, not sure how to take Finn's comment. He states observations as plain facts, without the layers of meaning I'm used to decoding. In Hollywood, compliments always come with hidden agendas. Out here, perhaps words are just words.

Breaking camp is a rush of activity—collapsing tents, packing gear, filling water bottles. Finn moves like he was born to this, quick and sure. I fumble with my tent until he appears beside me, helping me roll it properly. "Tuck the poles in the middle," he says, demonstrating. "Makes for better weight distribution."

"Thanks," I say, observing so I can do it myself next time.

When everything is packed and the campsite restored, we set off. Today's route will take us higher into the mountains, following a ridge trail toward what the maps call Blackwater Basin. The morning air still carries a chill, but the rising sun promises heat.

The first hour passes well enough. My body, though sore, finds a rhythm with the trail. My pack is more familiar now. Finn sets a pace that challenges without overwhelming us, stopping to point out landmarks or interesting plants.

"Cow parsnip," he says, showing a large-leafed plant with white flowers. "Native. Edible if you know how to prepare it."

"*Heracleum maximum*," I say without thinking, then regret it when his eyebrows rise. And a little flicker of something—pride? *ridiculous*—warms me that the name came so easily. "I think that's what it's called."

"You studied botany?"

"Picked things up here and there," I say, quickening my pace to avoid more questions.

By mid-morning, what started as mild discomfort in my heel has become real pain. Each step sends jolts up my leg, and I alter my walking to compensate. Finn notices and calls for an early break at a small clearing.

"Let me look at your foot," he says as I sit on a fallen log.

"It's fine," I say, though it isn't. "Getting used to the boots."

He crouches in front of me, ignoring my protest. "Boots shouldn't hurt. Take it off."

The cameras film. Elliott hovers nearby, excited at capturing wilderness adversity. I force a strained expression through gritted teeth, playing up the drama for the audience. "This is part of the adventure, right?" I say as I unlace my right boot, wincing as it pulls against tender skin.

Finn helps me remove the boot, then the sock. Three angry blisters have formed—one on my heel, one on the side of my foot, and another at the base of my big toe. All have burst, leaving raw, weeping skin.

"Why didn't you say something earlier?" Finn asks, his voice low enough that the microphones won't catch it.

"Didn't seem important."

He shakes his head, reaching for his pack. "Suffering isn't heroic, it's foolish." From his first aid kit, he produces antiseptic wipes, ointment, and moleskin. His hands are gentle as he cleans the wounds. The antiseptic stings, but I bite my lip to keep quiet.

And then the forest around me changes. The pine scent sharpens, the bird calls shift, and I'm not in Alaska anymore. I'm ten years old, sitting on a porch step, my small feet in my

grandmother's lap. My soles are raw and blistered from
following her through mountain meadows all day, basket in
hand, collecting herbs and roots for her remedies. The humid
Tennessee air, thick with the smell of honeysuckle and damp
earth, feels a world away from this crisp Alaskan air.

"Always tell me when your feet hurt, *niña*," she says, her
voice a low, comforting rumble as she applies a strong-
smelling, dark green salve to my blisters. "The plants will still
be there tomorrow." Her hands are dark and callused from
decades of digging in the earth, her knuckles gnarled, yet her
touch remains gentle as she bandages my feet with soft strips
of old cotton. The afternoon sun filters through the heavy
leaves of the grapevines trellised over the porch, casting
dappled shadows across the worn, grey floorboards.

"*Manzanilla* for inflammation," she says, her accent
wrapping around the Spanish word for chamomile like a
familiar hug. "*Calendula* for healing. Always respect the
plants that heal you, Magdalena. They give their life for your
comfort." I nod, breathing in the herbal scent that clings to
her clothes, a mix of dried herbs, wood smoke, and the faint,
sweet smell of the pipe tobacco she sometimes smoked in the
evenings.

"Lena?" Finn's voice pulls me back to the present. His eyes
are on my face, concerned. I've gone still, my breath caught in
my throat.

"Sorry," I say, blinking away the memory, the shift back to
the sharp Alaskan air almost dizzying. "It hurts."

He regards me longer than necessary, then returns to his
task. "These boots don't fit properly. The Second Chance
selection isn't perfect. We should have spent more time
breaking them in."

"Not your fault," I say. The words come without thought,
but I mean them. He tried to help me prepare. I rushed
through the shopping trip.

"We'll wrap them for now," he says, carefully applying moleskin to each blister. "At camp tonight, we'll air them out."

He glances up. "You'll want to change your socks more often going forward—midday at least. You can rinse a pair in the creek and let them dry overnight. Rotate through them."

I nod, watching his hands work. They differ from my grandmother's—larger, paler, but equally capable. I'm trapped between past and present—the girl who learned plant names in two languages, and the woman I became by burying her.

Elliott edges closer, camera rolling.

"All part of the experience, right?" I say with a camera-ready expression. "No pain, no gain."

Finn's mouth tightens, his gaze dipping for a beat—disappointment, maybe, or something close—but he says nothing. He finishes securing the moleskin, then pulls a clean pair of socks from his pack.

"Wear these," he says. "They're extras. Thicker. Will help with the pressure points."

"Won't you need them?"

"I've hiked these trails for twenty years. I came prepared." He hands them over. "Take them."

The socks are warm from his pack and soft, despite their practical nature. I pull off both boots, strip the damp socks from my feet, and replace them with his. They're a little big, but thick and comforting. I lace my boots loosely.

"Better?" he asks as I stand to test it.

It is. The thick socks cushion, and the moleskin protects the raw skin.

"Much. Thank you."

He nods once, then turns to the group. "Ten more minutes, then we move out. Five miles to lunch."

Five miles. Yesterday, that distance would have seemed

impossible. Today, despite the blisters and muscle aches, I am determined. I can do this.

As we hike, I walk behind Finn, observing how he navigates the trail. In my head, my grandmother's voice joins his explanations of the landscape. *Manzanilla. Calendula. Respect the plants that heal you.*

The trail steepens, winding through spruce and fir. Despite my foot pain, I notice details I missed yesterday— wildflowers between rocks, different bark textures, how certain plants grow together.

"What's that one?" I say at a switchback, pointing to a cluster of small white flowers.

Finn looks where I'm looking. "Yarrow. Good medicinal plant. Helps with bleeding, inflammation."

"*Achillea millefolium*," I say, the Latin name emerging unbidden, as familiar as my own. *Where did that come from?* At his sharp expression, I add, "You mentioned it yesterday, remember?" He hadn't, and we both know it. But he lets it pass, nodding and continuing up the trail.

By lunchtime, we've reached a high meadow covered with wildflowers. The view extends for miles—snow-capped peaks in the distance, the valley we've come from a green ribbon below. The crew films, capturing my communion with nature's majesty. I play my part, marveling with appropriate expressions.

When the cameras turn away, I sit on a sun-warmed rock, removing my boots to check the blisters. The moleskin holds, and Finn's socks have helped, but new hot spots form on my other foot.

Finn appears beside me, offering jerky and trail mix. "Change both socks," he says. "And drink more water. You're dehydrated."

"How can you tell?"

"Your lips are dry. Your pace is slowing. The way you hold your head."

"You observe me that closely?" I hadn't meant the question to sound personal.

His eyes meet mine, unwavering, giving nothing away. "Observing everyone is my job. Getting you all back alive is the goal."

"Alive seems like a low bar." I try to joke away the tension.

"In the wilderness, alive is the only bar that matters." He hands me a tube. "Lip balm. Has sunscreen in it." Our fingers touch as I take it, a brief warmth in the cool mountain air.

"Thanks."

He nods, then moves to check on the others. I watch him go, uncertain why I am so off-balance around him. He is unlike the men I know—no artifice, no agenda beyond keeping us safe and completing the job.

I apply the balm, change my socks, and eat despite my lack of hunger. Food is fuel out here, Finn has explained. The body needs energy regardless of appetite.

The afternoon brings steeper climbs and narrower trails. My blisters throb with each step, but I find a rhythm that reduces the pain—placing my weight carefully, adjusting my stride to suit the terrain. To distract myself, I catalog the plants we pass, remembering their names in English and Latin, sometimes in Spanish, when my grandmother's voice echoes in my memory. Fireweed. *Epilobium angustifolium*. Wild roses. *Rosa acicularis*. Lupine. *Lupinus arcticus*. Names my grandmother taught me before she died—before Momma said we had to leave that life, before I learned to erase that girl.

The mountain doesn't care who I pretend to be. Each step is real, each breath earned.

When we reach that night's campsite—another flat area near a stream, this one against a dramatic rock face—I am tired beyond anything I've known. Bone-deep exhaustion that

58

somehow seems earned. We've covered twelve miles of difficult terrain, climbed nearly two thousand feet, and survived. A wilderness success.

Setting up my tent goes better than yesterday. I only need Finn's help once, when a stubborn stake refuses to drive into the rocky ground. The cameras capture my improvement, Elliott's direction turning a simple task into a narrative of growth. "Perfect," he says after I secure the rain fly. "Now appear as if you're appreciating your accomplishment."

I do as instructed, though a flicker of pride surfaces. Yesterday I was helpless, today I am merely incompetent. Progress.

After camp is established, Finn gathers everyone for a refresher on wilderness cooking. "We'll be using the portable stoves again today," he says, demonstrating how to connect the fuel canisters. "Fire risk is too high for open flames." He shows us how to prepare a one-pot meal—dehydrated vegetables, instant rice, and preserved meat that I choose not to identify too closely. Despite its appearance, the result tastes good, or hunger enhances the flavor.

As we eat, gathered on rocks and logs, the crew shares stories of other remote shoots—a sandstorm that destroyed their equipment in Morocco, the flash flood that stranded them in Costa Rica, the angry moose that chased their sound guy in Canada. I stay quiet, listening. My world of controlled sets and catered lunches seems extravagant by comparison. These people routinely face difficult situations to capture images that others will view from comfortable sofas. There is authenticity in that which I've pretended to embody on screen.

"What about you, Finn?" one of the crew says. "What's the worst situation you've guided people through?"

Finn pauses, his face lit by our camp lanterns. "Winter of

'18. Group of four got caught in an early blizzard. We were three days from the nearest outpost when it hit."

We lean in, captivated. "Temperature dropped to negative twenty. Wind gusts of sixty miles per hour. Visibility perhaps ten feet. Had to dig snow caves and wait it out."

"How long were you stuck?" Elliott asks.

"Four days." Finn takes a sip of tea. "Used body heat to keep warm. Melted snow for water. Rationed the remaining food. When the storm broke, we had to navigate through three feet of fresh powder. Took us nearly a week to reach safety."

"Were you scared?" I ask, the question escaping before I can stop it.

His eyes meet mine across the circle. "Not scared. Respectful. Nature isn't malicious, only indifferent. Fear clouds judgment. Respect keeps you alert." It wasn't a platitude. For him, it was clearly a fundamental truth, something he lived by. Respect, not fear. I consider this as the conversation continues around me.

After dinner, I go to a flat rock near the stream to tend to my blisters. The evening air cools, the sky darkening toward night, stars appearing above. I remove my boots and socks, wincing as the fabric pulls from tender skin. The original blisters have improved thanks to Finn's treatment, but new ones have formed. I search my small first aid kit for something useful, finding only basic bandages that won't help much.

"Use this." Finn's voice startles me. He stands nearby, holding a small tin container.

"What is it?" I ask as he sits beside me on the rock.

"Wilderness salve. My mother's recipe. Works on blisters, cuts, burns, insect bites. Most things that happen out here." He opens the tin, revealing a greenish ointment that smells of herbs. The scent triggers another memory—my grandmother's porch, her aged hands, the precise way she measured dried plants into her mortar.

"What's in it?" I ask, steadying my voice.

"Plantain leaf, yarrow, comfrey, calendula. Other things."

Calendula for healing. I take the tin, keeping my expression neutral despite the turmoil inside. "Thanks."

He watches as I apply the salve to each blister, then helps me wrap them with clean gauze from his first aid kit. We work in silence, the stream gurgling nearby.

"Why'd you come here?" he says after a while, his voice low enough that the others can't hear.

"For my career. I told you that."

"There are easier ways to rehabilitate an image than hiking through the Alaskan wilderness."

I focus on wrapping my foot, avoiding his eyes. "I never agreed to hike. My agent said I'd stay at the lodge and take glamour shots with mountains in the background. Perhaps pose with a fishing rod near a stream. All staged."

"And you always do what your agent suggests?"

The question pricked at something raw. I lift my head, ready to snap at him, but the curiosity in his expression stops me. He isn't challenging me—just trying to understand.

"This time I did," I say. "I didn't have many options after the Martinez incident."

"What happened there? Rumors reached even here, but never the full story."

I pause. The official version is rehearsed—a momentary lapse in judgment, stress from a demanding role, sincere regrets. But here, miles from Hollywood, that version feels as useless as designer boots on a mountain trail.

"I lost my temper," I say. "The director, Martinez, kept pushing for more revealing shots, more skin, more sexuality in every scene. I'd spent years trying to break away from being the sexy vampire girl, and here was this acclaimed 'artistic' director doing the same thing, with fancier lighting." Finn listens, his face unreadable in the approaching darkness. "When I

61

objected, he said I should be grateful—that my appearance was the only reason I had a career. That I wasn't talented enough to make it any other way." I lower my head, staring at the mess wrapped around my feet.

"I threw my drink at him. It was in a crystal champagne flute, and it hit his face. Required twelve stitches."

"He deserved it," Finn says.

A surprised laugh escapes me. "That's not the usual reaction."

"What's the usual reaction?"

"That I'm unstable. Difficult. A liability."

He shrugs. "Standing up for yourself isn't being difficult. Though next time use plastic cups."

My laugh is real. "I'll remember that."

We fall silent. I should feel lighter, having said it out loud. But all it does is dredge up more—things I've buried for years. After Martinez, it wasn't only work that dried up. The decent guys stopped calling. The rest treated me like a walking head-line. Eventually, I stopped hoping for anything real. So, when that bouquet came flying at Timber and Kane's wedding, I flinched like it was a grenade. Because catching it would've meant I still believed in something. And I'm not sure I do.

In the distance, the crew retreats to their tents, exhaustion claiming even the most energetic. The stars fill the sky, bright against the darkness.

"I should sleep," I say, handing back his first aid supplies. "Early start tomorrow, right?"

Finn nods. "Dawn. Another big day ahead."

I stand carefully, testing my bandaged feet. The salve has numbed the worst pain. "This stuff works."

"Told you."

"Your mother taught you about plants?"

His face changes. "Some. But mostly it was May. She's the

closest thing to a doctor in Port Promise. Takes care of everyone with her herbs and salves."

The simple statement says volumes about their community. I want to ask more, to learn about this place where wilderness knowledge passes from person to person out of necessity, but his expression tells me to leave it for now.

"Thank you," I say. "For helping with my feet. And for not filming it for the show."

He appears surprised. "Some things aren't for cameras."

As I walk back to my tent, it strikes me—this is the most honest conversation I've had in years. No performance, no agenda, only two people talking in the darkness. My grandmother would have liked Finn, I think. They share the same competence, the same respect for the natural world, the same directness. The thought hits like a fist in my chest—this ache for a life I threw away.

In my tent, I remove the three bottles of skincare products from their protective wrap. The ritual comforts me—cleanse, apply serum, moisturize. Each step connects me to the controlled world I've left behind. But as I settle into my sleeping bag, my grandmother's voice speaks of plants and healing and respect. And I don't silence the memory.

Chapter Six

FINN

THE RAIN STARTS AT DAWN, fat drops drumming against my tent. Not unexpected for early summer in the Alaskan mountains. I've studied the weather patterns enough to know the signs—the drop in temperature, the wind shift, the way the clouds stacked up over the western peaks last night. I pull on my rain gear before stepping outside to assess our situation. The campsite is a slick mess—everything soaked within minutes.

Elliott emerges from his tent, rain pelting his inadequate jacket. "Is this going to be a problem?"

"Depends on how long it lasts," I say, assessing the heavy clouds. "Seems settled in."

"We're scheduled to film at the ridge overlook today. Can we still make that work?"

I nod. "We can reach it. Whether you'll make out anything through this is another question."

Slowly, the rest of the crew emerge, hunched against the rain, huddled together under a hastily erected tarp. No sign of Lena yet.

"Someone should check on our star," Elliott says, directing his attention to her tent.

I trudge across the soggy ground and call her name outside the tent flap. No response. I try again, louder.

"I'm awake," she finally answers, her voice rough with sleep. "Is it raining?"

"Has been for hours," I say. "We need to break camp soon if we're making the ridge today."

A rustle of movement, then her head appears through the tent opening. Her hair sticks out in several directions, her eyes puffy. When she registers the downpour, her expression sinks. "Seriously?"

"Welcome to Alaska," I say. "Breakfast in fifteen minutes."

No campfire this morning. We huddle under tarps, eating cold protein bars and passing around a water bottle. Lena sits silent, wrapped in her rain jacket, looking miserable but making no complaints. That surprises me. I'd expected dramatic protests about the weather, filming conditions, anything. Instead, she stares straight ahead, shoulders tight.

"We'll reach a more sheltered area by midday," I say as we pack up the soaked tents. "The forest is thicker there. Less exposed to the elements."

Elliott approaches with his clipboard sealed inside a plastic bag. "Change of plans. We want to capture Lena gathering edible plants in the clearing west of here before heading to the ridge."

"In this weather?" I indicate the driving rain.

"Perfect authenticity," Elliott says. "Survival skills in adverse conditions."

Lena joins us, her pack secured, rain jacket zipped to her chin. "What's the plan?"

"We'll start with the western field," Elliott says. "Need footage of you gathering plants."

"In a monsoon?"

"Dramatic backdrop," he says, unaffected by her skepticism. "The audience will love witnessing you persevere through natural challenges."

We set off single file through the glistening forest. Rain slickens every surface, making the trail treacherous. The crew struggles with their equipment, stopping every few minutes to wipe lenses and adjust protective covers. Lena walks directly behind me, following my footsteps with careful precision.

Through the trees, I can see the open expanse—a wide stretch of tall grasses and wildflowers, now bent low under the weight of the rain. No shelter here. We'll be completely exposed.

"Perfect!" Elliott declares, directing the camera operators into position.

Lena pulls her hood tighter around her face. "What am I supposed to gather in this?"

"I'll show you," I say, leading her into the grassland. Despite the downpour, several edible plants remain identifiable—wild onions, fireweed shoots, young ferns that will taste like asparagus when cooked. I point them out, demonstrating proper harvesting techniques while the cameras roll. Lena listens attentively, repeating my motions with unexpected skill. When she thinks I'm not looking, she names each plant under her breath as she gathers it. Not only the common names, but scientific ones.

An hour into filming, the rain intensifies. Water streams from the brim of my hat, and even quality rain gear has its limits. Lena's hands are red from cold and pruned from the constant wet as she digs for edible roots.

"We need enough for a proper segment," Elliott calls when I suggest wrapping up. "Twenty more minutes!"

The terrain slopes gently downward toward its northern edge, where the ground drops more steeply into a ravine. As we work our way in that direction, I keep a careful eye on our proximity to the edge. The rain has turned much of the field to slick mud.

"Stay back from the edge," I warn, aware the soil grows increasingly unstable. "Footing isn't reliable."

Lena nods, but Elliott directs her closer to get better framing against the dramatic backdrop of mountains disappearing into mist. "We need you right at this spot," he insists, pointing to an area near the edge where the ground drops away. "The composition is perfect."

Damn fool. She could fall. "That's too close!"

"It'll be fine," Elliott dismisses. "Quick shot, then we're done."

Lena steps carefully to the spot he points to, clutching her basket of gathered plants. The camera operator circles, capturing her from multiple angles while rain courses down her face. She forces a game expression for the shot, playing her role despite the miserable conditions.

That's when it happens. The rain-saturated soil gives way beneath her right foot. One moment she stands posing for the camera, the next, her leg disappears into a sudden depression, throwing her off balance. The basket flies from her hands as she pitches sideways, sliding toward the ravine edge.

I move without thinking, lunging across the muddy ground. My hand closes around her arm as her body goes over the edge, the abrupt weight nearly pulling me down after her. My boots dig into the mud as I brace against her fall. Lena dangles halfway down the steep incline, clutching my arm with both hands, her rain jacket snagged on protruding rocks. Below her, the slope grows steeper, dropping twenty feet to a rain-swollen creek.

"Don't move," I say, shifting my weight to better anchor myself. "I've got you."

Fear has wiped the camera-ready expression from her face. This is no performance.

"Pull me up," she says, voice tight.

I reposition, planting my feet more securely, and begin hauling her upward. The mud makes everything treacherous. *Damn it, she's slipping. Dig in. Pull. Harder.* Her rain-slick jacket slips in my grasp.

Elliott and one of the crew members hurry to my side, reaching down to help. Together, we pull Lena back onto level ground. She collapses onto the wet grass, breathing hard.

"Are you hurt?" I ask, checking for injuries.

She shakes her head, then winces. "My ankle twisted when the ground gave way."

I examine her right ankle, removing her boot. No obvious deformity but already swelling. A sprain, most likely, not a break.

"Can you walk?" I ask.

She tries to stand, pales, and sits back down. "Perhaps?"

"Got it all on camera," the second cameraman announces, a note of pride in his voice. "Amazing footage."

I turn to glare at him. "Put that down and help me get her back to level ground."

We create a makeshift seat with our arms and carry Lena away from the edge, back toward the more stable center of the meadow. The rain continues, soaking through layers of clothing.

"We need to get her dry," I say to Elliott. "The ridge is out of the question now."

He checks his waterlogged notes. "We can't fall behind schedule. Perhaps she could rest at camp while we—"

"No one's splitting up," I state. "And we're not making the ridge today. Not in this weather, not with her injured."

Elliott looks ready to argue, then sighs. "What do you suggest?"

I assess our surroundings, calculating. "There's an old Forest Service cabin about two miles from here. Basic shelter, woodstove. We can reach it before dark if we go now."

Lena looks down at her ankle, her expression full of doubt. "Two miles?"

"I'll help you," I say.

We fashion a quick compression wrap for her ankle using an elastic bandage from my first aid kit. Rain has plastered her hair to her face, water running in tracks down her cheeks. Despite everything, she manages a determined nod when I ask if she's ready.

With her arm around my shoulders and mine supporting her waist, we begin the slow journey toward the cabin. The crew follows, equipment protected as best they can manage, spirits dampened by the weather and change of plans. Progress is painfully slow. Lena tries to hide her discomfort, but each step on uneven ground brings a sharp intake of breath. The rain shows no sign of letting up, the temperature dropping as afternoon progresses. What should have been a forty-minute hike stretches to two hours.

When we finally hit the clearing with the small log structure tucked in the pines, the tension in my gut eases a fraction. The cabin stands weathered but solid, its metal roof keeping out the rain.

"Not exactly the Ritz-Carlton," Lena says as we approach.

"Better than a tent in this weather," I say.

The door creaks open to reveal a simple one-room shelter—wooden floor, small window, cast iron woodstove in the corner. Dusty but dry. The crew files in behind us, equipment cases creating an obstacle course in the limited space.

"Home sweet home," Elliott says, assessing our cramped accommodations. "Can we get a fire going?"

I ease Lena onto a bench along the wall, then check the

woodstove. "Wood's here, but it'll be damp. Might take time to catch."

While the crew organizes their gear, I focus on creating a fire. The cabin grows crowded as we all shed wet outer layers, hanging them from every available projection. Soon a thin line of smoke curls from the stovepipe, promising warmth.

Lena sits with her injured leg propped up, her face pale beneath smudges of mud. Her entire body trembles.

"You need to get out of those wet clothes," I say, digging through my pack for dry spares. "Your core temperature is dropping. Nothing to mess around with."

"I'm fine," she says, though her chattering teeth contradict her.

Elliott peers over. "We should capture this. The reality of wilderness survival."

"Camera stays off." My tone leaves no room for debate. "She changes in private."

The small cabin offers little in the way of privacy, but the crew moves outside to retrieve the rest of our gear, giving Lena a chance to change. I hand her my dry thermal shirt and a pair of wool pants. "They'll be too big, but they're warm," I say. "I'll step outside."

"Wait," she says, gripping my arm with icy fingers. "I can't … my hands won't work right." Her fingers have turned white with cold, unable to grasp the zipper of her jacket. The cold's hitting her hard.

"Let me help," I say, keeping my voice calm.

She nods, embarrassment coloring her cheeks as I help her remove the soppy rain jacket. Beneath it, her clothes have soaked through despite the supposed waterproofing. I work with forced focus, unzipping, unbuttoning, helping her arms free of the clinging, cold fabric. When necessary, she leans against my shoulder for balance, her skin cold where it touches mine.

"I don't need help with..." she gestures vaguely downward when we reach base layers.

"I'll turn around," I say. "But don't try standing on that ankle alone." I face the door, listening to the rustle of fabric, ready to catch her if she falls.

When the rustling stops, I wait until she speaks. "Okay."

I turn to find her swimming in my clothes. The sleeves hang past her fingertips, the pants roll multiple times at the ankle, but color is returning to her face.

"Better?"

She nods. "Thank you."

I help her back to the bench, examining her ankle again. The swelling has increased, skin taut and discolored.

"Bad?" she asks.

"Swollen," I say. "You'll need to stay off it for a day or two. Ice would help, but..." I gesture toward the rain-lashed window. "Cold compress coming up," I say, heading to the door.

Outside, rain continues to fall in sheets. I fill a small stuff sack with the cold rainwater, returning to place it on her swollen ankle.

"The crew?" she asks.

"Setting up tarps for the equipment," I say. "They'll be in soon."

She leans back against the rough wooden wall, exhaustion evident in every line of her body. "This isn't what I signed up for."

"No," I agree. "It's not."

Our eyes meet, and for a moment, something unspoken hangs in the air. "Thank you. For catching me."

"Part of the job."

"Is it?" A faint, tired smile touches her lips. "Hauling entitled actresses out of ravines?"

"Not usually included in the lodge owner contract," I

admit. "Nash handles the professional guiding. I'm the backup plan."

The stove generates actual heat now, filling the cabin with the scent of burning pine. Lena extends her hands toward it, palms out. "I've never been this cold," she says, her voice low.

"Wet cold is the worst," I say. "Especially when you're not moving."

"How do you stand living here?"

"You prepare for it," I say. "Respect it. The land isn't trying to kill you, but it will if you don't take it seriously."

She considers this, eyes on the glowing stove. "I never took anything seriously enough. That's what my grandmother used to say."

The mention of her grandmother registers. Another small insight behind the Hollywood façade.

The door bursts open as the crew returns, bringing a rush of cold air and the smell of rain. They crowd into the cabin, creating an instant chaos of wet gear and competing voices. Elliott reworks the shooting schedule, while the camera operators dry their equipment.

"We should check our food supplies. We might be here longer than planned if this weather holds."

Inventory reveals a solid amount—enough to last the trip when combined with what we'd planned to forage and catch along the way. The cabin has a crude rainwater collection system that will provide drinking water. Basic, but we'll survive comfortably enough.

As evening approaches, the rain transforms from a downpour to a steady drizzle. The crew sprawls across the cabin floor, exhausted from the day's ordeal. Lena remains on her bench, ankle elevated, wearing my oversized clothes. She's a far cry from the polished actress who arrived at my lodge days ago.

I sit beside her, offering a bowl of reconstituted stew. "Not gourmet, but it's hot."

She accepts it, a grateful look in her eyes. "I feel ridiculous."

"Why?"

She gestures down at herself. "Wrapped in clothes ten sizes too big, covered in mud, ankle swollen to twice its normal size. If people could see me now..."

"They'd find someone who hiked miles through a storm with a sprained ankle without complaining," I say. "That's not ridiculous."

Her head tilts, surprise flickering across her face. "Was that a compliment, Finn Hollister?"

"Observation," I say. "You're tougher than you let on."

"Don't tell anyone," she whispers conspiratorially. "It would ruin my reputation."

Despite everything—the rain, the injury, the change of plans—I appreciate this version of Lena. No performance, no calculated responses for the camera. A woman facing down the hard realities thrown at her.

Outside, darkness falls under the heavy clouds. The temperature drops, wind picking up to rattle the cabin's single window. Inside, the woodstove provides a bubble of warmth and light.

Elliott approaches with his ever-present clipboard. "We should discuss tomorrow's revised schedule."

"Tomorrow depends on the weather," I say. "And her ankle."

"We can work around both," he insists. "If the rain stops, we film her recovery narrative. If not, we capture the challenge of waiting out a storm. Either way, we need to make progress."

Lena says nothing, turning the empty stew bowl in her hands, her face drawn with fatigue.

"We'll assess in the morning," I say. "For now, everyone should rest."

Figuring out sleeping arrangements in the small cabin was

a puzzle. The crew spreads their sleeping bags across the floor in a tight formation. I insist Lena keep the bench, padding it with extra clothing to create a makeshift bed. I will take the floor nearby, within reach, if she needs help during the night.

As the others settle down, complaints about hard floors and cramped quarters filling the cabin, I step outside to check the weather one last time. The rain has stopped, but heavy clouds promise more to come. The air smells of wet earth and pine, crisp with dropping temperatures.

When I return, most of the crew has fallen asleep, exhaustion overcoming discomfort. Lena lies awake on her bench, looking at the low ceiling.

"How's the ankle?" I ask, my voice low as I settle into my sleeping bag.

"Throbbing," she admits. "But better than earlier."

"The cold compress helped. We'll try another in the morning."

She's quiet for a beat, then exhales. "I didn't expect to actually get hurt. Injury wasn't even on my radar." She glances at the ceiling, then back at me. "In Hollywood, everything's staged. Controlled. If someone's bleeding, there's a medic off camera." She touches her hair, limp and tangled from the day. "I knew this wouldn't be glamorous. I didn't realize how real it would get." Her eyes sweep over the cabin, confirming the crew is asleep before she leans closer. "You can't tell anyone this," she whispers, "but none of this is real. The blonde hair, the perfect skin. Hollywood magic."

That catches me off guard. "What do you mean?"

"My real name is Magdalena Reyes-Johnson. My grandmother Socorro taught me about plants—she was my dad's mother. My mom was raised to be a Southern belle, the kind of girl who made her debut in a white dress and pearls. Then she fell in love with a Mexican mechanic and got disowned before I was born." She gives a small, tired laugh. "The granddaughter of a Mississippi debutante and a Mexican immigrant doesn't sell as many movie tickets as blonde, blue-eyed Lena Kensington."

The revelation hangs between us in the quiet cabin. I see her differently now, catching traces of the woman she describes beneath the carefully constructed image.

"Magdalena suits you better," I say, my voice low. "Thank you for telling me."

She nods, looking both relieved and vulnerable. "Get some sleep," I add. "Things often look better in the morning."

"Even in Alaska?"

"Especially in Alaska."

She closes her eyes, pulling my borrowed jacket tighter around her shoulders. Within minutes, her breathing deepens into sleep. I remain awake longer, listening to the cabin sounds —creaking wood, soft snores, the occasional pop from the dying fire in the stove.

My thoughts keep returning to the moment at the ravine edge, her hand gripping mine, fear flickering in her eyes—raw, unguarded, and real. In that instant, all the Hollywood polish had fallen away. We were simply two people, one falling, one catching. Raw and real.

Through the cabin's single window, darkness presses against the glass. The rain has stopped, but clouds still block the stars. Tomorrow will bring challenges of its own—wet trails, slippery footing, and once the sun dries things out, the mosquitoes will return with a vengeance. Alaska's summer residents always make their presence known after a good rain.

I add another log to the stove and allow myself to sleep.

Chapter Seven

FINN

I WAKE before dawn in the cramped Forest Service cabin and stoke the small woodstove that barely kept us warm through the night. Through the single window, patches of blue push through thinning clouds. Yesterday's rain has passed, but the trail ahead will be wet and rough— mud, loose rock, and miles of it. Not great for a sprained ankle.

While the others sleep on the wooden floor around me, I slip out to scout the area around the cabin, searching for what I need. The streambed nearby has a stand of willows, their branches bending in the light breeze.

When I return, Lena is still asleep on the narrow bench where we made her bed. She looks better than yesterday—less like a drowned rat, not shaking from the cold anymore after that fall at the ravine.

Elliott crawls out of his sleeping bag, blinking hard, his hair a flattened mess on one side. "Schedule for today?"

"We need to reassess the situation," I say, my voice low, not wanting to wake the others. "The rain has made the upper trails dangerous."

"We need to keep moving," he insists. "The network has deadlines."

"The network isn't carrying anyone down a mountain with a broken leg." Elliott opens his mouth to argue, then closes it when I level my eyes at him. "Two hours," I say. "Everyone needs to eat and rest. Then we'll decide." He retreats to his corner of the cabin, muttering about production schedules and all the shots they were losing.

I set the branches I've gathered beside the stove. My mother started teaching me their uses when I was barely tall enough to reach them—how the pale inner bark could ease pain like aspirin, how the leaves made a poultice to bring down swelling. May built on that knowledge over the years, always saying, *"Our job is to remember the lessons."*

A soft groan draws my attention—then the sound of rustling. Lena is awake.

I move toward her bench, branches in hand. "Morning. How's the ankle?"

She pushes up on her elbows, hair tangled from sleep. Her eyes, rimmed with fatigue, still carry a clarity that catches me off guard. No performance. Just her. And despite looking like she's been through hell, there's a quiet strength I'm starting to recognize.

"It hurts," she says simply.

"Mind if I look? I might have something that could help." I hold up the branches. She hesitates, then shifts to make room for me on the edge of the bench. The scent of damp clothes and the faint trace of her shampoo hang between us.

She stretches out her leg. The ankle is swollen, purpled and angry.

"That's a nasty one," I say, leaning in without touching. "Can you move your toes?"

She does, with a wince.

"That's a good sign. Likely just a sprain."

I set the branches between us. "Willow bark eases pain—same compound as aspirin, but easier on the stomach. The leaves help with swelling."

"What are they called?" she asks, eyeing them.

"The Athabascans call it K'aii. Been using it for generations—long before pharmacies ever existed."

Her expression shifts—subtle, but not lost on me. "Does it actually work?"

"I wouldn't offer it if it didn't."

I strip bark while she watches, then crush the young leaves between two smooth rocks I'd gathered earlier. The rhythm of the task grounds me.

"Thanks for catching me yesterday," she says quietly. "At the ravine. I don't think I said that."

"Anyone would've done the same."

"Not everyone would've caught me in time."

"There's no need for thanks." I keep my hands busy, setting some bark aside for tea and handing her a smaller piece to chew. "My mom taught all six of us to live off the land. When I was five, she showed me which berries were safe—probably a hundred times before I got it right. Good thing she did. That knowledge saved my life a few years later."

"What happened?" Lena asks.

"When I was eight, I got separated from her while picking blueberries. I spent a night alone in the woods before they found me." I continue working the willow paste as I speak. "I was scared out of my mind, but I remembered what she taught me. I found shelter under a fallen log, made a bed from spruce boughs, and even ate some berries without poisoning myself."

"What happened when they found you?"

"My mother hugged me so tight I thought my ribs would crack. Then she made me recite every decision I'd made while I was lost, correcting the bad ones and praising the good ones." I smile at the memory. "After that, she took me out every weekend, teaching me more about survival. She said if I was determined to wander off, I'd better know how to survive."

"That knowledge stuck with you," Lena notes.

"It did. Years later, when my parents gave me the plot where Crystal Creek now stands, those skills helped me survive while building the lodge. I constructed it myself with help from my brothers. Took nearly two years of living in a tent on the property while we worked." The willow paste is ready. I hold it up. "This goes directly on the swelling. It will be cool at first, then warm."

She extends her foot, and I apply the paste with light touches, taking care not to press the tender areas.

"Your mother sounds remarkable," she says, watching my hands work.

"She was extraordinary." The 'was' hung in the air for a moment. "She taught all of us her wilderness knowledge, but each of us took to different parts of it. Kane, the oldest, runs a commercial fishing troller—supplies most of the county and probably half the restaurants in Juneau. Nash became the hunting guide. The twins, Rhys and Reid, handle the dock and the deep-sea charters. Eliza, my little sister, followed in Mom's footsteps as a teacher, though she's home full-time now with her child. I was always the plant kid."

"My grandmother was the same way," Lena says, her voice low. "She could look at a hillside and name every growing thing on it."

I glance up, nodding. "She taught you well."

"Some." Her voice grows guarded. "She made the best stew—wild onions and these little roots she'd dig up. I don't remember what they were called."

I wrap her ankle with strips of clean cloth, securing the willow poultice. "Some of that knowledge must be in your blood, then. That's a good heritage to have."

"I suppose it is."

"Now we need to prepare the tea," I say, changing subjects. "The bark needs to steep. The flavor isn't much better than over-the-counter pills, but it works equally well."

She makes a face.

"Doctor's orders," I add.

A small smile touches her lips. "Are you a doctor now?"

"In the wilderness, I'm close enough to one." I hand her the prepared bark chips to chew while I fetch water to boil on the woodstove. When I return, she's making a sour face but working the bark between her teeth.

"It's bitter," she says.

"Medicine often is," I reply.

Around us, the cabin starts to wake up—grumbles from sleeping bags, complaints about stiff backs and the cold floor. Elliott cuts through the noise, barking out ideas for the day's shoot.

I pour hot water over prepared bark in a metal cup and bring it back to Lena. "Elliot wants to capture your struggle with the injury," I say. "Talking about the best angle for sympathy."

"Of course he does." A bitter edge sharpens her voice. "Suffering sells to viewers."

"You don't have to give him what he wants."

She lifts her head, a question in her eyes.

"Your ankle needs rest. Forcing you to hike on it would make it worse. Better if you stay here in the cabin while I take the crew ahead to scout the trail. We would come back for you tomorrow when the swelling has gone down." I hand her the steaming cup.

"He'll never agree to that," she says. "The whole point is getting footage of me suffering."

"Let me worry about dealing with Elliott."

Something in my tone makes her study my face. "Why are you helping me so much?"

The question catches me off guard. Why am I? Two days ago, I'd seen her as nothing but a spoiled actress playing at wilderness adventure. Now... "Because you're trying harder than most would in your situation," I say at last. "Few people would keep going after what you've been through these past few days."

"I haven't been through anything compared to a real survivalist."

"That's my point. You're not trained for this kind of expedition, but you're still putting one foot in front of the other. That takes courage, and I respect that."

She looks down at the willow paste on her ankle, then back at me. "I'm so hungry I could eat pinecones right now."

The abrupt change of subject startles a laugh out of me. "It might come to that, but let's try something more digestible first." I reach into my pack and pull out an emergency ration bar. "This contains nuts, dried fruit, and honey. No cameras are watching us right now."

She hesitates, then takes it, turning the package over in her hands. "Why does Elliott's approval matter so much to you?" I ask as she unwraps it.

Her fingers still. "My entire career depends on this show being successful."

"One television show can't determine your whole career."

"This one can." She takes a small bite, chewing. "You already know what happened. Let's say I don't get a lot of second chances."

"By being shown as helpless in the wilderness?"

"By proving I can change and grow." She takes another bite, larger this time. "From Hollywood party girl to resilient survivor. That's the story they want to sell to viewers."

"But that's not your actual story, is it?"

Her eyes meet mine, something unguarded in them. "No one wants to hear my story."

The hell they don't, I think, a sudden sharp urge to protect that unguarded look in her eyes rising in me. Before I can speak, Elliott's voice cuts across the cabin.

"Lena? We need to get moving!"

I watch it happen—the mask slamming back into place, her vulnerability vanishing. "Coming!" she calls back, voice pitched in that too-bright tone she reserves for performances.

Elliott heads our way, his eyes narrowing as he takes in the scene: Lena's wrapped ankle, the willow branches, my proximity.

"What's going on here?" he asks, stepping into our corner of the cabin.

"I'm providing medical attention," I say, rising. "Her ankle's worse this morning than it was yesterday."

"We need to stick to the schedule," he says, tone already climbing. "The network—"

"The network isn't here right now," I cut in, turning to Lena, noting the shadows under her eyes, the way she's trying to mask the pain. Dammit, she's running on fumes and pretending she's fine. "I am. And I'm saying she needs a day off her feet to recover—really recover, not push through for some damn camera shot."

"That's impossible. We have to get usable footage today."

"You'll get footage of a medical evacuation if you push her too hard on that ankle."

Elliott's expression sours. "Lena, we need you out there. The viewers want to see you overcoming challenges, pushing through pain. It's the narrative we've established for the show."

I watch Lena's face, seeing the conflict play across it. Part of her wants to refuse, to listen to her body's need for rest. But the other part—the part tied to her career, her public image— is calculating how to give Elliott what he wants.

"I can hike today," she says, though her voice lacks conviction.

"No." The word comes out sharper than I intend. Both of them look at me in surprise. "This isn't a discussion," I continue, moderating my tone. "As the wilderness guide responsible for everyone's safety, I'm making a judgment call. Lena stays here today with a camp attendant. The rest of us will scout ahead and return tomorrow."

"You can't decide that on your own," Elliott sputters.

"Actually, I can. It's in the contract you had me sign. Safety decisions rest with the guide." I haven't read the entire document, but I'm betting Elliott hasn't either. "Page six, paragraph three, subsection B, if you want to check the paper-work." Elliott glowers, but uncertainty flickers in his eyes.

"Who stays with her, then?"

"Carlos," I say. He's the quiet one who seems more inter-ested in capturing nature footage than Lena's discomfort. "He can get footage of camp life, medicinal plant preparation, whatever narrative you need for the show."

Elliott's eyes narrow. "Carlos is one of my best operators. I need him on the trail with us."

"He's also the least intrusive with his camera work," I counter. "Lena needs rest, not someone hovering with a camera in her face all day." I keep my voice low enough that only Elliott can hear. "Unless you'd prefer I stay instead? Then you'd have no guide at all for today's shoot."

Elliott considers, clearly calculating which asset he can spare. Carlos is by the window, capturing the morning light filtering through the trees, focused on his craft rather than the drama Elliott keeps manufacturing.

"Fine," Elliott concedes. "One day. We'll get B-roll of the trail and wilderness shots today. Tomorrow she's back on her feet, adversity narrative in full swing."

Once he's stepped away to brief the others, Lena releases a

long breath. "How did you manage to convince him like that?"

"People like Elliott understand two basic languages—money and liability. I spoke to him in both."

She smiles, a real one that reaches her eyes. "Thank you for standing up for me."

"Drink your tea." I give a slight nod to the steaming cup. "And rest that ankle today. I'll have Carlos bring you food throughout the day."

As I turn to gather my gear, she catches my sleeve. "Finn?" I pause.

"Be careful out there." Something in her tone makes me look back. The mask is gone again, revealing something softer.

"I'm always careful."

Outside, I take a moment to breathe in the mountain air, centering myself. The interaction has left me oddly unsettled. Which version of Lena is real? The determined woman who's hiked miles on a sprained ankle without complaint? The vulnerable one who's shared a fragment of memory about her grandmother? Or the calculated performer who can switch personalities to please a producer? Maybe all of them. Maybe none.

As I organize the day's expedition, I plan what edible plants to show her when I return. Things that might trigger more memories of her grandmother's cooking. Plants that might bridge the gap between Lena Kensington, Hollywood actress, and Magdalena Reyes-Johnson, the woman she keeps hidden.

I'm not sure why it matters to me so much. But somehow, it does.

Chapter Eight

LENA

SOLITUDE IS a shock after days of constant company. The Forest Service cabin suddenly feels vast and empty, with only Carlos and me rattling around in it while the others are out there, facing who-knows-what on the trail. I've spent the morning on the narrow bench, my foot propped on a folded sleeping bag, watching dust motes dance in the shafts of sunlight that stream through the cabin's single window.

Carlos proves to be what Finn promised—unobtrusive. He moves around the cabin, now and then filming when I change my willow compress or sip the bitter tea, but mostly he stays focused on capturing time-lapse footage of clouds rolling past the window. Unlike Elliott, he never asks me to "look more pained" or "emphasize the struggle." The silence between us is comfortable rather than awkward.

"Finn left instructions for lunch," Carlos says around noon, the first full sentence he's spoken all day. He sets about heating water on the woodstove, adding packets from his pack with careful precision. The resulting meal is ... technically edible. Dehydrated vegetable-like substances and some kind of mystery meat that has me seriously re-evaluating every life choice that led me here. I eat by rote, more out of obligation than hunger.

"Not as good as when Finn makes it," I say without thinking.

Carlos nods. "He adds things. Plants from outside."

I glance toward the window. Beyond the glass lies a world of green I've been trudging through for days, seeing but not truly looking. A world my grandmother understood—plants that healed, nourished, protected. Knowledge I buried, along with my real name.

"Has the swelling gone down?" Carlos asks.

I rotate my foot. The willow poultice has worked better than I expected. The purple has faded, and I can move it with only moderate discomfort. "It's better," I admit. "His plant medicine works."

Carlos gives a knowing nod. "Finn knows things. Old things."

His simple words land harder than I expect. Finn knows things—more than survival skills or backcountry shortcuts. He moves through the world with a quiet kind of certainty, like he's reading a map I can't see. Like he understands things I've never learned to name.

As afternoon bleeds into evening, every creak of the cabin door makes me startle, half-expecting the steady rhythm of his boots. The silence that follows each time is a hollow thud in my chest. Missing him—actually missing that maddening, unexpectedly thoughtful mountain man—feels like stepping onto uneven ground I didn't know was there.

Three days ago, he was the grumpy guide I had to tolerate. Now I catch myself wondering what he'd say about the clouds stacking over the ridge, or which impossible-to-pronounce plant he'd point out with that maddening confidence.

When Carlos hands me dinner—another foil-packed science experiment—it's not the blandness that gets me. It's what's missing. The low hum of Finn's voice, the dry commentary, the way he made everything—somehow—feel like a story worth telling.

The stories that came with each meal, making even trail food connected to this place.

Night falls, the temperature dropping with the sun. Carlos banks the fire in the woodstove before retreating to his sleeping bag in the far corner. The cabin settles into creaks and whispers. I lie awake in the darkness, wondering where Finn is sleeping tonight. If he's looking at the same stars I can see through the small cabin window. If he's thought of me at all today. The idea that I want him to think of me sends a dangerous little thrill through me. This isn't in the script. Finn Hollister isn't supposed to matter. He's a temporary guide through a temporary experience—a means to rehabilitate my image, nothing more. And yet ... the memory of his hands gently wrapping my injury lingers. The quiet confidence in his voice when he stood up to Elliott. The way his eyes crinkle at the corners when he almost smiles. I pull his borrowed jacket tighter around me, breathing in the scent of pine and something uniquely him.

Sleep comes, and my dreams are filled with willows bending in the wind and strong hands guiding mine toward healing.

Morning arrives on a breeze of golden light and birdsong, the kind of scene that would look great on a postcard but forgets to mention the lack of indoor plumbing. I wake more rested than I have in days. The pain still hums beneath the surface, but at least it isn't screaming. I manage the wobbly shuffle to the outhouse without waking Carlos, using the cabin wall like a patient dance partner. He helped me the day before—bless him, and also never again—so the fact that I can pee without supervision is like a personal triumph. An unglamorous one, but I'll take it.

Back inside, I remove the willow poultice, marveling at how much of the swelling has subsided. The herbs have drawn out most of the inflammation, leaving only a dull ache. The trip to the outhouse confirms what I suspected—it's healing, though each step still sends a warning twinge up my leg.

Carlos stirs, checking his watch. "They should be back soon."

I nod, self-conscious about my appearance. I haven't seen a proper mirror in days, but there is grime on my skin and tangles in my hair. In Los Angeles, I wouldn't have let anyone see me like this—especially not a man whose opinion shouldn't matter but somehow does.

Using water from the rain barrel outside, I manage a makeshift sponge bath and change into my last clean shirt. I'm working a comb through the snarls in my hair when I hear voices outside.

The door swings open, and there he is—Finn, silhouetted against the morning light, his tall frame filling the doorway. Behind him, Elliott and the crew trudge up the path, looking more bedraggled than when they left.

"How's the ankle?" Finn asks, his eyes finding mine.

"Better," I say, surprised by the breathlessness in my voice. "Your willow remedy worked."

Something in his expression alters—relief, maybe, or quiet satisfaction. In three long strides, he's across the cabin, kneeling beside me. His hands are gentle as he inspects the injury, his touch sending a surprising jolt across my skin.

"Good," he says, his fingers warm where they touch. "You followed instructions."

"I can be taught," I reply, aiming for light humor but hearing something else entirely in my voice.

His eyes lift to mine, and for a moment, everything else disappears—the cabin, Carlos packing his equipment, the sound of the crew approaching. There is only Finn, his calloused hand cupping my heel, his eyes—*God, those eyes*—seeing straight through the Lena Kensington disguise to someone I'd almost forgotten existed.

Then Elliott bursts through the door, breaking the moment with his perpetual energy and clipboard. "Perfect timing!" he exclaims. "How's our star patient? Ready for a triumphant return to the wild? We're thinking a 'rising from adversity' narrative for today's shoot."

Finn stands, putting space between us that is both necessary and disappointing. "She can walk, but we take it slow," he says, leaving no room for debate. "And we change the route. No steep descents."

"But—" Elliott begins.

"Those are the conditions," Finn cuts him off. "Or we stay another day."

I watch the exchange with a newfound appreciation for Finn's authority. He hasn't asked my opinion, which would typically infuriate me, but somehow, I don't mind. He's protecting me—not because I'm a celebrity client, but because he cares about my wellbeing. A surprising warmth spreads through my chest that has nothing to do with the morning sun now streaming through the window.

"We leave in thirty," Finn announces to the room at large. "Pack up. Eat something."

As the crew bustles around gathering their gear, Finn returns to my side, holding out a familiar silver-wrapped bar. "Breakfast," he says. "Then we'll see how that ankle handles walking."

Our fingers brush as I take the offering, and I imagine the way his linger for a moment longer than necessary. "Thank you," I say, my voice low. "Not only for this. For yesterday. For making Elliott let me stay."

A hint of a smile touches his lips. "He's not the boss out here."

"No," I agree, locking eyes with him. "He's not."

The truth settles between us—out here, without Hollywood gloss or city comforts, the rules are different. The hierarchy is real. And Finn Hollister, with his competence and unwavering principles, outranks any clipboard-wielding producer by miles.

As I prepare to rejoin the expedition, lacing my boot over my tender ankle, I realize something has shifted during our day apart. The script I've been following—the one where I endure this adventure as a necessary career move—no longer feels right. I'm writing new pages now, and I have no idea where the story might lead.

Chapter Nine

FINN

THE AIR FEELS CLEANER after yesterday's rain. I shoulder my pack and watch Lena try to hide her wince as she shifts weight onto her injured ankle. When she bends to pick up her pack, I move faster.

"I'll take that," I say, lifting her pack before she can protest.

"I can carry my gear," she says, reaching for the straps.

I hold it away from her grasp. "Your ankle needs time to heal. No sense pushing it with unnecessary weight."

"I'm not an invalid," she insists, though she doesn't put full pressure on her injured foot.

"I'm not saying you are. But there's a difference between tough and foolish." I secure her pack on top of mine, adjusting the balance.

She stares at me, arms crossed. "You know, in Hollywood, we have these amazing inventions called porters. They carry things and don't make sarcastic comments."

"In Alaska, we call those bears. They carry things too, but mostly into their caves to eat later."

The corner of her mouth twitches. "Are you saying you're the bear in this scenario?"

"I'm saying porter service includes attitude in these parts."

Elliott approaches, clipboard in hand as always. "Are we ready to move out? We've lost a full day of filming."

"We're ready," I confirm, glancing at Lena. "Like I said, we take it slow today."

She nods, a grateful expression on her face, though I can see determination in the set of her jaw. Typical. Even injured, she's pushing herself harder than necessary.

The trail leading away from the cabin winds through dense forest before descending toward Crystal Creek—not the same one that runs behind my lodge but named for the same quality of usually-clear waters. Today, it runs muddy and swift.

Carlos eyes the rushing water. "Was it like this before?"

I shake my head. "No. It's risen since we crossed it a few days ago." The simple log bridge we built still spans the creek, but water now laps at its underside. What had been a gentle stream is now a churning current, swollen with runoff from higher elevations. "Snowmelt and yesterday's rain," I explain. "All that water works its way down from the mountains."

Elliott frowns at the torrent. "Is it safe to cross?"

I weigh our options. Going around would add at least a day, maybe more, with this terrain. The logs *look* stable enough. It's a risk, but losing another day is a bigger one for the production, and for getting Lena's ankle properly looked at, eventually. "We'll go one at a time," I decide. "Step where I step and use the guide rope."

I secure a rope across the makeshift bridge—three sturdy logs lashed side by side—and demonstrate the crossing, stepping on the center log while keeping one hand on the guide rope. On the other side, I tie off the rope to a tree and signal for the first crew member to follow. One by one, they make their way across.

As I help the next person over, I notice two of the cameramen moving into position—clearly intent on filming the rest of the crossings from both sides.

Lena watches, her jaw set with determination, though there's a flicker of apprehension in her eyes. When her turn comes, she moves with surprising grace despite her injury, testing each step before committing her weight.

"Not bad for someone who showed up in Alaska wearing designer heels," I say when she reaches my side. "Those logs are a long way from the red carpet."

"The red carpet is a glorified log with better lighting," she replies, brushing dirt from her palms. "And I walked it in six-inch stilettos after three glasses of champagne. This was practically a sidewalk."

"Ah, yes, the natural predators of Hollywood—champagne flutes and paparazzi."

"Don't forget directors with wandering hands," she adds under her breath. "I'm full of surprises," she continues, her eyes meeting mine. "Most of which aren't in my IMDB profile."

I turn to watch Carlos cross, the last in our group. His camera equipment is distributed between a large backpack and a waterproof case he clutches to his chest. The creek has risen in the time it took everyone to cross, water now splashing over the logs in places.

"Be careful with your footing," I call as he steps onto the first log. He moves slowly, the heavy pack affecting his balance. Halfway across, he adjusts the case he carries, his attention divided between his equipment and the treacherous footing.

"Carlos, focus on crossing first, equipment second," I call, not liking how the logs bob under his weight.

"Almost there," he replies, eyes still on his case rather than his feet.

"Eyes forward, Carlos," I say, my voice firmer. "The equipment can be replaced. You can't."

His head snaps up, but the movement throws off his already precarious balance. His right foot slips on the wet bark, arms windmilling as he fights to stay upright. The heavy pack shifts, pushing him off-center.

"Drop the case!" I shout, moving toward the bank. But Carlos clutches it tighter, unwilling to sacrifice his expensive equipment.

With a startled cry, he topples sideways into the rushing water, the case still clutched in his hands. *Damn it!*

"Carlos!" Lena shouts, already moving, a blur of motion toward the bank before I can even bark out a warning for her to stay put.

The current sweeps him downstream, the weight of his equipment pulling him under momentarily before he surfaces, sputtering and gasping. He keeps the camera case above water with one arm while thrashing with the other.

"Drop the case and swim to the edge!" I yell, running along the bank. But the shoreline quickly grows steeper, the rocks slicker from the recent rain. I can't get close enough to reach him.

"He's heading for the rapids," Elliott shouts.

"I can see that," I growl, searching for a spot to intercept him.

Carlos seems to realize the danger he's in. He releases the case, letting it dangle from the strap around his neck, and attempts to swim toward shore. But the current is too strong, pulling him toward a section of rapids thirty yards downstream. The crew races along the bank, shouting useless encouragement. I scan the terrain, calculating distances, trying to find a place where the creek narrows enough that we might reach him. But the bank grows steeper, the current faster. We'll never get to him in time.

Then Lena does something unexpected. "Give me your rope," she commands, her voice cutting through the panic.

Without hesitation, I hand her the coil of rope from my belt. Her fingers fly, a blur of motion, creating a complex series of loops and knots I recognize from my training but hadn't expected her to know. She isn't fumbling or guessing—these are the movements of someone who's tied these knots hundreds of times.

"Hold this end," she instructs, thrusting the rope back into my hands. Then she fashions a makeshift harness around her waist and chest. "When I give the signal, pull hard."

Before I can ask what she's doing, she scrambles down the bank toward a boulder jutting into the creek, upstream from the rapids. Carlos is getting closer—still fighting the current, still losing.

"Carlos!" Lena shouts. "Grab my hand when I say now!" She positions herself on the rock, secured by the harness she rigged earlier, and extends her arm over the water. As Carlos sweeps toward her, she leans out, far.

"NOW!" she yells.

Carlos lunges for Lena's outstretched arm. Their hands connect, fingers locking tight. His momentum nearly yanks her off the ledge, but the lines absorb the shock, tension snapping through the rig instead of her shoulder.

"Pull!" she calls to me.

I heave on the rope, muscles straining against the creek's pull, amazed at how effectively her knot system works. It gives us the mechanical advantage we desperately need. *Where the hell did she learn this?* With a final effort, we haul them onto the bank, both soaked and gasping.

Carlos collapses on the muddy shore, coughing up creek water, while Lena unwinds the rope harness with calm, efficient hands.

"That was..." Elliott begins, for once at a loss for words.

"Unbelievable," finishes one of the crew members, staring at Lena with new respect.

She shrugs, self-conscious as everyone gapes at her. "It was nothing. Basic rescue knots."

"Basic rescue knots?" I repeat. "That was a textbook swiftwater rescue harness. Where did you learn to tie something like that?"

She glances up, something vulnerable flickering across her face. "My grandfather. He was a fisherman." Then, as if catching herself revealing too much, she adds, her tone lighter, "Plus, I had to play a Coast Guard officer in that movie... You know, the one with the hurricane."

"*Rough Waters*," supplies Elliott. "You had, what, three scenes before your character got killed off?"

"Four," she corrects. "But who's counting?"

I study her, noting the way she avoids my eyes as she coils the rope with efficiency. Those weren't movie knots. Those were skills someone lives by, passed down, the kind that settle deep in your bones.

Meanwhile, Carlos has recovered enough to check his camera equipment, dismay tightening his features as water pours from the expensive case. "My footage," he moans. "Everything from yesterday is on these memory cards."

"At least you're alive to shoot more," Lena points out, wringing water from her hair.

"Elliott's going to kill me," Carlos groans, not seeing his boss standing three feet away, arms crossed.

"I haven't decided yet," Elliott says. "Depends on how salvageable those cards are."

I help Lena to her feet, noting she's re-injured her ankle in the rescue. "That was quick thinking," I say in a low voice. "You saved him."

"We saved him," she corrects, wincing as she puts weight on her ankle.

"You're hurt again," I observe.

"It's fine."

"It's not fine," I counter. "You've re-injured it."

She shrugs. "Better a sore ankle than a dead cameraman."

I can't argue with that logic. But I also can't ignore the fact that our journey suddenly got a hell of a lot more complicated.

We now have a cameraman with potentially ruined equipment, Lena with a freshly injured ankle, and a creek crossing that is growing more dangerous by the minute.

"We need to make camp," I announce to the group. "Carlos needs to dry out, and we need to reassess our route."

Elliott's face clouds. "We've lost a day. We can't afford another delay."

"We can't afford a drowned crew member either," I point out.

"I'm fine," Carlos insists, though his teeth are chattering from the cold water.

"You're not fine," I state. "You need dry clothes and a thorough check of that equipment. And everyone needs a break after that excitement." I turn to Elliott. "Besides, this gives you footage of a real rescue. Much better television than whatever you had planned for today."

That gets his attention. Elliott's expression changes from frustration to calculation. "You're right. We'll play up the danger angle. Lena rising to the occasion, saving a crew member. It's perfect for her redemption narrative."

Of course, that would be his takeaway.

While Elliott recalibrates his production plans, I help Lena to a fallen log where she can sit and elevate her ankle. The rest of the crew busies themselves setting up a hasty camp. Carlos strips off his wet clothes and wraps himself in an emergency thermal blanket, looking like a giant baked potato.

"I owe you," he says to Lena, teeth still chattering. "I thought I was dead for sure."

"Just doing what needed to be done," she replies, though I catch the smile she doesn't hide from the cameras this time.

I kneel beside her to examine her ankle again. Her boot is laced tight, but I can see the strain in the leather and the way she holds herself—favoring it more than before. The swelling's likely returned, undoing all the progress from her day of rest.

"We need to wrap this well and get some willow bark tea in you."

"Is that your solution for everything? Tree bark tea?" she asks, though there's no real bite in her words.

"Only for things that work," I reply, pulling medical supplies from my pack. "Can't fix stupidity with tree bark, though. Otherwise, I'd be making gallons for some of these crew members."

She laughs, a sound that catches me off guard.

"And here I thought you were all gruff mountain man with no sense of humor."

"I save it for special occasions." I unlatch her boot and ease it off. "Like near-death experiences and sprained ankles. Also, solar eclipses and when moose wander into my yard."

"Lucky me." She winces as I probe the tender area.

"Do the moose appreciate your humor?"

"Hard to tell. They've never left a Yelp review, but they keep coming back. Unlike my human guests."

"I can't imagine why," she deadpans, then hisses through her teeth as I find a tender spot.

"The good news is it's not worse than before," I tell her. "The bad news is we've undone most of the healing from yesterday."

She nods, accepting the diagnosis without complaint. "What's the plan now?"

I glance toward the creek, which continues to rise as we speak. The logs that had formed our bridge are now submerged, water rushing over them with increasing force.

"We're not crossing back soon," I say. "We'll camp here tonight and see if the water level drops by morning."

"And if it doesn't?"

"Then we find another way around," I say. "There's always another path if you know where to look."

While I wrap her ankle, Elliott approaches with his ever-present clipboard, now speckled with water stains from the creek. "Finn, I need to speak with you privately." His tone is serious.

I finish securing Lena's wrap. "Rest. Don't put weight on it." She nods, and I follow Elliott a short distance from camp. He glances back to make sure no one can overhear us.

"I got off the satellite phone with the network," he says. "They love what we have so far—especially the early footage of Lena struggling with the terrain. But they want more interpersonal drama."

I stare at him. "Someone nearly drowned today. That's not dramatic enough?"

"Physical danger is great television," Elliott acknowledges. "But viewers also want emotional stakes. They're suggesting we play up the tension between you and Lena."

"There is no tension," I say flatly.

Elliott's eyebrow lifts. "Really? Because everyone else sees it. The classic wilderness-guide-versus-city-slicker dynamic. The network wants more of that. Conflict, then gradual mutual respect, maybe even a hint of attraction."

"No," I cut him off. "I'm not performing for your cameras. I'm here to keep everyone alive and get them back. That's it."

Elliott sighs. "Look, I'm not asking you to fake anything. Don't hold back. If she annoys you, show it. If you're impressed by her, show that too. Be authentic, that's all."

"I'm always authentic," I say. "That's the difference between us."

He opens his mouth like he wants to argue but thinks better of it. "Just think about it. This show could bring a lot of business to your lodge. The right kind of tension on screen translates to bookings in real life."

He has me there, and he knows it. I need the money from this expedition, and future bookings would help keep Crystal Creek afloat. But I'm not about to manufacture drama for ratings, especially not at Lena's expense. She's been through enough.

"I'll be myself," I say at last. "Take it or leave it."

Elliott nods, knowing it's the best offer he'll get. "Fair enough."

When I return to camp, Lena has changed into dry clothes and is attempting to help set up the cooking area, hopping on one foot.

"Sit down before you fall down," I tell her, taking the pot from her hands.

"I'm not completely useless," she protests.

"I'm not saying you are. But you performed a water rescue with a bum ankle. You've earned a rest." I guide her back to the log. "Besides, I don't trust your cooking. You probably think pine needles are a garnish and tree sap is artisanal maple syrup."

She snorts. "Like you're Julia Child. I've seen what you call cooking. The MREs in your pack have expiration dates from the previous presidential administration."

"Those are collector's items," I defend. "And they taste better with age. Like fine wine or that weird cheese with the mold that probably costs more than my Polaris."

"Roquefort," she supplies. "And yes, it costs more than your Polaris."

"Luxury wilderness stew," I say, gesturing to the pot. "Only the finest dehydrated ingredients for Hollywood royalty. If you close your eyes and use your imagination, it's practically Spago's."

"If I close my eyes and use my imagination, I'm eating literally anywhere else," she counters, but takes the offered spoon. "How considerate," she drawls, but settles back onto the log. "Though after today, even tree bark sounds appetizing."

"Don't tempt me," I warn. "I know seventeen different ways to prepare bark as food."

"Of course you do," she laughs. Her laugh. I find myself listening for it. I shouldn't. For a moment, the tension of the day's events fades, and we are two people sharing a joke beside a creek in the wilderness.

But as I glance toward the rising water, I know our journey has become more complicated. The rain might have stopped, but its effects are still building as runoff continues to feed the creek. We are cut off from our original route, with a wounded team member and Lena's re-injured ankle to consider. For the first time on this trip, concern, sharp and unwelcome, pierces me. Not only about completing the journey, but about the responsibility of keeping these people safe —especially the woman who's revealed herself to be far more capable than anyone had given her credit for.

I watch Lena as she looks at the rushing water, her expression thoughtful rather than fearful. Not the Hollywood version, but the real woman. The one who tied those knots and pulled off that rescue like it was second nature.

She catches me looking and raises an eyebrow. "Something on your mind, Finn?"

"Wondering what other surprises you might be hiding," I say honestly.

Her expression closes, the vulnerability disappearing behind her mask. "I told you—I'm full of them."

What she doesn't say, but what I'm understanding, is that the biggest surprise is the real woman under the act. I need to figure her out.

Chapter Ten

LENA

"I NEED you to appear more terrified," Elliott demands, circling me like a vulture eyeing its next meal. "Remember, you're about to watch Carlos get swept away to his death."

"Except he didn't die." I cross my arms, struggling to balance on my good ankle. "He's sitting right there, eating beef jerky, and cataloging which memory cards survived."

The morning sun beats down on our makeshift camp beside the still-swollen creek. After yesterday's rescue drama, I'd hoped for a quiet recovery day. Instead, I'm being asked to recreate my "emotional journey" during Carlos's near-drowning—with more panic and less competence.

"The audience needs to feel the stakes," Elliott insists. "The network specifically requested more vulnerability in your journey."

"I tied a proper rescue harness and helped save a man's life," I say, my patience, already frayed, having snapped. "How is that not vulnerable enough?"

Elliott's expression shifts to the condescending smirk I recognize from countless Hollywood meetings. "Listen, we appreciate your quick thinking yesterday. Impressive. But it doesn't fit our established narrative arc."

"What narrative arc?"

"You know ... fish out of water, struggling city girl slowly learning wilderness skills." He gestures. "The audience is invested in watching you overcome your helplessness."

"I'm not helpless." The word grates, a throwback to a version of me I'm rapidly shedding. Or maybe, a version that was never me at all.

"Of course not." His patronizing tone makes my skin crawl. "But your character arc—"

"My character arc?" I repeat, heat rising to my face. "This isn't a scripted drama, Elliott. Carlos nearly drowned. I used skills I possess to help save him. That's the reality."

"Reality needs reshaping sometimes to fit audience expectations," he says with reasonableness. "Give me thirty seconds of looking terrified, perhaps call for Finn to help you, and we'll move on."

My fingers curl into fists at my sides. I take a deep breath, trying to contain the anger building in my chest. "No."

Elliott blinks, surprised. "No?"

"No reshoot. No pretending I was helpless when I wasn't." I straighten my spine, ignoring the throbbing in my ankle. "Use the footage you have or none at all."

A shadow falls across us. Finn stands nearby, arms crossed over his chest, observing our confrontation. I hadn't registered his approach, but judging by the tight set of his jaw, he's heard enough.

Elliott sees him too and pivots. "Finn! Perfect timing. Perhaps you can help explain to Lena why this reshoot is so important for the show's continuity."

Finn's expression doesn't change. "Sounds like she understands."

"Then you can explain why it's in her best interest to cooperate," Elliott tries again. "The network—"

"The network isn't here," Finn interrupts. "Lena made a choice. Respect it or don't, but we're not spending the morning staging fake distress when we have a real creek crossing to figure out."

Elliott's face reddens. "I need to remind both of you that you signed contracts. I have production requirements to meet."

"And I have safety requirements that take priority," Finn counters. "The water's still rising. We need to scout an alternative route, not waste time with theatrical performances."

Elliott shifts his eyes between us, aware he's outnumbered. "Fine. We'll use what we have." He stalks away, muttering into his satellite phone.

When he's out of earshot, I turn to Finn. "Thank you."

"Don't thank me yet," he says. "He'll find another angle."

"Why did you stand up for me?" I ask. "It would have been easier to let me handle it alone."

His eyes meet mine, clear and direct. "Because you were right."

The simple statement catches me off guard. In my world, people rarely take sides based on principle alone. There's always an agenda, an angle, a favor to be repaid later.

"And because we have bigger problems," he continues, pointing to the creek with a nod. "That water won't be crossable today, perhaps not tomorrow either. We need a new plan."

Predictably, Elliott slips his producer's mask back into place.

"Slight change of plans. Since we can't move forward today, we'll use the time to capture some background footage of camp life. Lena, I want to film you trying to start a fire, perhaps struggling with setting up your tent again." I open my mouth to refuse, but he's already moving on, directing the camera operators into position.

Something about his sudden shift in focus raises my suspicions. "I thought he'd push harder about the reshoot," I say to Finn.

"He's planning something," Finn agrees. "Stay sharp."

Throughout the morning, cameras follow my every move around camp, focusing on moments when my injured ankle causes me to stumble. Elliott directs with exaggerated patience, asking me to repeat simple tasks until exhaustion makes mistakes inevitable. By midday, frustration has me wound so tight I think I'll break. I retreat to a fallen log at the edge of camp, elevating my throbbing ankle while the crew breaks for lunch.

Carlos approaches, looking uncomfortable. "How's the ankle?" he asks, clutching his camera equipment.

"Been better," I admit. "How's the gear?"

"The memory cards survived." He checked over his shoulder, then lowers his voice. "But that's not what I wanted to talk about. I need to show you something." He seems so nervous that alarm bells immediately ring in my head.

"What is it?"

He sits beside me, opening his camera's viewing screen. "Elliott had me compile footage for a rough-cut last night. I thought you should see what he's planning to show the network."

The small screen flickers to life. Me, trudging through mud, face a mask of pain. My pain, yes, but amplified, isolated. Cut to me fumbling with the tent. He left out the part where I figured it out. Cut—dropping the pot. Once, after hours of exhaustion. Cut—slipping on a log. It's a carefully crafted ballet of my misery and incompetence.

"I don't remember being that bad," I say, frowning.

"You weren't," Carlos confirms. "He's cherry-picking

moments, editing them together out of sequence." He scrolls through more footage. "And this is how he's cutting yesterday's rescue."

The screen shows me looking panicked as Carlos falls into the water. Then Finn rushing forward, taking charge, directing me to hold the rope while he performs the actual rescue. The footage has been manipulated to make it look like I was a helpless bystander following Finn's instructions, not the person who created the rescue system.

"That's not what happened," I say, anger building.

"I know." Carlos looks miserable. "I was there. You saved me. But Elliott wants the narrative of you being helpless so your transformation later will seem more dramatic."

"Let me guess—the transformation happens when we reach the final filming location?"

He nods. "Where you'll become capable after Finn's expert guidance. Elliott calls it your 'wilderness awakening' moment."

"It's all a lie," I say, the realization sinking in like a lead weight. "This whole show is built on making me seem incompetent and then 'fixing' me."

"That's reality TV," Carlos says with a shrug. "They hired you for your name recognition and your recent reputation problems. It was never about showing the real you."

The words hit like a physical blow. In my desperation to salvage my career, I've allowed myself to become a caricature— the helpless city girl who needs a rugged mountain man to rescue her from herself. It's not only manipulative, it's insulting to everything my grandmother taught me, everything I've worked to become despite my constructed Hollywood image.

"I'm sorry," Carlos adds. "I shouldn't have shown you, but it didn't seem right."

"No, I needed to see this." I hand back his camera. "Thank you for being honest with me."

He nods, then returns to the main camp area. I remain on my log, watching the crew through fresh eyes. The cameras that have followed me aren't documenting my journey. They're manufacturing a story at my expense. I lift my eyes to the mountains beyond camp. My grandmother would be ashamed of me now—not for being caught in this situation, but for allowing others to erase who I am. For forgetting the strength she tried to instill in me.

The sound of approaching footsteps gets my attention. Finn appears, carrying a steaming mug that smells of herbs. "Willow bark tea," he says, offering it to me. "For the ankle."

I accept it, the bitter aroma triggering memories I've spent years suppressing. "Carlos showed me what Elliott's been doing with the footage."

Finn's expression darkens. "How bad?"

"Bad enough." I take a sip of the tea, grimacing at the taste. "They're making me look completely helpless. Even yesterday's rescue is being rewritten so it seems I stood there while you did everything."

He sits beside me, his presence solid and reassuring. "Does that surprise you?"

"It shouldn't," I admit. "But I thought this was supposed to help my image, not destroy the last shreds of my dignity."

"Reality TV has never been about reality."

"No, it's always been about creating whatever story sells best." My focus is on my tea. "And apparently, the story that sells is me being an incompetent princess who needs a big strong mountain man to save her."

Finn says nothing, but his silence feels supportive rather than judgmental.

"You know what's ironic?" I continue. "They're working so hard to create this narrative of me being helpless in the wilderness, and meanwhile, they're completely missing the real story."

"Which is?"

"That every summer growing up, I learned from my *abuela*—my dad's mother. She moved to Tennessee from the mountains of northern Mexico. Taught me how to find edible plants, how to treat a fever, how to read the wind. She was proud of who she was, even when I wasn't." I pause, the words catching at the back of my throat. "For a long time, I was ashamed of that part of me. Her accent. Her remedies. The way she made something from nothing. I wanted to fit in, to be shiny and smooth. So, I let Hollywood gut me and rewrite the rest."

My eyes lift to his. "But out here ... with no one watching, I keep hearing her voice again. And I think—I think you can try to bury who you are, but it doesn't stay buried. Not forever."

The admission hangs between us. I've told no one in Hollywood about those summers, about the knowledge I deliberately buried to fit the image my agents created.

"Why hide it?" Finn asks, his voice low.

"Because no one sees it," I say, my voice soft. "I've got blonde hair, blue eyes—on paper, I'm exactly what they want. Marketable. *Safe.* No one questions my background because I don't look like someone with roots that stretch deep into a different culture." My attention returns to my tea, willing the words to come out right. "But inside? I'm not simple. I'm not polished. I'm a girl who learned to crush herbs in a stone bowl and tie knots that hold through a storm. I'm half a world no one sees—and sometimes I wonder if I buried it so well that I forgot how to claim it."

Finn is silent for a long moment. "So what are you going to do about it?"

His simple question hits me with unexpected force. *What*

am I going to do? Keep fading into the version of me that sells —or finally show the one who survived?

"I don't know yet," I answer, my voice honest. "But I'm done letting them manipulate me."

His expression shifts—just a trace of a grin. "Good."

That night, long after the camp has fallen silent, I lie awake in my tent, thinking about choices and consequences. The satellite phone is with Elliott—I could ask to use it, call my agent, demand extraction from this disaster, fight the narrative he's building. But running away solves nothing. It only confirms what they already believe—that I'm a diva who can't handle challenges.

Sleep eventually claims me, pulling me into dreams filled with my grandmother's voice. We're in her small garden behind the house in Tennessee, her hands guiding mine as we crush herbs in a stone mortar. *Estas plantas son tu herencia, Magdalena.* These plants are your heritage. Knowledge passed from mother to daughter for generations. *Never forget who you are.*

I wake to shouting. For a disorienting moment, I think I'm still in my grandmother's garden, but the voices outside my tent are urgent, panicked. Nothing like the peaceful morning I'd expected.

"The water's rising too fast!" someone yells—Carlos, I think.

"Get everything to higher ground now!" Finn's voice cuts through the chaos, commanding and tense in a way I haven't heard before.

I scramble out of my sleeping bag, wincing as pain shoots through my ankle. When I unzip my tent, the scene that greets me steals my breath. Where our camp had been is now a churning pool of muddy water. The creek has swollen during the night, breaking its banks and advancing toward our tents with frightening speed. The crew scrambles to save equipment, their movements frantic in the dim pre-dawn light.

And then I see it—hear it first, a low rumble like an approaching freight train—the massive wall of muddy water and debris tearing its way downstream toward us. Tree trunks, branches, what looks like shattered pieces of a bridge, all churning in a surge that will obliterate everything. My blood runs cold.

"Flash flood!" Finn shouts, his eyes finding mine across the chaos, stark with urgency. "Get to the ridge!"

I have seconds to decide—my pack is still in the tent, and the water is already lapping at the entrance. The debris wall is maybe thirty seconds from hitting camp. My ankle screams in protest as I turn to grab my pack. Knowledge is heritage. Identity is power. And sometimes, survival depends on knowing what to leave behind.

Chapter Eleven

FINN

THE FLASH FLOOD tore through camp, leaving a wreck. Everyone made it to the ridge—that's something. Most of our gear didn't. Some tents ripped to shreds, cameras soaked, food gone. I stand at the edge of the devastation, tallying the damage while the crew pokes through the mud for anything worth saving. Not much left.

"We're down to half rations," I announce, finishing my inventory. "Four tents saved out of seven, most sleeping bags intact but soaked. One satellite phone still working, and our water purification equipment survived."

Elliott paces, his clipboard abandoned in favor of his satellite phone. "The network is going to lose their minds when they hear we're behind schedule."

"The network will be more concerned about keeping their star alive," I counter, my attention on Lena across the clearing. She works alongside Carlos, dabbing water from soaked camera cases, her movements quick and efficient, removing memory cards and batteries from the equipment that might be salvageable.

"At least we got incredible footage of the flood," Elliott

says, already focused on ratings. "Lena's reaction when she saw that wall of debris coming was priceless. Pure terror, what we needed."

I turn to face him. "You understand we're in actual danger here, right? This isn't a performance."

He has the decency to look embarrassed. "Of course. Safety first. But we might as well capture interesting footage while we're at it."

We move toward the center of our makeshift camp, grateful no one had been inside the tents when the flood hit. The ground is saturated now, which eliminates the risk of wildfire—good, because we'll need heat fast. Carlos and Javier shake out wet sleeping bags, searching for a place to dry them. We have to get a fire started—the sooner we generate enough heat, the faster we can dry what's left of our gear. With eight people and only four shelters, we'll need to double up tonight, relying on body heat to keep warm when the temperatures drop.

My attention drifts to Lena as she checks the tent poles, her hands now steady and sure, making quick work of the task. There's no hesitation, no need to prove anything—quiet skill and focus. The realization hits me hard—how much I've misjudged her. Not because she put on an act, but because I was too damn stubborn to see past the Hollywood bullshit.

Dave's shout slices through the clearing. "Hey, boss! Found a beehive the flood knocked down."

"Stay clear of it," I call back, moving toward him. "If the colony survived, they'll be aggressive."

Dave gives a nod but leans closer. "Think there's any honey? I've seen survival shows where they—"

"Dave, back away. Now." Too late. His startled yelp echoes through the trees as he stumbles back, swatting at his arms and neck. "They're on me! Get them off!"

I break into a run as he collapses to his knees, welts

blooming across his skin. Carlos throws the med kit my way. I tear it open and curse. No EpiPen. No antihistamines. Gauze, antiseptic, aspirin. The backup kit. The other one went downstream. Dave's breath comes fast, his skin flushed and swelling.

"I saw plantain by the creek," Lena says, her voice cutting through the rising panic. "I'll get it." Before I can even process what she's said, let alone give an okay, she's moving. Despite that ankle, she's running—favoring the leg, yeah, but fast. Plantain? How the hell does she know about plantain?

The rest of us huddle around Dave, trying to keep him calm. She returns minutes later, breathless, muddy, and clutching a bundle of broad green leaves.

"Here it is," she says, dropping to her knees. "I need water and a cloth. Honey if we have it."

Carlos passes her a canteen. Elliott pulls a bandana from his pocket. Someone hands her a honey packet from the salvaged food rations. She crushes the leaves between two flat rocks, adding water and honey until it becomes a thick green paste.

As she works, I can't help thinking the tin of salve May gave me—the one that worked wonders on bites—would've been perfect for this. But it's long gone, swept away with the rest of our gear in the flood.

She applies the paste to Dave's arms and neck, her movements deliberate and sure. "This should pull out the venom and calm the inflammation. Keep him upright and monitor his breathing."

Dave flinches at first but then lets out a shaky breath. The panic in his eyes fade. The welts stop growing. His breathing evens out.

"Thank you," he wheezes, his attention riveted on Lena with new respect.

"Don't thank me yet," she says, preparing a fresh batch of the poultice. "We need to leave this on and make you a tea from the same plant. The reaction could return if we're not careful."

While she works, I check Dave's pulse and airways, confirming what's already clear—he's out of immediate danger. The crew watches in silent amazement as Lena, covered in mud from the flash flood and working with primitive tools, continues to treat him with calm, steady hands.

As we lift Dave, Elliott regards her. "Where'd you learn to do all that?"

Lena doesn't hesitate. "Research for the role," she says with an airy shrug. The actress is back. Smooth deflection. But why deflect now, after yesterday?

As we haul Dave to one of the tents, I look over at her. "You know," I say, "you don't look like someone with a sprained ankle."

She doesn't lift her eyes. "Adrenaline's a hell of a drug."

I nod, but I'm not thinking about the adrenaline. I'm thinking about her—the Lena beneath the image, the one who ran on an injured leg to grab leaves she remembered seeing in a patch of mud. The one who moved like a woman trained by someone who loved her enough to pass down generations of knowledge.

"The apple doesn't fall far from the tree, huh?" I offer, trying to make it easy.

She huffs a soft laugh. "Oh, my mother was useless in a crisis. Perhaps that's why Memaw spent so much time with me. She wanted someone to carry it on."

"She picked the right girl."

She regards me, then turns away, busying herself with the poultice again. I let it go. For now.

Elliott's voice breaks the quiet. "Finn! How long before Dave can travel? We need to get moving if we're going to make up lost time."

I finally turn on him, the anger I've been swallowing since

the ravine incident boiling over. "The only reason we've 'lost time,' Elliott, is because you wouldn't listen to me. Lena's ankle, the flash flood, all of it—this entire mess is on you because you had to get your perfect shot," I say, leaving no room for argument. "We're staying put."

Elliott has the decency to flush, grumbling as he stalks away.

With Dave stable and the immediate crisis over, we turn our attention to making camp functional. The sun hangs low, casting long shadows across the clearing. Time to prioritize what matters most.

"First priority is fire," I say, gathering the driest kindling I can find. "Then we pack the remaining food and secure the perimeter."

Lena kneels beside me, arranging tinder. "I'll help. Once we get it going, we can start drying the sleeping bags."

Our fingers work in tandem, building a small tepee of twigs and strips of birch bark I'd collected earlier. Within minutes, we have a spark caught and nursed into a flame. Lena feeds it with patience, adding fuel with precision, surprising me with her skill.

"Girl Scouts," she offers, seeing my expression. "Plus, I've watched a few survival reality shows."

Carlos and Dave construct a makeshift rack near the growing fire, where saturated sleeping bags hang steaming in the heat. Elliott directs a camera operator to capture it all, the lens focusing on Lena's determined expressions as she sorts through the supplies, separating what can be saved from what cannot.

I turn back in time to see Lena kneeling by the stream, washing her hands with care. I join her, collecting water. "Dave's resting easier. Color's back."

She nods. "Keep giving him the tea. It'll help."

"I will. And thank you."

She shrugs. "Right plants. Right place."

"No," I say, my voice gentle. "That was you. That was knowledge."

She meets my eyes at last. "My grandmother always said the plants know what to do. You have to listen."

"Smart woman."

Lena's lips curve. "The smartest. But the world I chose didn't value her kind of wisdom."

"Perhaps you chose the wrong world."

She doesn't respond at first, but then, in a low voice, she says, "Perhaps I did."

A silence falls between us, warm and weighted. She lifts her hand from the water, droplets catching the sun. Without thinking, I catch one with my thumb. Her breath hitches. Our eyes meet and hold.

"Finn," she whispers.

"Lena! We need you for the recovery scene!" Elliott again, with his impeccable timing.

She pulls her arm away, rising with a wince.

"You should rest that ankle," I say.

"Some things are worth the pain," she says, brushing my hand as she walks past.

I watch her cross the clearing. The crew nods as she passes. Even Elliott regards her differently. Something changed today. Not in them. In her. The mask isn't gone, but it's thinner now. And I wonder if what's underneath might be worth risking everything for.

As I prepare our reduced rations, my attention keeps sliding her way. Once, our eyes meet across the camp, and she doesn't look away. A slight upturn tugs at the corner of her mouth—not the polished, on-cue smile she gives the camera, but something smaller. Quieter. *Real.* Warmth meant only for me. The realization hits with a dangerous jolt.

This expedition has enough complications without adding

117

unexpected feelings for a woman who lives in a different world. A woman who will return to Hollywood when this is over, slipping back into the role society expects her to play. Yet as she helps distribute the meal, stopping to check on Dave with concern, I find it difficult to remember why maintaining professional distance matters. Especially when her fingers brush mine as she accepts her portion, the contact brief but electric.

"Careful," she says. "It's hot." Her words could apply to more than the food and judging by the way her eyes linger on mine, she knows it too.

The sun drops behind the treetops, washing the sky in rust and fading gold. Around our fire, the sleeping bags finish drying, the last bit of steam gone from the fabric.

Elliott stands, clipboard in hand, assessing our four remaining tents. "Carlos, Dave and I will bunk with a crew member in three tents." His eyes move meaningfully between Lena and me. "That leaves you two in the fourth."

Lena rises from beside the fire, where she's been checking the dried sleeping bags. "You're sure that's the best arrangement?"

Elliott's lips curl into a smirk that doesn't reach his eyes. "Absolutely. Makes the most logistical sense." The way he says it makes it clear that logistics are the last thing on his mind. I recognize the calculation instantly. The casual suggestion, the manufactured proximity—it's the tension he mentioned wanting to "play up" for the cameras. The network's grand plan unfolding in real time.

"I'm fine with it if Finn is," Lena says, turning to me. "You're the wilderness expert, after all."

The crew exchanges knowing glances. Carlos finds his bootlaces fascinating. The others busy themselves with equipment, but not before I catch their raised eyebrows.

"Fine by me," I say, keeping my voice neutral. "We need to conserve body heat."

Elliott cannot hide his triumphant grin. "Perfect. The wilderness survival expert and the star sharing shelter. Very ... authentic."

Lena gives him a cool stare. "Practical, Elliott. The word you're seeking is practical."

But Elliott's expression tells me everything I need to know. This is what he wanted—physical proximity creating emotional stakes, the tension he promised the network. In his mind, the ratings are already climbing.

Night falls with unnerving speed across our makeshift camp. Stars pierce the darkness overhead—brilliant pinpricks through black velvet, untouched by city lights. The fire crackles, casting long shadows across tired faces as we finish our meager dinner and administer Dave's medicine.

"They all think we're waiting until they sleep before slipping away together," she says, voice low enough that only I can hear.

I poke the dying embers. "Elliott probably has a camera ready."

Her laugh comes soft in the darkness. "Wouldn't be the first time someone tried to manufacture a scandal around me."

"Is that what this is? Manufacturing a scandal?"

She meets my eyes, the firelight casting her features in gold. "No. This is surviving."

She registers my expression. "Stop looking like I surprise you by breathing. I'm capable of more than any of us thought, me included."

"I could sleep by the fire," I offer. "You don't have to sacrifice your privacy."

"My privacy?" The bitter edge in her laugh surprises me. "That commodity got sold years ago."

One by one, headlamps extinguish as people retreat to their assigned shelters, bodies craving rest after the day's trials. Professional boundaries be damned. We're in this situation together, and with each passing day, Lena Kensington is making it harder for me to remember why getting involved would be a terrible idea. The worst part? I'm starting not to care.

Chapter Twelve

LENA

Darkness in Alaska feels alive—a breathing, pulsing thing that presses against our tent walls. No streetlights or city glow to dilute it. Pure, undiluted night. I lie next to Finn, acutely aware of every inch of space between us, listening to his measured breathing.

The tent Elliott assigned us—no doubt with a leering internal chuckle—barely fits two people. With our sleeping bags still damp from the flood, we've spread them beneath us like makeshift, lumpy mattresses, huddling under scratchy emergency blankets that are clearly more 'emergency' than 'blanket' for actual warmth.

Finn's restlessness is palpable. I swear I could hear his thoughts churning.

"Stop thinking so loudly," I whisper, breaking the silence. "I can practically hear you cataloging all the disasters that might strike next."

"Force of habit," he replies, his voice low in the darkness. "Someone has to prepare for the worst."

"Mmm, and that someone is always you, isn't it?" I say, understanding rather than mocking. Men like Finn carry the weight of others' safety on their shoulders like it's nothing. Like it's expected.

I turn onto my side to face him, though I can barely make out his silhouette in the darkness. My body aches in places I didn't know could hurt, muscles protesting against another day of pushing limits.

"Get some sleep," he tells me. "Tomorrow won't be easy."

"None of the days have been easy," I counter. "But I'm still here."

"You are," he acknowledges, something like admiration in his voice. "Most Hollywood types would have called for emergency evacuation after the first blister."

I laugh, the sound filling our small shelter. "I'm made of tougher stuff than you thought."

"Yes, you are," he says, and the simple affirmation warms me more than it should.

The wind picks up suddenly, rattling the tent walls, and a fresh wave of cold air sweeps under the rain fly. An uncontrollable shiver wracks me.

"Cold?" Finn asks.

"Freezing," I admit, drawing my knees closer to my chest, trying to preserve what little warmth I have.

He hesitates for a heartbeat. "Body heat helps. Basic survival." Right. Basic survival. Like this whole ridiculous, freezing night is another entry in his wilderness manual. And I'm the shivering specimen. I consider his offer, weighing my rapidly dwindling professional boundaries against the very real possibility of turning into a Lena-cicle by morning. Survival, and the thought of his solid warmth, wins. I turn my back to him in silent invitation.

The mattress shifts as he moves closer. Then his chest presses against my back, his arm draping cautiously over my waist. Heat radiates from him, seeping through our layers of clothes and into my chilled skin.

"Better?" he asks, his voice strangely uncertain.

"Much," I whisper, relaxing into the unexpected comfort of his body. I've shared beds with costars during press tours, huddled with strangers in crowded subway cars, but nothing feels quite like this—Finn's solid presence against my back, his breath warming the nape of my neck. His nearness doesn't feel intrusive, but protective. Safe.

My thoughts drift to our larger situation. "Do you think we should continue to Painted Peaks?" I ask after a companionable silence. "After everything that's happened, maybe we should head back to the lodge instead."

I feel his chest expand as he considers his answer. "Turning back might be the safer option. But..."

"But our careers both depend on getting there," I finish for him, voicing what we both know. "You need the money from this production. I need the reputation rehabilitation."

"Yes," he admits. "And there's another route we can take. Longer, but safer."

"Then we push on," I say with quiet determination. "We didn't come this far to give up now."

I shift slightly, seeking a more comfortable position—and freeze when I feel something hard press against my thigh.

"Seriously?" I whisper, half-amused, half-embarrassed. The wilderness survival expert is still a man, after all.

His laugh rumbles through his chest against my back as he shifts to reach into his pocket. "Not what you think." He pulls out something small and metal. "Just survival gear."

"Of course," I say, embarrassment washing through me. "What else would it be?"

He clicks it on, and a narrow beam of light cuts through the darkness, creating strange shadows on the tent ceiling. "Thought you might want proper lighting for once, instead of moonlight."

I turn my head slightly. "What do you mean?"

"I've seen you doing your skincare routine," he says, and I can hear the smile in his voice. "No judgment. I thought you'd appreciate better lighting."

Instead of embarrassment, I feel a strange relief. One less secret. He doesn't comment on how I look without it, which is almost more unsettling than if he'd made a crack. "Well, it doesn't matter now. I lost all my products in the flood—they weren't in the bag I managed to save."

The admission stings more than it should—those small bottles were talismans, my armor from that controlled Hollywood life.

"Not all of them," Finn says, reaching toward the corner of the tent. He rummages briefly before pulling out a small, familiar tube. "Found this while we were salvaging gear. Thought it might be important to you."

In the harsh beam of the flashlight, I recognize my tinted sunscreen with SPF 50—the one product he'd insisted I bring. Something catches in my throat at the small gesture.

"You saved this?" I ask, taking the tube from his hand like it's something precious.

"It's important," he says simply.

Gratitude, sharp and overwhelming, punches through my carefully constructed defenses. He saved my sunscreen. It's ridiculous, and yet ... it means something. Before I can second-guess it, before the Lena Kensington filter kicks in, I turn fully in his arms, cup his face with both hands—his skin surprisingly rough against mine—and plant a quick, clumsy kiss on his lips. It's over in a second—impulsive, chaste, nothing like the calculated kisses I've shared on camera.

I pull back, suddenly realizing what I've done. "Sorry, I—"

"Don't apologize," he whispers.

We're face to face now, my hands still framing his bearded cheeks. His eyes reflect the small beam of light, studying me with an intensity that sets my pulse racing. I can feel his heart beating against my chest, matching the rhythm of my own. Time seems to stretch, thick with possibility. My thumb brushes across his cheekbone, feeling the rough texture of several days' growth.

"Finn?"

"Yes?" His voice sounds rougher than before.

"I—" I start, unsure what I even want to say, but I'm interrupted by shouting outside.

"Movement in camp! Everyone up!"

The moment shatters. Finn is already reaching for his boots, training taking over. I move with similar urgency, tucking the rescued sunscreen into my pocket like a treasure.

"What is it?" I whisper, fear tightening my chest.

"Not sure," he says, pulling on his jacket. "Stay here until I check."

"Not a chance," I counter, already lacing my boots. "We stick together."

He looks like he wants to argue but seems to recognize the determination in my voice. "Fine. But stay behind me."

As we prepare to exit the tent and face whatever new danger awaits, I catch his arm. "Finn, about what happened—"

"Later," he promises, his eyes meeting mine with unexpected warmth. "We'll figure it out later."

I nod, but the brief kiss lingers between us like an unfinished sentence as we zip open the tent and step into the noise and confusion of our makeshift camp.

The moment we exit, disarray greets us. Headlamps swing wildly in the darkness, creating disorienting beams of light that cut through the night. Elliott, clad in a ridiculous red thermal onesie, stands in the center of camp, pointing frantically toward the tree line.

"Over there!" he shouts. "I saw something moving!"

The crew clusters together, brandishing whatever

makeshift weapons they've found—a hiking pole, a frying pan, a tripod. Carlos looks absurd wielding his camera like a weapon, as if he plans to document whatever is about to eat us.

Finn's expression shifts to something I recognize—focused, alert, but not panicked. He scans the darkness methodically, one hand reaching back to position me behind him.

"Everyone calm down," he commands, his voice cutting through the noise. "Elliott, what exactly did you see?"

"Something big," Elliott says, his voice higher than normal. "Moving between the trees. Could be a bear."

Dave, still recovering from his bee stings, clutches his sleeping bag around his shoulders like a cape. "I heard branches breaking. Something's definitely out there."

Finn motions for silence, tilting his head to listen. I strain my ears too, trying to hear past the thundering of my heart. The forest around us seems to hold its breath.

Then I hear it—a low, huffing sound and the unmistakable crack of branches under heavy weight.

"Back away slowly," Finn instructs, his voice calm but firm. "No sudden movements. Get behind the fire."

The crew follows his directions, shuffling backward with surprising obedience. My ankle throbs as I step carefully, following Finn's lead without taking my eyes off the tree line.

A shadow moves between the trees, larger than a person and definitely more massive than a deer. My mind cycles through May's casual list of local predators—bears, wolves, lynx with "murder mittens." None of those options seem appealing right now.

"What do we do?" I whisper to Finn. "Play dead? Climb a tree? Start singing show tunes to scare it away?"

"It depends on what it is," he says back. "But making noise is good. Let it know we're here, so we don't surprise it."

"That I can do," I say, gathering my courage. Years of vocal training for roles has to be good for something in the real world.

Before I can unleash my Broadway-worthy scream, the shadow emerges from the tree line. In the firelight, I can make out the form of a large buck—taller than I expected, with an impressive rack of antlers that catches the moonlight.

"Holy—" I start.

"Don't move," Finn interrupts quietly. "It's a deer, but it could bolt if startled. Those antlers aren't for decoration."

The creature regards our camp with what seems like mild interest, its large eyes reflecting our fire as it surveys us. Its breath forms clouds in the cold air.

"Is it dangerous?" Elliott whispers, his clipboard clutched to his chest like armor.

"Not usually, but we don't want to spook it," Finn replies, not taking his eyes off the animal.

The deer takes another step forward, its movements cautious yet graceful. It pauses at the edge of our camp, examining the remains of our dinner with apparent curiosity.

"It's after the food," Carlos says, camera now raised to capture the moment.

I hold my breath as the animal lowers its head to sniff at our cooking area. It picks up something with its lips—maybe a piece of dropped jerky or a fragment of protein bar wrapper.

"Should we chase it away?" Dave asks, voice trembling.

"Just stay still," Finn says firmly. "Let it move on naturally."

For several agonizing minutes, the deer explores our camp with delicate steps. It nudges a pack with its nose, looks directly at Elliott, who visibly pales, and then, satisfied with its investigation, turns and bounds back into the forest with surprising speed and grace.

Collective breath releases around the camp.

"That was..." Elliott starts, then seems unable to find the right word.

"A deer," Finn supplies helpfully, a hint of amusement in his voice. "Completely normal wildlife encounter. Nothing to panic about."

"It was huge!" Dave exclaims. "Did you see the size of those antlers?"

"Is it gone for good?" I ask, still scanning the tree line nervously.

"Probably," Finn says. "Just passing through. The flood likely disrupted its normal routes."

Elliott's producer instincts kick in despite his lingering fear. "Did we get that on camera? That's gold footage! The celebrity, the wilderness expert, the dangerous wildlife encounter!"

Carlos nods, lowering his equipment. "Got it all. Great composition with the firelight silhouetting the deer."

I catch Finn's eye and see the subtle eye-roll he can't quite suppress. In the space of five minutes, we've transitioned from potential mortal danger to production opportunity. Elliott's resilience would be admirable if it weren't so annoying.

"Everyone back to sleep," Finn announces. "We have an early start tomorrow. New route to scout."

Reluctantly, the crew disperses to their respective tents, excitement gradually giving way to exhaustion. Elliott lingers, glancing between Finn and me with undisguised curiosity.

"You two settling in okay? I could rearrange the assignments if there's a problem—"

"We're fine," I cut him off before he can make the situation more awkward. "This works."

Elliott's smile is too knowing. "Of course it does. Sleep well, you two."

As we crawl back into our tent, the previous moment of intimacy feels both distant and painfully present. Finn zips the door closed, sealing us once again in our private bubble of darkness.

I settle onto my side of our makeshift bed, acutely aware of every movement, every breath. The small tube of sunscreen presses against my hip where I tucked it into my pocket—a physical reminder of the spontaneous kiss that now hangs unaddressed between us.

"Sorry about that," Finn says, his voice low as he arranges his portion of the blanket. "Deer encounters are common this time of year."

"Is everything in Alaska trying to kill people, or does it only seem that way?" I ask, aiming for lightness despite the lingering tension.

He settles beside me. "It's not out to get you. It's simply ... not on your side either."

"That's comforting."

"It should be," he says, and I'm surprised to hear actual conviction in his voice. "It means nothing out here is personal. No malice. No judgment. Only life doing what life does."

I consider this perspective, so different from Hollywood's calculated ecosystem of favor and spite. "I've spent my entire career in an industry where everything is personal. Every critique, every rejection, every success—it's all filtered through this lens of who likes you, who's jealous, who's pulling strings."

"Sounds exhausting," he observes.

"It is." I pull the blanket closer around my shoulders, suddenly feeling the cold again. "Maybe that's why I find this —" I gesture vaguely at the wilderness beyond our tent "— oddly refreshing. It's trying to kill me, but at least it's honest about it."

His soft laugh warms the space between us. Without discussion, we gravitate back toward our earlier position, my back against his chest, his arm around my waist. This time, the arrangement feels less like survival necessity and more like chosen comfort.

"About earlier," I start, then falter. How do I explain an impulsive thank-you kiss that felt like something more?

"The deer?" he asks, though I'm certain he knows that's not what I mean.

"No," I whisper. "Before that."

His arm tightens slightly around my waist. "You don't need to explain."

"I think I do," I counter, gathering courage. "I kissed you."

"I was there. I remember."

"It wasn't ... I mean, I wasn't trying to..." The words tangle in my throat. I'm never at a loss for lines, but without a script, I'm floundering.

"Lena," he says, his voice gentle in a way I've rarely heard from him. "It was a thank-you kiss. For rescuing your sunscreen from certain doom. I understand."

But *did* he understand? Did I? It had started as gratitude, but in that moment when my lips touched his, something else had sparked—something unexpected and terrifying in its potential.

"Right," I say finally. "A thank-you kiss." The definition feels insufficient, but it's safer than the alternatives.

"Though as thank yous go," he continues, his voice dropping lower, "it was very effective."

My pulse quickens. "Was it?"

"Very." His breath warms the back of my neck. "Much better than a handshake."

A laugh escapes me, breaking the tension. "I'll keep that in mind for future expressions of gratitude."

We fall into comfortable silence, the warmth between us building like a cocoon against the wilderness night. His heartbeat is steady against my back, his breathing gradually slowing toward sleep.

I should be exhausted, but my mind races. Everything is changing—not just this unexpected connection with Finn, but something deeper within me. The woman I've pretended to be for so long feels increasingly distant, like a character I once played rather than my true self.

As sleep claims me, my grandmother's voice drifts through my mind, whispering the words she repeated every summer when we'd gather herbs at dawn. *Las raíces más profundas sobreviven cualquier tormenta. The deepest roots survive any storm.*

For years I've been a tree without roots, bending to whatever direction Hollywood demanded. But here, pressed against Finn's solid warmth, I feel something long-dormant stirring beneath the surface—not the polished Lena Kensington, but the wild, stubborn heart of Magdalena who knows the names of plants in three languages and remembers how to tie knots that hold against rushing water.

The woman who might be strong enough to finally stop running from herself.

Chapter Thirteen

FINN

I WAKE to the sound of voices outside the tent. Lena's curled against me, breathing with a steady rhythm. The cold air seeps through the tent's thin walls, but between our shared body heat and the emergency blanket, we've avoided freezing during the night. I'm acutely aware of my body's reaction to her curled against me—a reaction that would likely make Lena Kensington bolt, even if the real woman beneath the image might understand. A ghost of a smile touches my lips, remembering her embarrassment last night when she felt my flashlight through my pocket.

Professional boundaries. I need to remember those. I shift away from her, trying not to wake her. She needs the rest, especially after yesterday's flash flood and the deer incident. Four tents for eight people—not ideal, but we're working with what we have. Elliott's voice carries through the morning air, directing his crew. I slip into my boots and jacket, leaving Lena asleep. Time to check our situation and figure out our next move.

I unzip the tent and step out. The first thing I see is Elliott directing Carlos, who has his camera aimed at our tent.

"Perfect timing," he says to Carlos. "Get Finn emerging from the shared shelter. The rugged guide and the actress forced together by disaster—viewers will eat this up."

"Put the camera down, Carlos," I say, but my attention is on Elliott. My voice comes out harder than intended, but I don't care.

"But this is gold! The wilderness forcing proximity—"

"I said, put it down. You're not filming our sleeping arrangements."

Elliott's expression shifts between disappointment and calculation. "The audience connects with authentic moments. This expedition is about Lena's transformation, and your role in—"

"This expedition is about surviving and completing the journey to Painted Peaks," I cut him off, my voice harder than I intended. "Not manufacturing drama."

I turn away from Elliott, jaw tight, and crouch by what's left of our gear, sorting through the salvaged supplies and checking the fire ring for dry kindling. The silence stretches, broken only by the rustle of trees and a distant bird call.

The tent rustles behind me as Lena emerges, hair in a practical braid, her expression alert despite the early hour. Her eyes land on Carlos's camera, and her expression hardens. "Seriously, Elliott?" She shakes her head.

"There are actual disasters to film. The flood destroyed half our camp. Focus on that rather than whatever narrative you're trying to construct."

Elliott signals Carlos to lower his camera, though not with good grace. "Fine, fine. Trying to capture real moments."

"Real would be filming our actual situation," Lena says, stepping fully out of the tent. "Like how we're going to continue with half our supplies gone."

She's right. Yesterday's flash flood tore through the valley, washing out trails, destroying bridges, and sweeping away gear. We're lucky no one was injured or worse.

"We need to decide," I say, addressing the group gathered around the dying fire. "Our planned route is gone. We have two options—head northeast on higher ground to reach Painted Peaks or turn back toward the lodge."

"Northeast adds three days," Elliott protests, checking his water-damaged clipboard. "The network has a timeline—"

"The network isn't out here making life-or-death decisions," I cut him off. "This isn't about ratings. It's about getting everyone home."

I survey the group. Carlos's camera equipment looks half-ruined. The others look exhausted from yesterday's ordeal. Only Lena seems steady, focused.

"We push forward," she says, surprising me. I watch her, trying to find any trace of the Hollywood princess who first arrived at my lodge. That woman has vanished. In her place stands someone I barely recognize—mud-streaked and disheveled, but somehow more present, more real, and beautiful.

"You sure about that?" I ask.

Her eyes meet mine without hesitation. "We didn't come this far to quit now."

Elliott brightens. "Exactly! The show must go on!"

"This isn't about the show," Lena says firmly. "It's about finishing what we started. On our terms."

Our terms. When did this become about us instead of her versus me? Not sure, but I recognize the shift. It's as real as the destroyed landscape around us.

"Okay," I decide, nodding to her before addressing the group. "We head northeast. Everyone pack only what they need. We travel light and fast."

The group disperses to pack what's left of their gear. I turn toward our tent, but Lena is breaking it down with surprising efficiency. Not the clumsy fumbling from our first days on the trail.

"You don't have to do that alone," I say, joining her.

"I'm not helpless," she replies, but without the edge her voice used to carry. "Besides, I've been watching you do this for days. About time I pulled my weight."

"How's the ankle today?" I ask, seeing she's moving with more ease than yesterday.

She rotates her foot. "Almost good as new. Your willow remedy worked wonders."

"Glad to hear it," I say, surprised by how much her recovery matters to me. "Still, let me know if it gives you trouble on the climb up."

She nods, then turns her attention back to the valley below. "It's beautiful," she says, her voice low. "Even like this."

I follow her line of sight. The mountains rise beyond the valley, snow-capped peaks catching the sunlight. Wildflowers dot the slopes with color. Even the destruction has its beauty —nature's raw power.

"Alaska doesn't try to be beautiful," I say. "It is."

Her attention is on my face. "You love it here, don't you? It's not only a business for you."

The observation catches me off guard. "The lodge is more than that. It's home. A connection to my mother, to the land."

"I envy that," she says, her voice soft, almost wistful. "Having roots somewhere."

Her words hit a nerve. Roots. She feels rootless. And here I am, taking mine for granted. Before I can find the words to respond, Elliott interrupts from across the camp.

"If we're doing this, we need to get moving. What's the plan, wilderness man?"

I pull out my map, spreading it across a flat rock. Lena leans in beside me, her shoulder brushing mine as she examines the contours. "If we head this way," I say, tracing a route with my finger, "we can follow this ridge line. Steeper but safer than the valley, especially with more rain coming."

"What about this area?" she asks, pointing to a formation on the map. "It looks like it might be sheltered, and is that a water source nearby?"

"That's Crystal Basin," I confirm, impressed she spotted it. "Sharp observation. It's a natural shelter with a spring. Would make a good camp for tonight." I'm surprised by her attention to map details. "How did you pick that out from the contour lines?"

She shrugs, but I catch a flash of pride in her expression. "I pay attention to important things."

"Like escape routes?" I can't help teasing.

"Like survival," she corrects, something softer in her voice. "My grandmother would be disappointed if I didn't."

The mention of her grandmother gets my attention. Every time she talks about her, it feels like a gift—a glimpse behind the Hollywood façade.

"Crystal Basin is our best option," I agree. "Though it'll be a rough hike up."

"Nothing has been easy since I stepped off that plane," she says with a wry smile. "Why start now?"

As we finish packing, Elliott approaches, watching our interaction with that producer's calculation I've come to recognize. "Everything okay with you two?" he asks, trying to sound casual.

"Fine," Lena answers before I can. "Discussing the best route forward."

"Interesting," Elliott muses. "The audience will eat up this developing dynamic. The friction at the start, now this growing partnership... It's gold."

Lena's jaw tightens. "We're not characters in your show, Elliott."

"Of course not!" he backpedals. "Just appreciating the journey."

When he moves off, Lena mutters, "He's still pushing that helpless angle."

I don't respond. We've been over it. She already knows I see through it too.

"He wants a rescue story," she adds, quieter now. "Doesn't matter if it's true."

I want to tell her she's not the story he's trying to sell. But I don't.

Instead, I check my timepiece. "Ten minutes. Pack smart."

The morning passes in hard work. The trail—what's left of it—climbs through dense forest. Conversation dies as we conserve energy. Sweat soaks my shirt despite the cool air. I set a pace that balances progress with caution, monitoring Lena's injured ankle. Every so often, I stop to check our bearings against the map, calculating distance and terrain.

During one break, Lena comes beside me, offering a piece of jerky from her dwindling stash. "You need to eat too," she says.

I accept with a nod of thanks, aware I've forgotten my hunger in the focus of leading the group. "Smart thinking."

"Following your advice," she says, sitting beside me on a fallen log. "Food is fuel out here. The body needs energy regardless of appetite."

Hearing my words repeated back brings an unexpected hint of amusement to my face. "You've been paying attention."

"I'm a quick study." She looks out across the valley we've been climbing away from, the flooded creek now a distant ribbon below. I follow her line of sight, seeing the landscape through a new perspective. The storm-swept valley, the peaks beyond, the sky stretching endless blue overhead.

"This place gets into your blood," I say, understanding

what she's feeling. "Makes everything else seem small in comparison."

"Is that what happened to you?" she asks, turning to study my face. "Alaska got into your blood?"

"My family's been here for generations. We're part of this land as much as it's part of us."

She nods, something wistful in her expression. "Must be nice, having that kind of belonging."

"You don't have to play a part for Elliott," I say, hearing something forced in her tone. "The real you is..." I hesitate, searching for the right word.

"Is what?" she asks when I don't finish.

Better. Stronger. More interesting. More beautiful. All these answers come to mind, but none seem right. "Is enough," I finally say.

Something flashes in her expression—surprise, perhaps gratitude—before she rises from the log. "Thanks for the pep talk, wilderness man. Let's get this show on the road."

The afternoon brings tougher hiking. The path grows steeper, rockier. Recent rains have turned solid ground to treacherous mud. I reach back to steady Lena on the worst sections, and she accepts the help without comment—a quiet shift from the woman who once bristled at needing it.

By mid-afternoon, dark clouds gather on the horizon. The metallic scent of approaching rain fills the air. We need to reach our camping spot before the weather turns.

A call comes from behind. "How much farther?" one of the crew asks, breathing hard from the climb.

"Two miles," I estimate, checking the ridge ahead. "We can make it before dark if we keep moving."

The first raindrops hit as we crest the final ridge. The clearing sits nestled between protective rock formations—a natural shelter that will protect us from the worst of the weather.

"Perfect timing," Elliott says as the rain intensifies.

I direct the setup of our four remaining tents, positioning them where they'll get maximum protection from the elements. No one questions the arrangements anymore—necessity has overcome modesty. Dave and Carlos take one tent. Elliott and Miguel another. The two other camera operators take the third, leaving Lena and me to share the fourth.

While the others rush to unpack before the rain soaks everything, I see Lena examining the surrounding vegetation with interest. "Something catch your attention?" I ask, joining her at the edge of the clearing.

"Wild chamomile," she says, pointing to small flowers nestled among the rocks. "Good for inflammation, helps with sleep. And over there—" she gestures to another plant "—alpine arnica. My grandmother used it for muscle aches and bruises."

I regard her with new appreciation. "Your grandmother taught you well."

"I wish I'd paid more attention," she admits, a hint of regret in her voice. "I was so focused on becoming someone else that I discarded a lot of valuable knowledge."

The honesty in her confession surprises me. "It's not lost," I say. "You still have it. It's part of you, even if it was buried for a while."

Her eyes meet mine, something vulnerable and questioning in her expression. Before she can respond, the skies open, sending sheets of rain down around us. We dash to the shelter of our tent, laughing despite the soaking we're getting in the process.

Inside, I catch myself thinking about boundaries again. Professional. Practical. Necessary. But as I watch Lena wring water from her hair, those boundaries seem increasingly meaningless. The woman before me isn't a client or a responsibility. She's something more complicated, more important.

And that realization is more dangerous than anything we've faced so far.

Chapter Fourteen

LENA

RAIN HAMMERS AGAINST OUR TENT, turning the thin fabric into a drum. The temperature drops with the sunset, chasing away the day's warmth and replacing it with a damp chill that settles deep in our bones. I wring water from my hair, watching droplets splash onto the tent floor.

"Some shelter," I say, shivering as cold air finds its way under my collar.

Finn rummages through his pack, efficient even in our cramped quarters. "Better than nothing. This storm would've been miserable without the tents."

The close confines of our shelter force an intimacy neither of us expected. When we shared a tent before, exhaustion made it simpler—two bodies needing warmth in icy darkness. But now, awake and aware, every shift is amplified. Every accidental brush of skin, every shared breath, feels like a live wire in the small space. The touch of his arm against mine as he unrolls his sleeping bag. The subtle scent of pine and sweat clinging to his skin. The way his eyes meet mine, then shift away like he's not sure he's allowed to linger.

"Here," he says, offering me a small towel. "It's not much, but it's dry."

Our fingers brush as I take it, a brief touch that shouldn't mean anything. Yet I find myself aware of the roughness of his hands, the small calluses earned through work. Real hands. Hands that build things, fix things, save people.

"Thanks." I pat myself dry, suddenly conscious—again—of my bare face. Days on the trail have stripped away every trace of makeup, and though I've grown used to the feel of clean, unpainted skin, the self-awareness still flares up when I least expect it.

No foundation to blur imperfections. No contour carving out cheekbones. No mascara lifting my eyes. In L.A., a whole team manages my face—makeup artists, hairstylists, dermatologists with their injectable miracles. My contracts even forbid bare-faced photos.

I touch my cheek, skin chapped and a little windburned. I know what I must look like—blotchy, tired, hair frizzed from the rain. A PR disaster. And yet, sitting here, after everything we've faced, it feels ridiculous to care.

That realization isn't new—but it still catches me off guard. Vulnerable. Free.

"You're shivering," Finn observes, unfolding an emergency blanket. "Wet clothes in dropping temperatures is how hypothermia starts."

"What's your professional recommendation?" I ask, aiming for lightness despite my chattering teeth.

"Change into whatever dry clothes you have left. I'll turn away."

He moves to face the tent wall, giving me as much privacy as possible in the small space.

I dig through my pack, finding a thermal shirt and leggings that are mostly dry. Changing in the narrow tent takes the agility of a yoga instructor, but I manage—barely—knocking into the canvas more than once.

"You can turn around now," I say when I'm decent.

Finn has changed too—into a dry flannel shirt that's seen better days. The sleeves are pushed up to his elbows, revealing forearms corded with muscle. A different kind of strength. Useful. Capable. Earned.

"Better?" he asks.

I nod, though the chill hasn't left my bones. "Getting there."

Outside, the wind picks up, driving rain against the tent in rhythmic waves. The temperature continues to drop as night deepens around us. Despite my dry clothes, I can't stop shivering. Finn sees it, of course. He notices everything.

"Your body temperature is still down," he says, his voice matter-of-fact. "The sleeping bags are damp from the flood, but body heat is still the most efficient way to warm up."

Last night's arrangement—my back against his chest, his arm around my waist—flashes through my mind. The memory brings warmth that has nothing to do with temperature regulation. "Practical survival," I say, the words a shield I'm throwing up, mostly against myself. "Don't get any ideas about this being a romantic wilderness moment." Liar. My heart is doing the cha-cha.

He smiles. "Wouldn't dream of it."

We arrange ourselves side by side, shoulders touching, the emergency blanket spread over both of us. It crinkles with every movement, sharp and cold against the rain's steady beat.

"Better?" he asks again.

"Getting there." The warmth radiating from his body already makes a difference. "So. Here we are."

"Here we are," he agrees.

Silence stretches, not uncomfortable, but like we were both waiting for something. Being this close, we'll have to talk eventually, yet neither of us starts. There's safety in silence—no revelations, no vulnerabilities exposed.

"Why Alaska?" I ask at last, curious. "When there's an entire world out there, why stay in one small corner of it?"

He considers the question with the seriousness he gives everything. "Hard to explain to someone who's spent their life chasing the next horizon. It's not about staying in one place—it's

about knowing a place deeply. Understanding its seasons, its moods. Belonging somewhere."

"Not even in Hollywood? You seemed to fit with all that glitz."

I laugh, the sound sharper than intended. "That's the ultimate pretend game. Everyone's playing a part, hoping no one notices the cracks." I draw the blanket tighter around me. "I was better at the game than most."

He's quiet for a moment. Then, softly: "Did you ever feel seen there?"

The question catches me off guard with its simplicity.

"Fame? Money? Neither is worth much when you're alone in a room at night, wondering if anyone would recognize you without the mask."

Lightning flashes outside, illuminating the tent for an instant before thunder crashes overhead. I flinch, moving closer to Finn. His arm slips around my shoulders, a gesture so natural it doesn't register as crossing a boundary.

"What about you?" I ask, settling against him. "Ever been married? Almost married? Tragic love story I should know about?"

Now it's his turn to laugh, a low rumble that vibrates through his chest to mine. "Nothing tragic. One serious relationship in college. Sara. We were together three years before she got a job offer in Seattle. She wanted me to leave Alaska, but I couldn't imagine living anywhere else."

"You chose Alaska over love?"

"I chose being true to myself over compromising what matters most. Sara would have been miserable here eventually, and I would have resented giving up my home. Sometimes love's not enough if you're not walking the same road."

His words hit me with surprising wisdom. How many times have I compromised myself for what I thought was love? How many pieces of my identity have I sacrificed at the altar of approval?

"What about you?" Finn asks. "Are Hollywood romances as manufactured as the rest of it?"

I think about my dating history—selected relationships that benefited both our public images, coordinated by publicists and captured by conveniently placed paparazzi. "Most of it," I admit. "There's someone for every career stage. The up-and-coming actor to create buzz. The established name to cement your status. The strategic breakup for sympathy. It's all calculated."

"Sounds exhausting."

"It is." I look at the tent ceiling, watching shadows dance across the canvas. "When you spend your whole life performing, you forget where the role ends, and you begin."

Another crash of thunder, closer this time. The storm settles over us like a living thing, wild and unpredictable. I move closer to Finn, drawn to his steady presence.

"Cold?" he asks, voice low.

"A little," I lie. The truth is more complicated. I'm drawn to his warmth, yes, but it's more than physical heat I'm seeking.

He adjusts the blanket, tucking it around us both. His arm remains around my shoulders, neither of us acknowledging this is no longer about survival.

"Can I ask you something personal?" he says after a while.

"More personal than sharing a tent in the wild?"

His amusement is audible in his voice. "Fair point. Why did you bury Magdalena? You didn't only change your name —you erased everything she was."

No one has ever asked me this. The question pierces through layers of constructed defenses. In the darkness, with rain isolating us from the rest of the world, truth feels safer than usual.

"I was nineteen," I begin, the memory sharp despite the years. "Fresh out of a community theater program with big dreams and a name no one could pronounce correctly. After my hundredth audition rejection, one casting director finally told me the truth. He said, 'You're talented, but with that name and that background, you'll only ever be cast as the maid or the gang member's girlfriend.'"

Finn's arm tightens around me. "Sounds like an ass."

"He was," I agree. "But he wasn't wrong. Hollywood has boxes, and I didn't fit in the ones that get leading roles. So, I created someone who would."

"Lena Kensington."

"Born in a small town in New England, daughter of academics who summered on the Cape. Prep school, a semester abroad in France for 'culture,' then straight to a prestigious drama program. Enough vague polish to be whoever they wanted."

"And it worked."

"It worked. Three months after the reinvention, I landed my first actual role. Six months later, a recurring part on a network show. Then the vampire series that made me famous." I pause, remembering those early days of success. "The more Lena succeeded, the more Magdalena needed to stay buried."

"And your family? Did they understand?" This question cuts, touching a wound I rarely examine.

"My mother encouraged it. She saw my transformation as

practical—maybe even redemptive after the choices she'd made. My father had left by then anyway, so his opinion didn't matter."

"And your grandmother? The one who taught you about plants?"

"She died before I became 'Lena.' Sometimes I think that's a blessing. She wouldn't have recognized who I turned into."

Finn is quiet for a long moment, his hand moving in small circles on my shoulder. Not pushing, listening. The simple acceptance in his touch loosens something tight in my chest.

"I hadn't spoken Spanish in years before this trip," I confess. "Not since my last visit home. But out here, with the plants and the wilderness, my grandmother's voice keeps coming back to me. All the things she taught me that I pretended to forget."

"Perhaps they were waiting for the right moment to be remembered," he suggests.

An especially powerful gust of wind rocks the tent, pressing the canvas inward before retreating. The storm's intensity matches something building inside me—a restlessness, a yearning for honesty I've denied myself for too long.

"My turn for a personal question," I say, shifting to study his face in the dim light. "Are you happy here? Actually happy, not simply content."

He doesn't answer at once, considering the question with characteristic thoughtfulness. "Most days," he says. "The land feeds something in my soul nothing else can. But there are moments—winter nights when darkness lasts twenty hours—when I wonder if there's more I should be experiencing. Different challenges, different perspectives." In the low light, his eyes meet mine. "What about you? Are you happy in Hollywood?"

The question deserves honesty. "I was. For a while. When success first came, it felt like vindication. Like proof I'd made

147

the right choice in becoming someone else. But lately..." I search for words to describe the emptiness that's been growing. "Lately it's hollow. Like I'm going through motions because I don't know what else to do."

Our faces are close now, bodies angled toward each other in the small space. I'm aware of his breath, warm against my cheek. Of his hand, resting on my shoulder. Of how right this is—how easily I slip into this version of myself when he's nearby. The tent feels smaller, the air thick with something more than the storm's electricity.

His eyes linger on my mouth before meeting mine again, a silent question in them. I shift, and something firm nudges my thigh. A smile tugs at my lips—last night's awkward moment flickering back.

"Is that the flashlight again?" I ask, raising an eyebrow.

His cough sounds like a suppressed laugh. "Not this time."

The admission hangs between us, honest and unembellished. No Hollywood games, no calculated moves. Just raw attraction, plain and simple between us.

I lean forward, closing the distance, my hand finding the nape of his neck. When our lips meet, it's not hesitant or questioning. I'm taking what I want, kissing him with a hunger that surprises us both. His hands find my waist, pulling me closer as I deepen the kiss, my fingers threading through his hair.

Everything falls away—the storm, the cameras, the separate worlds we inhabit. There is only this moment, this connection, pure and uncomplicated.

When we break apart, both breathless, I am dizzy with awareness. This wasn't in the script. Not for the show, not for my planned image rehabilitation. Not for the life I've constructed so meticulously.

"That was..." Finn begins.

"Yeah," I agree, understanding.

He traces my cheekbone with his thumb, a gesture so tender it makes my chest ache. "This complicates things."

"Everything about Alaska has been complicated," I say, resting my forehead against his. "Why stop now?"

His amusement is something I sense rather than see in the darkness. "Fair point."

Outside, the storm subsides, rain softening from violent drumming to gentle patter. Inside, something shifts and settles between us—an acknowledgment, a possibility neither of us expected to find here.

I reach for the hem of his flannel shirt, my fingers slipping beneath the fabric to trace the ridges of muscle across his abdomen. His breath hitches at my touch, and I feel powerful in a way that has nothing to do with fame or image. This is raw, honest desire—no performance, no calculation.

His hands capture mine, stilling them against his chest. "Lena." His voice carries something I don't recognize at first— restraint. "I don't want you to start something you might regret tomorrow."

The words hit me like cold water. *Regret. Tomorrow.* The assumptions buried in his careful tone make my stomach clench. He thinks this is impulse. Adrenaline. The kind of mistake people make when they're scared and seeking comfort.

My hands go limp against his chest. The heat that has been building between us dissipates, leaving me exposed in ways that have nothing to do with the clothes we're still wearing. He's being noble. Chivalrous. Protecting me from myself.

And he's probably right.

I pull back, creating space between our bodies that feels arctic despite the sleeping bags' warmth. The tent that had felt intimate now feels cramped, suffocating. I can't meet his eyes.

"You're right," I whisper, hating how small my voice sounds. "This is ... this isn't..."

"Hey." His finger finds my chin, tilting my face toward his. "It's not that I don't want—" He stops, runs his hand through his hair. "You've been through hell. We both have. I won't take advantage of that."

I turn away, curling into myself, the sting of rejection mixing with grudging respect for his control.

As we finally settle to sleep, his arms around me now without any survival necessity, I wonder about choices. About paths taken and abandoned. About which version of myself is real—the constructed Lena Kensington or the Magdalena Reyes-Johnson who keeps resurfacing in this wilderness. Perhaps Finn is right. Perhaps they were never separate. Perhaps all the knowledge, all the heritage, all the parts of myself I buried, have been waiting to be remembered.

Against Finn's chest, I listen to his heartbeat, steady and strong. Like the land he loves, he is solid, unchanging, true to himself in a way I've forgotten how to be. I've spent years cutting myself off from my roots. Maybe it's time to discover if any remain, waiting to grow again.

Chapter Fifteen

FINN

THE STORM PASSED during the night, leaving behind a landscape scrubbed raw by rainfall. Beside me, Lena sleeps, her slumber peaceful and deep. Last night's kiss hangs in my mind. Not part of the plan. Not professional. But I can't bring myself to regret it. I ease away, not wanting to wake her. The flood cost us valuable time. If we're going to reach Painted Peaks according to Elliott's precious schedule, we need to push hard today.

Outside the tent, frost coats the ground. The temperature has dropped sharply after the rain. I check the sky—boundless blue, which means good hiking but cold conditions until the sun rises higher. My first thought is getting everyone warm and fed. Elliott's, no doubt, is how to spin last night's storm into more 'drama.' Better get water boiling for coffee before waking everyone.

By the time I've got the camp stove running, Elliott emerges from his tent, clipboard in hand. "Morning," he says, sounding surprisingly cheerful for a man who slept on the ground. "Weather's perfect for filming. How far to Painted Peaks from here?"

"We've still got a solid two days. If we push, we can make the lower basin by nightfall," I say, measuring out coffee grounds. "But it's all uphill from here. Rough terrain."

"Excellent," he says, making notes. "The struggle will play well on camera. Is there a suitable camping spot at this lower basin?" *Called it*, I think as I pour the coffee.

"There's a protected clearing with a small spring nearby. Good visibility of the peaks, which I assume is what you want for your shots."

Elliott nods, pleased. "Perfect. Let's get everyone moving."

The others emerge, Carlos checking his equipment for moisture damage, the second cameraman comparing notes on light conditions. Dave comes out last, moving slowly. The bee stings from earlier should have improved by now, but he looks worse—face pale, movements stiff.

"You alright?" I ask him.

"Just tired," he says, but there's a wheeze in his voice that concerns me.

I hand him a mug of coffee. "Drink this. I'll check those stings after breakfast."

Lena appears as I'm distributing the remaining protein bars from my personal stash—the extra rations I carry despite my family's teasing. Nash especially gives me grief about the "unnecessary weight" whenever we hike together. "You're carrying rocks in that pack," he always says. But situations like this prove me right. You never know when you'll need the extra supplies.

"Morning," she says, accepting the coffee I offer. Our fingers brush—a brief touch that sends a spark right through me, something it has no business doing.

"Sleep well?" I ask, keeping my voice neutral for the benefit of the others.

A small smile plays at the corner of her mouth. "Better than expected."

Breakfast is quick. Everyone focuses on the day ahead. I check Dave's bee stings. The affected areas are hot to the touch, red streaks spreading from the original welts. Not good.

"These are infected," I tell him, my voice low. "And I'm worried about your respiration. Any tightness in your chest?"

He gives a reluctant nod. "Since last night. Figured it was the cold air."

I've encountered this before—delayed allergic reactions that develop into secondary infections. Out here, without proper medical supplies, it could turn dangerous fast. "You need antibiotics," I say. "And possibly steroids for the reaction."

"What do we do?" Dave asks, worry creasing his brow.

I weigh our options. Damn it. This is on me. I should have checked that backup kit more thoroughly after the flood. Can't send him alone. Can't risk the entire group turning back and losing the contract money either. But his breathing... The nearest medical help is May, back in Port Promise. At least a day's hike down, probably more given Dave's condition. But if he gets worse, he'll need a hospital in Craig. Sending him alone would be irresponsible, and splitting the group means fewer people to continue the journey.

"Let me think," I tell him. "Try to stay calm and breathe slowly. We'll figure out next steps."

We break camp. This expedition has at least taught everyone to move fast when they have to.

I take Elliott aside as the others pack. "Dave needs medical attention," I tell him. "Those bee stings have developed into something more serious."

Elliott directs his attention to Dave, who's struggling to roll his sleeping bag despite Carlos's help. "How serious are we talking?"

"Serious enough that I don't want him climbing higher. His lungs are compromised. The altitude will make it worse."

Elliott rubs his face, and I can almost see the calculations clicking behind his eyes. "What are our options?"

I glance up the ridge, then back toward the narrow switch-backs we climbed yesterday—loose shale, tree cover, nowhere near enough space for a chopper. "We're too high and too exposed for a safe landing. Closest flat terrain is back down." I pause, then lay it out. "I take him down to a clearing big enough for a helicopter pickup. The rest of you keep going to Painted Peaks with the directions I'll give you."

"Split the group?" Elliott looks skeptical. "Is that safe?"

"Safer than letting his condition deteriorate at a higher altitude. He needs medical attention, and I'll take the satellite phone if there's an emergency."

Elliott considers this, then nods with reluctance. "Alright. But what about the footage? The whole point of this expedition was to document Lena's wilderness journey with you as the guide."

"Carlos is an experienced cameraman. He can handle both his regular shots and cover what Dave would have filmed. The trail to the basin is well-marked on the maps. Lena's proven she can handle herself better than anyone expected." I pause, considering my next words. "Plus, staying with the group would mean delaying medical help for Dave by days."

Elliott weighs his priorities, the man's health winning out over production concerns. "Fine. We'll split up. But I need something for the narrative—some moment between you and Lena that bridges this separation."

Of course he does. Everything's about the story with Elliott, even medical emergencies.

"I'll talk to her," I concede, if only to get him moving.

Once the decision is made, things move. I pull out my maps, marking the route to the lower basin with precise directions for Elliott. "Follow the ridge line," I explain. "When you reach this rock formation that resembles a thumb, descend to your right. The lower basin opens up below—can't miss it. Good water source, protected camping area. I can probably get Dave to safety and rejoin you there in two days."

Elliott examines the map. "And if you don't make it back by then?"

"Continue to the high basin. The trail's straightforward—follow the valley up. Painted Peaks is a day's hike from there. We'll catch up or meet you on the return journey."

I gather the group to explain the plan. Dave looks simultaneously relieved and guilty, while the others shift at the thought of continuing without me.

"I'll guide them," Lena says, her voice clear. Everyone turns to regard her. "I've been paying attention to the maps," she adds. "And I've got a good sense of the terrain now. Between me and Elliott, we can manage." *Her, guide them?* A week ago, the idea would've been laughable. Now ... hell, she's probably right. She's got a calmness about her, a focus that wasn't there before. And she actually has been studying those maps.

Elliott brightens at this fortuitous plot twist. "Perfect! The student becomes the teacher. We'll get great footage of Lena using her newfound skills."

I can't help but be proud, watching her step up with quiet confidence. This isn't the woman who arrived in designer heels, afraid of the outdoors. This is someone discovering her capability, day by day.

"Can we talk?" I ask her as the others finish packing. "Alone."

We walk a short distance from camp, far enough for privacy but still within sight of the group. Morning sunlight catches in her hair, turning the edges gold. It strikes me again how different she looks out here—stronger, more present, more real.

"You don't have to take on the guide role," I tell her. "Elliott's responsible for everyone's safety."

"I know." Her eyes find mine. "But I want to. I can do this, Finn."

"I know you can." And I do. That's what surprises me most—the certainty that she'll get them there.

"Stick to the maps, keep to daylight travel, and monitor the weather. I'll keep the satellite phone since Dave might need emergency evacuation."

She nods, taking it all in. "How bad is Dave?"

"Infected bee stings, possible delayed allergic reaction. Nothing life-threatening yet, but it could head that way if untreated."

"Then you're making the right call." She hesitates, then adds, "About last night—"

"We don't have to talk about it," I interrupt, unsure what to say. Last night was simple in the darkness, two people connecting. In daylight, with reality reasserting itself, everything's more complicated.

"I want to," she insists. "I need you to know that wasn't ... I wasn't playing a part. That was real."

The admission catches me off guard. I'm used to guarding myself, keeping distance. But standing here with her, the morning light on her face—stripped of Hollywood makeup but somehow more beautiful for it—I find myself unwilling to maintain those barriers.

"It was real for me too," I tell her.

Elliott's voice carries across the clearing. "We should get moving if we want to reach the basin by nightfall!"

Time's running out. I reach into my pocket, pulling out the small brass compass I've carried since my mother died. The case is worn smooth from years of handling. The face is yellowed but still accurate.

"Take this," I say, pressing the heirloom into her hand. "It was my mother's. Hasn't failed me yet."

She looks at the compass, then back at me. "I can't take this. It's too important."

"Which is why I want you to have it." I close her fingers around it. Handing it over feels like letting go of a part of myself, a part of Mom. But looking at her, at the steady resolve in her eyes, it feels right. Like it's found its next keeper. "It'll guide you to the basin where I'll meet you in two days."

She tucks the small instrument into her pocket, understanding its significance without the need for explanation. "I'll return it personally," she promises.

Elliott is watching us with poorly concealed excitement, anticipating usable footage. Time to give him what he wants— but on our terms. I pull Lena close, not caring who is watching. Our kiss is brief, shorter than last night, but intensely felt —a promise of something more, not a goodbye.

When we separate, her eyes remain closed for a moment. Then she straightens, squares her shoulders, and nods. "Two days," she says. "We'll be at the basin."

"I'll be there," I promise.

The goodbyes are quick after that. Dave's condition makes delays unwise, and Elliott's eager to continue filming. I watch them depart, following the ridge line as I instructed. Lena walks with new confidence, occasionally checking the brass compass in her palm. She doesn't turn back.

"Just us now," I tell Dave once the others are out of sight. "Let's get you down to where a helicopter can land."

The journey back is slower than I'd like. Dave's condition worsens throughout the morning, his chest heaving with each labored breath as we descend. By midday, I'm taking most of his weight, his arm draped over my shoulders as we navigate the rugged terrain.

"Sorry about this," he pants during a brief rest. "Feel like I'm ruining the whole production."

"Your health matters more than TV," I tell him. "Besides, they'll get to the basin just fine. Lena's got a good head on her shoulders."

"She's changed," Dave observes between careful breaths. "Since we started. It's like she's becoming a different person out here."

Or perhaps becoming herself, I think but don't say.

We make slow progress through the afternoon, stopping often for Dave to rest. I keep him talking, monitoring for any worsening symptoms. The clearing I'm aiming for is hours away, and I'm concerned about reaching it before nightfall. As we walk, my mind drifts to Lena—her confidence as she stepped up to guide the others, the warmth in her eyes when she accepted my mother's compass, the feel of her lips against mine. Not supposed to happen. Makes everything messy. But watching her take charge, remembering the way she felt in my arms ... I find myself planning. For her. For us. Would upgrading that ancient kitchen at the lodge actually kill me? Lena might actually enjoy cooking in a space that wasn't built before the last ice age. Installing a proper internet connection? Definitely. Getting one of those fancy coffee machines that steams milk for the lattes she probably misses? Small price to pay. Small changes that might bridge our different worlds without sacrificing what matters about Crystal Creek.

I catch myself mid-thought. One kiss and I'm thinking about renovations. But the idea doesn't feel forced. It makes sense, wanting to build something new without erasing what matters. Perhaps Crystal Creek's overdue for a little change— same as the guy who runs it.

As darkness settles around us, I find myself looking in the direction of Painted Peaks. They're out there somewhere, making camp at a higher elevation. Following Lena's lead. I'll get Dave to May in Port Promise tomorrow—hopefully she can treat the infection and get his breathing back to normal.

I touch my pocket where the compass usually rests and find it empty. The absence is strange after years of carrying it close. But I know it's where it needs to be—guiding her while I can't. I've given her my most treasured possession, not as a tool but as a promise. A connection between us, spanning the mountain range that temporarily divides us. The real revelation of this wilderness journey isn't the TV show or the stunning landscapes. It's finding someone worth changing for. Worth fighting for. Worth waiting for.

Chapter Sixteen

LENA

THE WEIGHT of Finn's compass presses against my hip as we climb another ridge. I touch it through my pocket, something connecting me to him. Six hours since we separated, and the absence of Finn's steady presence is a physical ache, sharpened by Elliott's increasingly questionable navigation. Honestly, a squirrel with a head injury could probably find north faster than this guy.

He took charge after Finn left, declaring himself our leader with confidence. "I've organized expeditions in the Amazon and the Sahara," he'd boasted, dismissing my attempts to remind everyone that Finn had suggested I guide them. Now, after hours of hiking in what feels like circles, Elliott calls for yet another break, mopping sweat from his brow.

"Let me check the map again," he mutters, unfolding it with trembling fingers. He peers around, confusion plain on his face. "We should have spotted that thumb rock by now."

I pull out Finn's compass, checking our bearing. As I suspected, we've been traveling too far east. The thumb rock would be visible if we crested the ridge to our left. Okay, time to channel some of that Hollister directness. Waiting for

Elliott to figure this out could take us to Canada. "Elliott," I say, my voice firmer than I feel. "I think we need to adjust course. We're trending east."

"And how would you know that?" He doesn't hide his irritation. "An expert in wilderness navigation now, are we?"

I hold up the compass. "Because north is that way. The basin Finn marked is northwest from our starting point."

"Oh, I understand," Elliott's voice drips with sarcasm. "You've got a pretty little compass, so you know better than someone who's organized expeditions across four continents."

"This isn't about who knows better." I keep my voice level. "It's about finding the right path."

"And you think you know the right path?" Elliott laughs, the sound sharp and humorless. "The actress who showed up in designer clothes? The woman whose entire wilderness experience comes from a three-day crash course with a mountain guide?"

His words sting, but only because they align with what he believes—not with what's true.

Carlos clears his throat. "My GPS app says we're off course too, Elliott."

"You have a GPS app?" Elliott rounds on him. "Why didn't you mention this before?"

"Because it hardly works out here," Carlos shrugs. "And you seemed so ... certain."

Elliott looks from Carlos to me, then at the cameramen who have become fascinated with adjusting their equipment. The silence stretches. "Fine," he says at last, his voice tight with wounded pride. "Where do you think we should go, Lena?"

"Over that rise." I point to the ridge crest to our left. "If I'm right, we'll spot the thumb rock from there, and the basin beyond it."

Elliott gestures for me to lead, his expression a mixture of doubt and resentment. "By all means. Show us your newfound expertise."

I sense the cameras on me as I pick a path up the rocky slope, testing handholds before committing. The weight of Elliott's skepticism presses on me—if I'm wrong, I've confirmed his low expectations. But I'm not wrong.

We crest the ridge, and there it stands—a solitary spire of dark rock, jutting skyward like nature's idea of a thumbs up.

"The thumb," Carlos breathes beside me. Below it, the landscape opens into a broad natural basin, sheltered by mountains on three sides. A ribbon of silver water cuts through its center—the spring Finn mentioned.

"That's our camping spot," I say, unable to keep the satisfaction from my voice. "We should make it before sunset."

Elliott looks at the basin, then at me, his expression unreadable. "Lucky guess."

"Not luck," I counter, no longer willing to play small. "I spent summers with my grandmother in the Appalachians. She taught me a few things about finding my way. Not everything, but enough to know which way is north and what a map is supposed to look like right-side up."

"Your grandmother was an outdoorswoman?" Carlos asks, intrigued.

"She lived in the mountains." My lips curve, remembering her lined face and calloused hands. "Knew some plants, could predict the weather by looking at the sky. Practical knowledge that she passed down to me during those summer visits."

Elliott's eyebrows lift. "That wasn't in your bio, Kensington."

"Hollywood doesn't sell movie tickets with stories about actresses who can identify a few edible plants."

"But the whole premise of this show—" Elliott starts.

"Was to observe me struggle and fail," I finish for him. "To laugh at the pampered princess out of her element."

Elliott has the grace to look uncomfortable. "It tested better with focus groups."

"I'm sure it did." I turn away from him, starting down the slope toward the basin. "But that's not the show you're going to get."

We descend in single file, following a natural drainage path down the steep terrain. As we near the valley floor, I spot a patch of familiar plants growing beside a seep in the rock face.

"Wait," I call to the others, kneeling beside the greenery. "I think I recognize these."

"What are they?" Carlos asks, directing one of the cameramen to capture the moment.

"Yarrow, I think," I explain, touching the clusters of tiny white flowers. "My grandmother showed me this one. Good for cuts and scrapes, if I remember right."

Elliott watches with masked interest. "Anything else useful around here?"

"Those might be wild onions." I point to shoots growing nearby. "But I'd need to check with Finn before eating any of them. Gram always said, 'When in doubt, go without.'"

As we continue toward the spring, I point out a few more plants that look familiar, though I'm careful to admit when I'm uncertain. Carlos captures everything on camera, prompting me to explain things.

"This is good content," I overhear him telling Elliott. "Authentic."

Elliott's producer instincts override his wounded pride. "Could be interesting. City starlet turns out to know her way around the wild. No one sees it coming."

When we reach the basin, shadows stretch across the valley floor. Mountains rise around us, their peaks catching the waning sunlight. In two days, Finn will join us. The thought warms me.

"Let's set up camp near the spring," I suggest, careful not to sound commanding. "We'll want easy access to water."

Elliott hesitates, then nods. "Carlos, get the cameramen to capture some establishing shots of the basin. The light's perfect right now."

I lead the way to a level area near the spring but elevated enough to stay dry if it rains again. Carlos helps me examine the ground for rocks and depressions while the cameramen begin unpacking their equipment. Elliott watches from a short distance, consulting Finn's map. I can almost see his mental calculations—weighing his pride against his desire for compelling footage.

"Need help setting up your tent?" I ask him casually.

"No, I've got it," he replies, though the uncertainty in his voice suggests otherwise.

Ten minutes later, I find him wrestling with a tangle of tent poles, his face flushed with frustration. "These things are designed by sadists," he mutters, attempting to force a pole into a sleeve that's not meant to receive it.

"May I?" I hold out my hand for the pole. Elliott surrenders it with a sigh. "Fine. Show me your grandmother's ancient Appalachian tent-raising wisdom."

"My grandmother slept under the stars or in a cabin she built herself," I say, sorting out the poles. "This I learned from Finn, day one."

"You're never going to let me forget this, are you?" Elliott asks as I assemble his tent.

"Depends how pleasant you are for the rest of the trip." I secure the rain fly with a final stake. "There. Rainproof, at least."

"What about bears?" Elliott's voice rises an octave. "Are there bears here?"

"I'm told there are bears everywhere in these mountains."

I enjoy his discomfort more than I should. "But they avoid humans unless we give them a reason not to."

Elliott peers at the tree line. "What kind of reasons?"

"Food left out. Approaching their cubs. Standing between them and an escape route." I pause for effect. "The usual."

By the time the sun sinks behind the mountains, we've established camp. I remember Finn showing me how to secure our food supplies, and I try to reproduce what he did, using a high branch to suspend our provisions away from curious wildlife.

"My grandmother told me to be alert for bear signs," I explain as I work. "Claw marks on trees. Overturned rocks. Droppings with berries or pine nuts."

"Droppings?" one of the cameramen asks.

"Bear poop," I clarify, unable to suppress a chuckle at his grimace. "That's about the extent of my bear knowledge, I'm afraid."

"Let's talk about something else during dinner," Elliott suggests, looking queasy.

While the others filter water and prepare our dehydrated meals, I walk the perimeter of our camp, searching for any signs of wildlife. I hear birds calling and the rustle of small animals in the underbrush. It reminds me of those summer evenings on Gram's porch, listening to the forest sounds as darkness fell. Finn's warnings about proper food storage echo in my mind. Out here, an improperly secured camp is an invitation to wildlife—particularly bears.

I'm examining some tracks in the mud near the spring when Carlos approaches. "Elliott wants to talk to you," he says. "I think he's coming around."

I follow Carlos back to camp, where Elliott paces beside the unlit campfire area, clipboard in hand.

"There's been a development," he announces as I approach. "I've been considering our narrative options, and I believe there's a compelling story in your unexpected knowledge."

"You don't say."

"The audience will respond to authenticity—your connection to nature revealed through this journey." He gestured broadly. "We pivot from 'fish out of water' to 'return to roots.' It's perfect."

I resist the urge to roll my eyes. "I'm not interested in performing a role, Elliott—not even one closer to the truth."

"I'm not asking you to perform. I'm asking you to share what you know on camera." His eyes gleam with renewed ambition. "Show them a side of Lena Kensington they've never witnessed before."

Carlos comes to stand beside me. "It could be good, Lena."

Perhaps he's right. Perhaps there's value in showing people that women contain multitudes—that the same hands can apply lipstick and build a fire.

"Fine," I agree. "But on my terms. No manufactured drama. No staged reactions."

"Absolutely." Elliott's enthusiasm borders on manic. "We film as events unfold. Pure documentary." I doubt his commitment to authenticity will survive the first dull hour, but it's a start.

After dinner, we gather around the small campfire for warmth. Elliott seizes the opportunity for an impromptu interview, positioning one of the cameramen to capture the firelight on my face.

"Lena," he begins, slipping into interviewer mode. "Tell us about your grandmother and how she influenced you."

I stare into the flames, memories surfacing. "My parents divorced when I was eight. Mom had to work double shifts, so I spent summers with Gram in the Appalachians. She and my grandfather built a cabin there before he passed. He was still around when I was little—taught me how to tie knots, build fires, basic survival stuff. After he died, Gram kept the place going on her own."

"That must have been quite an adjustment for a city kid," Elliott says.

I chuckle at the memory. "I hated it at first. No television, no shopping malls, no indoor plumbing. Mountains and silence and my grandmother's expectations that I pull my weight."

"What changed?"

"I did." I raise my eyes from the flame to the camera lens. "Gram didn't coddle me. She taught me what she knew. How to identify a few useful plants. How to read basic weather signs.

How to move through the forest without tripping over every root."

"And yet you chose acting—about as far from the wilderness as one can get."

"Did I?" I challenge him. "Or did I choose another form of survival? In Hollywood, you learn to read people instead of weather. You navigate social terrain as treacherous as any mountain. You figure out which masks protect you and which leave you exposed." And I mastered those masks. But what did it cost me? What part of Magdalena got lost in the construction of Lena?

Elliott blinks, thrown off script. "I hadn't thought of it that way."

"Most people don't." I feed another small branch into the fire. "But all survival requires the same fundamental skills—observation, adaptation, persistence. Whether you're facing a blizzard or a bad review."

The interview continues, different from anything I've done before. I speak plainly about the contradictions I've lived with—the mountain-taught child inside the polished actress.

About the freedom I feel out here, away from expectations and appearances.

Later, as the others sleep, I sit alone outside my tent, Finn's compass open in my palm. The needle points north, unwavering despite the mountains around us. I think of Finn and Dave, making their way down to safety, and hope they've reached the helicopter clearing without incident. Two days until we reunite. Two days to lead this group and prove—to Elliott, to the audience, to myself—that I am more than anyone has allowed me to be.

Morning arrives with a crisp clarity that makes the mountains seem close enough to touch. I wake before the others, building a small cooking fire and setting water to boil. As steam rises from the pot, I notice movement at the edge of the basin—a flash of russet fur disappearing into the tree line. Fox, perhaps. Or marmot. My lips curve, thinking how Gram would have known what animal it was from a brief sighting.

One by one, the others emerge from their tents. Carlos starts checking his equipment, while the cameramen examine the magnificent landscape for establishing shots. Elliott emerges last, looking refreshed until he tries to stand upright. "Ow," he gasps, clutching his lower back. "What did I sleep on, a rock?"

I bite back a chuckle. "Probably. Did you check your tent site before setting up?"

"I thought that's what the sleeping pad was for," he groans, attempting to stretch.

"Try rubbing the sore spot," I suggest. "Finn showed me that heat helps with muscle pain. If there's a smooth rock around here, we could heat it in the fire, wrap it in a shirt, and use it as a hot compress."

Elliott regards me with suspicion. "You're not going to rub dirt in it or suggest some strange plant poultice?"

"I'm an actress, not a shaman," I laugh. "My knowledge has limits. But I do know basic first aid."

He attempts another stretch. "I'll try your rock idea if it gets worse. For now, I'll complain loudly and make everyone uncomfortable."

"That's the Hollywood way," I agree, which earns a grudging upturn of his lips.

After a breakfast of instant oatmeal and coffee, we pack up camp. Elliott, emboldened by his slightly improved back and yesterday's successful navigation, approaches me with a different proposition.

"I want to point out a few spots along the route to the high basin," he says, scanning the trail ahead. "The terrain changes should make for compelling footage, especially as we gain elevation."

"We need to make progress," I remind him. "That's still the goal, right?"

"Of course, but we have time. According to Finn's timeline, we're ahead of schedule since we reached the basin yesterday." He's not wrong. The maps show a relatively straightforward route from here to the high basin and then to Painted Peaks—a gentle ascent up the valley, then a steeper climb to the alpine meadows.

"A few hours of filming won't hurt," I concede. "But we pack up and move by noon. I want to make good progress today."

We spend the morning exploring the lower basin. I show them the few plants I recognize with certainty—some edible greens my grandmother taught me to identify, a birch tree whose bark tastes like wintergreen, a few berries that are safe to eat when ripe.

"I'm no expert," I admit when Carlos asks about a flower I

don't recognize. "My grandmother knew hundreds of plants, but I only remember the ones we used regularly."

Elliott watches with growing satisfaction. "This is gold," he whispers to Carlos. "Straight from the source with camera-ready delivery. We couldn't have scripted it better."

"That's because it's not scripted," I remind him, overhearing. "I remember these things."

"And they said you couldn't act and be smart," Elliott jokes, then looks contrite. "Sorry. Old Hollywood habits."

"At least you recognize it," I concede, touched by his self-awareness.

By midday, we've packed camp and begun our journey toward Painted Peaks. The valley narrows as we ascend, the spring we camped beside growing into a proper stream fed by mountain runoff. The terrain grows rockier, but the path remains clear—a natural route carved by water and wildlife.

We've been hiking for perhaps two hours when I notice a change in the bird sounds around us. The cheerful chatter falls silent, replaced by warning calls. I stop, raising my hand to halt the group.

"What is it?" Elliott asks, coming alongside me.

"Something's spooked the birds." I sweep my eyes over the slopes on either side of us. "We should be cautious."

Carlos lowers his voice. "Bear?"

"Possibly." I keep my tone calm, though my heart races. "Let's make noise as we walk. Talk, call out. Let any wildlife know we're coming."

We continue along the path, making conversation to alert any wildlife to our presence.

Elliott perks up. "So, we should sing? I know all the words to 'Oklahoma'—"

"Perhaps something less theatrical," I suggest. "Simple conversation is fine."

The cameramen walk closer together, watching the rocky

slopes above us. The warning in my gut sharpens as we round a bend in the valley. A musky scent drifts on the breeze— distinctive and unmistakable. I stop again, this time with more urgency. "Everyone stay still."

Ahead, perhaps fifty yards up the trail, a massive golden bear stands on its hind legs, front paws dangling as it tests the air. Even this far off, I could see his coat, a magnificent honey-gold in the sun.

"Holy shit," Elliott breathes. "Is that—"

"Grizzletoe," Carlos whispers in awe. "The legendary Golden Bear of Port Promise. Locals claim he's been ranging these mountains for twenty years."

The bear drops to all fours, turning his massive head in our direction. My heart hammers, but I force my breathing to remain steady. "Don't run," I whisper to the others. "Whatever happens, do not run."

"Should we play dead?" Elliott's voice quavers.

"Not yet. Right now, we need to look big and back away slowly." I raise my arms above my head, trying to make myself appear larger than the terror currently shrinking me from the inside out. "Hey, bear!" I call, amazed my voice comes out firm, channeling Gram's calm authority. "We are aware of you! We're passing through!"

The bear observes us, curiosity in its posture. I continue talking, my voice loud but not threatening, as I slowly step backward. The others follow my lead, arms raised, faces pale with fear.

Grizzletoe lumbers a few steps closer, nose twitching as he tests the air. My mouth goes dry, but I keep talking, voice shaky but steady enough. "Easy, big guy. We're a couple of humans passing through. No trouble. We know this is your place."

For a heart-stopping moment, the bear continues toward us. Then, with imperial indifference, it turns aside, ambling

171

down to the stream where it begins to overturn rocks, searching for food beneath them.

"Keep backing up," I instruct. "Around the bend, out of sight."

We retreat until the curve of the valley conceals us from the bear. Only then do I lower my arms, my shoulders aching with released tension.

"That," Elliott says shakily, "was the most terrifying moment of my life."

One of the cameramen raises his hand. "I got it all on film."

Elliott looks at him, then at me, then back at the cameraman. A wide expression spreads across his face. "You filmed Grizzletoe? The legendary bear? With Lena facing him down like a woodland goddess?"

The cameraman nods. "Every second."

"Even the part where Elliott almost wet himself?" Carlos adds with a chuckle.

"I did not!" Elliott protests, though his face suggests otherwise.

"Your voice went up about three octaves," I point out. "You sounded like you were auditioning for a boys' choir."

"Fine, I was terrified," Elliott admits. "Anyone would be. That thing was enormous."

"And magnificent," I add, the adrenaline dissipating. "My grandmother saw a grizzly once. Said it was like witnessing the mountain come to life."

Elliott looks as if he might faint from joy. "Do you have any idea what this footage is worth? Wildlife channels will pay a fortune for licensing. This is—" he seems at a loss for words "—this is beyond perfect."

"The best part is how Lena took charge," Carlos says. "Natural leadership in a crisis. That's your story right there."

"It is," Elliott agrees, regarding me with new respect. "You knew what to do."

The truth is, I wasn't calm. I was terrified. But fear and action can coexist—another lesson from my grandmother. "Courage isn't about not being scared," she'd say. "It's about doing what needs doing despite the fear."

"We need to take a detour," I say instead of explaining. "Give Grizzletoe a wide berth. There should be a parallel route up the western slope."

Elliott doesn't argue. His newfound respect is evident in how quickly he defers to my judgment. "Lead the way."

We climb the western slope, finding a game trail that runs parallel to the main valley. The going is harder, but the path takes us past the bear's location. By late afternoon, we've rejoined the main route, continuing toward Painted Peaks.

As we make camp that evening, I sense a shift in the group dynamic. The others turn to me not only for guidance but with respect. Even Elliott, plotting the narrative possibilities of our bear encounter, treats me as a collaborator rather than talent to be managed.

"Something occurs to me," Elliott says as we sit around our campfire. "You could have told us about your grand-mother from the beginning. You could have avoided playing the helpless city girl. Why didn't you?"

The question deserves honesty. "Because everyone is more comfortable with me in that role. The glamorous actress who needs rescuing. It's what you expected—what you wanted for your show."

"But it's not who you are," Carlos observes.

"It's part of who I am," I correct him. "I do love beautiful clothes and comfortable hotels. I enjoy filmmaking and the escape it provides to audiences. But it's not all of me."

Elliott stares into the fire, his jaw working. "I suppose I got what I thought I wanted." His voice carries disappointment—

not in me, but in himself. "The easy story. The predictable narrative."

"And now?" I ask.

"Now I'm wondering what else I've missed by not looking deeper." He meets my eyes across the flames. "In this project. In others."

As night settles around us, I take out Finn's compass again. The needle points north, unwavering in its purpose. I run my thumb over the worn brass case, tracing the subtle impressions left by countless hands before mine. Finn's hands. His mother's.

For the first time in years, I am myself—not the constructed persona I present to the world, but the woman shaped by summers in the mountains and a life in the spot-light. Both aspects real. Both valuable. The true journey hasn't been across this wilderness, but back to me. The destination worth the climb.

Chapter Seventeen

FINN

FIRST LIGHT HITS the windows at the lodge as I finish packing supplies. The helicopter evacuation yesterday went smoothly—Dave was delivered straight to Craig Medical Center, an IV already pumping antibiotics into him. By the time we got him to the valley, he was past the point of May being able to help, so they took him directly to the hospital. I hiked back to Port Promise.

Getting back to the lodge and resupplying took longer than expected. Now I'm behind schedule.

The lodge is unusually alive for this early hour. I spot boots by the door that aren't mine—worn hiking boots I recognize.

"Didn't expect to find you back so soon." Nash stands in the kitchen doorway, coffee mug in hand. He's supposed to be deep in the mountains on a week-long guided hunt, not here at the lodge.

"Could say the same to you," I respond, cinching my pack closed. "Thought your hunting trip lasted through Friday."

"Got cut short." The tired lines around Nash's eyes tell me

more than his words. "Had some trouble with those eco-activists again."

"Anybody hurt?"

"Not this time." Nash takes a long swallow of coffee. "But they crossed a line, Finn. Left death threats pinned to our gear. Slashed the tires on our ATVs. A clear message they wanted us gone." Eco-activists. Exactly what I needed. Another damn fire to put out, and these ones play dirtier than most.

I stop what I'm doing. Nash isn't the kind of man who flinches—he's spent too many seasons carving paths through untamed land. The tension in his stance tells me everything.

"You report it?"

"Yeah. State troopers took statements, but you know how it goes. By the time anyone investigates, the trail's cold." He sets his mug down, watching me pack. "TV crew done filming?" he asks.

"Not yet. They ran into some delays. I told them I'd catch up—meet them further in."

Nash raises an eyebrow but doesn't comment.

I shrug and reach for my pack. "They've got three weeks scheduled for the shoot," I say, adjusting the weight across my shoulders. "And either way, the contract guarantees rental income for the full summer. That should cover what I need."

Nash grunts. "With what they're paying, you ought to have it under control." He picks up one of the bank notices pinned under a smooth rock on the kitchen table. "Found these while I was making coffee."

My stomach tightens. I'd meant to put those away somewhere safer before leaving with the expedition.

"Forgot they were there," I mutter, reaching for the notices.

Nash holds them out of reach. "Three months behind, Finn? Why didn't you say something?"

"It's under control."

"Doesn't look that way to me." Nash gestures around the empty lodge. "Still haven't recovered from the avalanche repairs, have you? Not to mention that windstorm last winter."

"I know my business," I snap, then regret the tone. Nash means well.

"Your business is about to belong to First Alaskan Bank unless you accept some help," he counters. "I'd be happy to contribute, and I'm sure Reid, Rhys, and Kane would come through too."

"I don't need handouts." The words come out harsher than intended.

"It's not a handout." Nash's voice remains even. "It's family helping family. Hell, even Dad would pitch in if you'd swallow your pride long enough to ask."

That got under my skin. The lodge sits on land my parents gave me, but everything else—every nail, every board, every window—I built with my hands. Taking their money now feels like admitting failure.

"I built this place," I say, adjusting my pack. "I'll fix it."

"You built it on family land—with help," Nash reminds me. "No shame in needing it again. That avalanche would've bankrupted businesses twice your size."

He's not wrong. Between the avalanche that took out two cabins and the windstorm that damaged the main lodge roof, Crystal Creek hasn't had a chance to recover. But accepting help means admitting I can't do it alone, and that's a truth I fight admitting.

"I need to think about it," I say, shouldering my pack. "After I get back."

"From meeting the actress." Nash gives me that steady look of his, all quiet assessment.

"What's her name again?"

"Lena. Lena Kensington."

"Right."

"You good on gear?" he asks.

"I've got the satellite phone," I say. "We're covered."

"Which route you taking to Painted Peaks?" Nash leans against the counter.

"Raven's Spine."

The coffee mug in his hand pauses halfway to his mouth. "That's not a trail. That's a climbing route."

I adjust the straps on my pack. "Cuts six hours off. I need to make up time."

I don't like leaving them with nothing. No backup. No second way out if something happens. And the longer I'm gone, the worse that sits with me. So yeah—Raven's Spine is steep, narrow, and not exactly friendly. But it's the fastest way back. And right now, that's what matters.

"Or break your neck trying." Nash sets his mug down with enough force to slosh coffee. "The main trail would get you there tomorrow morning. Safe and whole."

"I promised Lena today." The words come out with more force than intended.

Nash watches me for a long moment, something changing in his expression. "She must be some actress."

I don't answer. Can't explain what I don't understand myself—this pull toward Lena, this need to keep my promise at any cost.

"Be careful," Nash says. "Dad would kick my ass if I let you kill yourself on that ridge."

"Not planning on dying today." I head for the door. "And we'll talk about those bank notices when I get back."

"And the activist problem," Nash calls after me. "Reid heard they're getting more organized. Might be someone new pulling the strings."

I nod, filing the information away. Lodge finances and eco-drama will have to wait. Getting back to Lena can't.

The morning air bites cold as I hit the trail out of Crystal Creek. The path climbs through forest before opening to alpine terrain. I push hard, muscles still tired from yesterday's descent with Dave, but I ignore the discomfort. Every minute counts if I'm going to reach Painted Peaks basin by nightfall.

By mid-morning, I reach the fork where the main trail continues its gradual climb toward the peaks. Instead of following it, I veer right onto a barely discernible game trail that climbs steeply up the eastern face.

Raven's Spine—named for the dark rock formations that jut like feathers along its crest. Few hikers attempt it, and for good reason. It's treacherous, demanding, and unforgiving of mistakes. But it's also direct. And right now, direct matters more than safe.

The first hour tests every muscle, the incline so steep I use hands as much as feet, loose shale sliding beneath my boots. I focus on each movement, each handhold, shoving away the image of Lena's face when I last saw her, the worry about the bank notices, Nash's damn knowing look. Up here, distraction gets you killed.

Midday finds me perched on a narrow ledge, catching my breath and checking my position against landmarks. The valley spreads below, the main trail a thin ribbon winding around the gentler slopes. I'm making decent time despite everything. If I maintain this pace, I'll reach the upper ridge by late afternoon, then down into the basin before dark.

I force myself to eat a protein bar, though hunger's nowhere in sight. The repairs after the avalanche nearly wiped me out. Taking loans for the windstorm damage pushed me to the edge. Now I'm hanging on by my finger-nails, refusing help out of stubborn pride. The lodge is mine —the thing I built, the legacy I created. Accepting money from family feels like giving that up. But Lena ... something's different there. She belongs in these mountains in a way I never expected. The thought sits, uncomfortable but right.

The climb becomes a punishing rhythm. One foot, one handhold at a time. Dad's voice echoes in my head—"The mountain doesn't care about your problems, son. It asks if you've got what it takes."

"By late afternoon, my muscles are burning. I reach the knife-edge that marks the final approach to the upper basin. The valley spreads below, and I can make out the distant glow of a campfire. Good, they made it to the upper basin as planned."

The descent demands as much focus as the climb—loose rock and steep drops waiting for any mistake. I pick my way down, using poles for balance. The basin grows larger with each switchback. Near the lower section of the trail, I reach for a handhold on a jagged outcropping. The rock gives way, sharp edges raking across my forearm as I fall forward. I manage to catch myself with my other hand, but not before slamming my side into the rocky slope. Pain flares hot along my ribs and arm. When I look down, blood seeps through my torn sleeve from a deep gash running from wrist to elbow. Not life-threatening, but deep enough to need attention. *Damn it.* Stupid mistake. Lost focus. Thinking about her smile when I gave her the compass. Thinking about her, when I should have been thinking about the damn rock.

I unzip my pack with one hand, pulling out the first aid kit. The wound needs cleaning and stitches, but all I can manage is a quick rinse with water from my canteen and a pressure bandage wrapped around my forearm. Blood seeps through the white gauze by the time I secure it. My ribs throb with each breath—bruised for sure, possibly cracked. Progress slows to a painful crawl. Each movement jars my injured side, each step requiring balance with my wounded arm held close to my body. But I push forward. The upper basin is close, perhaps an hour away at this new pace.

Shadows lengthen across the valley floor as the sun begins its descent behind the mountains. I'll be navigating the last section in twilight at this rate. Not ideal, but manageable.

I'm still a half-mile from the basin floor when I detect movement ahead—a figure on the trail below, moving upward with speed. Too far to make out details, but something in the way they move looks familiar. As the distance closes, recognition punches through the haze. Lena. Coming up the trail, alone, moving fast. What the hell is she doing out here by herself? At dusk?

She hasn't spotted me yet, her head swiveling as she scans the fading light, like she's searching for something—or someone. I try to call out, but my voice barely carries. I raise my uninjured arm instead, hoping to get her attention before she passes me by. The moment she sees me, her pace quickens, eating up the distance between us. I try to move faster to meet her, but each step sends fresh waves of pain through my ribs.

Lena reaches me, her expression shifting from relief to concern as she sees the blood-soaked bandage on my arm. "Finn! You're hurt." She moves to my side, assessing the injury.

"A rock broke loose on the descent," I say, the relief of finding her finally catching up with the pain. "The cut is deeper than I'd like. Where's everyone else?"

Still at camp," she says. "We made good time from the lower basin yesterday. Elliott's planning to push to high camp tomorrow." She hesitates, glancing up the steep ridge behind me, then back to my face. "But I had a feeling something was wrong. I couldn't sit around and do nothing."

"You came after me? Alone?"

She lifts a shoulder. "Told the crew I was turning in early, grabbed a light, and waited until they were distracted. Then I headed out."

I stare at her. "You left camp by yourself. In unfamiliar terrain. At dusk."

Her brow lifts, calm and unbothered. "Says the guy who free-climbed with a bleeding arm and no backup?"

That earns a breath of something like a laugh. It hurts. But it's worth it.

"Camp is about an hour from here," she says, stepping under my arm to support my weight.

"Too far," I mutter. "There's a shallow cave about a quarter mile ahead. Used it once during a storm. It'll do."

"Then that's where we're going," she says. "Once we get there, I'm checking that arm."

The conviction in her voice doesn't surprise me—not anymore. This isn't the same city woman who stepped off the seaplane a week ago, wide-eyed and unsure. This is someone who has found her footing in these mountains—and perhaps in herself. As we make our slow way toward the promised shelter, I realize something has shifted. We trust each other now, the respect moving in both directions. And whatever else is building—that unnamed pull that drove me across Raven's Spine with single-minded determination—that, too, seems to have only deepened despite my injury. Or maybe because of it.

The cave, when we reach it, is more an overhang than a true cavern, but it's dry and sheltered enough to give us a place to rest. Lena helps me sit with my back against the rock wall, then sets about gathering material for a small fire.

"You make that look effortless," I observe as she arranges kindling with ease.

"I've had plenty of practice on this trip," she says, striking a match. "Though I admit, doing it while worried about your arm makes my hands shake."

The fire catches, throwing warm light across her features.

In this moment—miles from civilization, blood seeping through my bandage, pain throbbing with every heartbeat—I'm struck by a simple truth, I don't want this journey to end. Not the expedition—that was always temporary. But this connection with Lena. This unexpected partnership that is both new and somehow familiar—like coming home to a place I didn't know I'd been missing.

Crystal Creek's financial problems haven't disappeared. The uncertainty of what happens when this expedition ends still looms. But as Lena kneels beside me to unwrap the bandage, her hands gentle, one thing becomes clear amid all the questions. Whatever comes next, I'm not letting Lena Kensington walk out of my life. Some trails, once taken, change your map forever.

Chapter Eighteen

LENA

The small fire that I built casts dancing shadows across the cave walls as I unwrap Finn's blood-soaked bandage. The gash on his forearm runs deep, angry red against his tanned skin. He doesn't flinch as I examine it, but the pallor of his face betrays his exhaustion and pain.

"This needs stitches," I say, turning his arm to assess the full extent of the damage.

"Not equipped for that out here." His voice is strained, heavy with fatigue, and fear, cold and sharp, clenches my stomach. He's trying to downplay it, but he's hurt, badly.

"We'll see about that," I say, more to myself than to him, already rummaging through the first aid kit. Finn, being an experienced guide, carries a decent medical kit. Among the supplies, I find a roll of medical tape. This is exactly what I need.

"Maybe not stitches, but we can improvise," I tell him, pulling out the tape and some gauze pads.

"What are you doing?" Finn asks, watching as I tear several strips of the tape.

"Making butterfly closures," I explain. "They won't be as good as stitches, but they'll help hold the wound together until we can get you proper medical attention."

Finn raises an eyebrow. "Where'd you learn bush medicine?"

"Believe it or not, from a failed TV pilot." If he only knew. Failed pilot, yes, but the hours in that ER weren't fake. Some things stick, even when you try to forget the role. I smile as I work, cleaning the wound with water from his canteen. "I played an ER nurse for three episodes before the network pulled the plug. Spent two weeks shadowing real trauma nurses for research."

"Hollywood training comes in handy after all," he says, watching me work with a mixture of pain and curiosity.

"They made us learn procedures for authenticity." I press the edges of the wound together, then apply the first impro- vised butterfly strip. "Though I never thought I'd be using it in a real emergency, especially in a cave."

Once I've closed the wound with the tape strips, I decide to add another element to the treatment. "Let me add some- thing my grandmother taught me." I reach into my jacket pocket and pull out the small bundle of yarrow I'd gathered during our hike the day before. The leaves and flowers are wilted now, but Gram always said that didn't matter much for their effectiveness. I select a few of the limp leaves and rub them between my fingers. Despite their withered state, the bruised leaves release their distinctive earthy scent.

Finn watches with interest as I work. "Yarrow," he says, recognizing it. "Good choice."

"My grandmother swore by it for cuts and scrapes." I place the bruised, lifeless leaves against the skin around the edges of the wound, careful to avoid the butterfly closures. "It's not as fresh as I'd like, but it should help with infection."

"Old-timers up here call it soldier's woundwort," Finn says, the pain in his eyes briefly giving way to curiosity. "Your grandmother knew her stuff."

I secure the yarrow leaves in place with the gauze as I wrap his arm. "She had names for everything that grew wild. Said the mountains speak in their own language—you just have to learn how to listen."

I can see the toll today has taken on him—the punishing climb up Raven's Spine followed by the fall and injury, all after yesterday's long trek getting Dave to medical help. He looked like he was running on sheer will, his body screaming for rest.

"You need to rest," I say, my tone leaving no room for argument. "You're exhausted."

"We should get back to camp," he protests, his voice weak. "The others—"

"Will be fine until morning. You can barely keep your eyes open." I remove my outer jacket and fold it into a makeshift pillow. "Lie down before you fall down."

To my surprise, he doesn't argue. He shifts, reaching for the canvas bedroll tied securely to the bottom of his pack. With a few movements, he unstraps it and spreads it across the flattest section of the cave floor, its wool lining creating a welcome barrier against the unforgiving stone. Then he eases himself down onto his uninjured side with a low groan that escapes despite his best efforts.

I place the folded jacket beneath his head, a pang going through me as I see how his body melts into the ground with relief. He's hurting. More than he's letting on.

"A short rest," he says, eyes already closing.

"Of course," I agree, knowing he'll be out until morning once sleep claims him. I add more wood to our small fire, grateful Finn had thought clearly enough to get us to this cave before collapsing. Outside, darkness has claimed the mountains, wind whistling past our sheltered alcove.

Finn's breathing has deepened, exhaustion pulling him under. I watch his face in the firelight, tension easing from his features as sleep takes hold. Hours pass. I keep vigil, adding wood to the fire now and then, checking Finn's bandage, watching the steady rise and fall of his chest. His color improves with rest, the lines of exhaustion softening.

Sometime in the darkest hours, he stirs, eyes opening to find mine in the firelight. "How long was I out?" His voice is rough with sleep.

"A few hours." I offer him water. "How's the arm feeling?"

He flexes it. "Better. Your butterfly strips are holding well."

"They should get you back to civilization." I check the bandage, pleased to see no fresh blood has seeped through. The temperature has dropped as night deepens, the mountain air growing bitter with cold. Despite the fire, I find myself shivering. Finn notices, his expression tightening.

"You're cold. Take your jacket back."

"I'm fine. You need it more than I do right now."

He looks at me for a long moment, then shifts position, making space beside him. "Come here."

I hesitate, uncertain.

"Body heat," he explains, his voice practical but his eyes saying something else. "Basic survival."

I move to his side, settling next to him on the bedroll, mindful of his wounded arm.

He lifts his good arm, wrapping it around my shoulders and drawing me against his side. The warmth of his body is a shock after the chill, and I find myself pressing closer.

"Better?" His voice has dropped to a whisper that vibrates through me.

"Much." The word feels small, barely touching the comfort of his solid presence. Yet here, in this cave, those neglected parts of myself have emerged when needed most.

The woman who can identify healing plants and build fires. The woman who doesn't need rescuing.

"My agent would have a heart attack seeing me like this," I say, attempting lightness. "She's spent years helping me craft my 'sophisticated cosmopolitan image.'"

"And how's that working for you?" Finn asks, cutting to the heart as usual.

I consider deflecting with humor, but something about the night and the way he's looking at me demands honesty. "It's worked as planned," I admit. "Got me the roles, the magazine covers, the brand endorsements."

"But?"

"But it never quite fit right." I poke at the fire, watching sparks rise. "Like someone else's clothes that you can wear but never feel comfortable in."

He's quiet for a moment, absorbing this. "And out here?"

"Out here is different." I meet his eyes. "I keep surprising myself with what I remember, what I know. Things I thought I'd forgotten."

"Or things you tried to forget?" His perception is unsettling.

"Maybe both." I hand him another drink of water. "Hollywood doesn't value wilderness skills and herbal remedies."

"Their loss." The simple certainty in his voice warms me more than the fire.

We sit in comfortable silence, the only sounds the crackling flames and the breeze outside our shelter. There's an ease between us that I've rarely experienced with anyone—a lack of performance or expectation. We're two people, all pretenses stripped away by everything we'd been through.

"The lodge is in trouble," Finn says abruptly, breaking the quiet. The admission seems to cost him, his expression tightening with what I recognize as pride.

I glance at him, keeping my voice soft. "You said it nearly bankrupted you."

He nods, eyes on the fire. "You already know the gist. Avalanche, windstorm. The repairs wiped me out. I'm still digging out from it."

I glance at him, struck by how much he's holding together with sheer will. "And you built it yourself."

"Every board, every nail." His uninjured hand makes a sweeping gesture. "My parents gave me the land, but Crystal Creek Lodge is mine. My dream. My responsibility." The possessive note in his voice tells me everything about what this place means to him. This isn't a business to Finn, it's his creation, his legacy. The thought of losing it must be unbearable.

"Your family offered to help?" He looks surprised that I guessed.

"Nash did, this morning. Said my brothers would pitch in too. Even my father."

"But you said no."

"Didn't say anything. Left it hanging." He stares into the fire. "Taking their money feels like I failed."

"Sometimes the strongest thing you can do is accept help," I say, my voice soft. "At least that's what my grandmother always said when I was young and stubborn."

"Did you listen?"

"Eventually." I smile at the memory. "I didn't always understand her then, but her words stuck. She used to say, 'Child, love isn't love if it doesn't have hands and feet.' Took me years to understand what she meant."

Finn is quiet for a long moment, absorbing this. "Your grandmother sounds wise."

"She was." I check his bandage again, pleased to see my makeshift butterfly strips holding. "And terrifying when cross. She would have loved these mountains."

"And what about you?" Finn asks, his eyes intent on mine. "Do you love them too?"

The question feels simple but carries weight—more than asking about scenery or wilderness. There's an invitation in it, a door opening to possibilities I hadn't let myself consider.

"I do," I answer, my voice honest. "More than I expected to."

Something shifts in his expression, warming despite the exhaustion still etched into his features. I become aware of how close we are, the firelight painting gold across his face. For a moment, I forget we're in a cave on a mountainside. Forget the expedition, the cameras, the show. Forget everything except the man before me and the raw, undeniable current between us.

Finn reaches out, his uninjured hand capturing mine. "Thank you."

"For what? The medieval first aid?" I attempt humor to defuse the sudden intensity.

"For coming to find me." His thumb traces small circles on my palm. "For knowing what to do when you did."

"Don't thank me yet," I say, voice softer than intended. "Let's see if you survive my nursing."

His smile deepens, crinkling the corners of his eyes. "I've faced worse odds."

A breeze slips into the shelter, curling around us with a whisper of cold. I shiver, not from the chill but from the current running between us. Finn notices, his hand tightening around mine.

"Still cold?" he asks, though his eyes tell me he knows better.

I shake my head, unable to look away from him. The air between us hums with tension, like the stillness before a lightning strike. Without conscious thought, I find myself moving closer. His hand releases mine, reaching up to brush a strand of hair from my face. The touch is gentle, reverent, sending a jolt straight to my core. My heart pounds so loudly I'm certain he must hear it, a wild drum against the quiet of the cave. "Lena," he says—my name raw and real, like something sacred. And in that sound, in his eyes, I see an answered need, a question I'm suddenly desperate to explore. Screw the scripts, screw the roles. I don't answer with words. Instead, I close the last bit of space between us, my lips finding his in the firelight.

The kiss is soft at first, more question than demand. His response is immediate. His hand slides to the nape of my neck, pulling me closer, his thumb brushing against my skin with a quiet possession. Time suspends. The cave, the mountains, the world—all fall away. There is only this moment, this connection, this discovery. The kiss deepens, changes from gentle exploration to something urgent. His lips part, and I follow instinctively, our breaths mingling—hot, ragged, real.

When we pull apart, still breathing hard, I see my wonder reflected in his eyes, now dark with a desire that matches my own. This wasn't part of any script. Any plan. This is something else entirely.

"I knew back at the consignment store," Finn says, his voice rough with emotion. "When you stood your ground and insisted on knowing why you needed the thermal underwear instead of taking my word for it." His fingers tighten, drawing me closer. "That's when I realized you weren't going to be what I expected."

"Really?" I smile, remembering our heated exchange. The memory carries a new kind of warmth now, more ember than spark. "I thought you found me insufferable."

"Challenging," he corrects, his thumb tracing the line of my jaw. "And now I'm grateful you listened. That thermal layer's keeping you warm in this cave." His focus shifts to my mouth, holding there a moment too long.

"Well, that and other things." I tilt my head toward his arm around me.

His smile deepens. "You're more impressive now, covered in dirt, treating wounds with plants, finding your way in the wild." His other hand finds my waist, his grip firm, possessive.

"The real me," I whisper, the admission both terrifying and freeing.

"The real you," he agrees, pulling me closer again until our bodies are almost touching, the heat radiating between us. Our second kiss carries the certainty the first one questioned. His hands find my shoulders, careful of his injured arm but eager for the solid strength of me. My palms press to his chest, splayed against the thick fabric of his shirt, where his heart hammers beneath. His arm wraps around my waist, eliminating what little space remains between us. Heat builds—not the kind from the fire crackling nearby, but something far more consuming. His lips leave mine to trace along my jaw, down to the sensitive skin of my neck. A soft sound escapes me, something between a sigh and a moan as his teeth graze my skin. He smiles against me, and I know it by the shift of his mouth, the way it changes the rhythm of his breath. Then he recaptures my lips. My fingers tangle in his hair, holding him there, like he might vanish if I let go. The kiss deepens—wet, desperate, a mess of tongues and need.

"We should stop," he whispers against my mouth, even as his arm tightens around me.

"Should we?" I whisper, letting my hand trail along the base of his neck, where skin meets hair.

His response is a groan that rolls through me. "If we don't stop now—"

"Maybe I don't want to." The words come out bold, unfiltered, and true.

Finn pulls back enough to search my eyes. Whatever he sees must settle the question, because the next kiss comes hard and certain, stealing the breath from my lungs. His hands leave my waist, fingers tracing heat as they slip lower, gripping my hips. His thumbs press into the small of my back, an anchor, pulling me flush against him until there's no doubt, no space, no thought left at all. His arousal is a hard, undeniable pressure against me, a stark truth even through the layers of our clothes. A sharp thrill shoots low in my stomach—a feeling so potent, so long denied, it's almost a shock. This is real. Not a performance. Not a conquest. Just ... this. Him. Me. It's terrifying. It's exhilarating. It's impossible to ignore.

Outside, the wind picks up, a cold breeze gathering force —rising, pressing, like something awakening. Inside our shelter, protected from the elements but not from this fierce drawing together, we surrender to a different kind of wilderness—uncharted, unexplored, irresistible.

His hand finds the edge of my thermal shirt, hesitating for a heartbeat that thunders in my ears before slipping beneath. *Oh.* His fingers, calloused and surprisingly warm, skim over my bare skin—a shock, a brand—and goosebumps prickle my arms, chasing away the last of the chill. My breath catches, a ragged sound in the tiny tent, as his palm presses against my side, the heat of his touch not searing, but claiming.

"Are you sure?" he whispers, voice rough, his lips hovering above mine.

Instead of answering, I glance down, my hand brushing gently over the gauze on his arm. "What about you?" I ask, breathless. "Your injury..."

He leans in, mouth grazing mine with a smile I feel more than see. "Adrenaline's a hell of a drug," he says—my words thrown back at me, low and wicked and so damn tender I could fall apart.

That's all it takes. I guide his good hand to my breast, my hand covering his, pressing him closer. A soft moan escapes me as his thumb brushes over my nipple, already tight and aching beneath the thin fabric of my bra.

I arch into his touch, instinct taking over—a raw, untamed hunger awakening deep within me. The world shrinks to the touch of his hands on my body, the taste of his mouth on mine, the frantic rhythm of our breathing in the small, fire lit space.

Chapter Nineteen

FINN

THE SOFT, breathless sound she makes as she arches against my hand is the only answer I'll ever need. It's a complete surrender, a total giving-over that mirrors the desperate, aching need clawing its way up my throat. In that instant, every one of my carefully constructed walls evaporates. The world, the cave, the mountain itself—all of it falls away until there is only the feel of her beneath my hand and the thunder of blood in my ears.

The need to feel her, all of her, becomes an ache so sharp it's a physical pain. Our kiss is no longer a question, but a sealing of a pact made without words. I pull back, only an inch, my good arm shaking with the effort of restraint. I breathe her name against her lips, a raw sound of surrender. "Lena."

She meets my eyes, dark and wide with a trust that steals my breath. Then, with fluid grace, she helps me shrug out of my thermal shirt, her fingers brushing against my heated skin, leaving trails of fire. I toss it aside.

In the flickering light, her focus traces the scars across my chest and shoulders, but there's no pity in it—only a

195

profound, heart-stopping acceptance. Then, her hands go to the hem of her shirt, and she pulls it over her head.

Stripped of everything she usually wears—the makeup, the polish, the distance—she's still beautiful. More than that. She's real. And I can't look away.

The firelight throws shadows across her skin, catching on the curves of her chest, the dip of her waist. She's soft in all the places I'm not. Strong in ways that sneak up on me.

Something pulls tight in my chest. Not nerves. Something heavier.

I reach for her, slow, careful. My hand hovers for a second, like touching her might shatter whatever this is. Then I do—fingertips brushing her collarbone, down between her breasts, over the flat of her stomach. Her skin's warm. Soft. She shivers beneath my touch, and I swear I feel it everywhere.

She watches me, her eyes wide—open. There's vulnerability there, yes. But something else too. Power. Like she knows exactly what she's giving me in this moment.

She shifts, her movement bringing her closer. Her hand reaches out, not for my unmarred chest, but for the jagged, puckered scar along my ribs—the worst one, a souvenir from a fall years ago. Her fingers trace its length with a feather-light touch that has me holding my breath. I expect a wince, a question. Instead, she leans forward, and the gentle, unhesitating press of her lips against the damaged skin sends a shockwave straight through my soul. It's not a kiss of passion, but of acceptance. Of healing. It's the most intimate thing I've ever felt, and a groan escapes me.

That single, selfless act breaks the last tether of my restraint. Her hands slide around my back, pulling me down until our bare chests touch. The contact is a brand, a jolt of lightning. I shift over her, bracing my weight on my good forearm and keeping my injured arm tucked carefully against my side. She moves onto her back, drawing me into the cradle of her thighs. The world narrows again to this space, to her. Skin against skin, new and familiar all at once. I brace myself above her, every part of me focused on her—on this. She looks up, eyes locked on mine, open and steady. No fear. No hesitation. Just her, trusting me with all of it.

And as I sink into her, the world stops.

It's not just physical—it's something deeper. A jolt that shoots through me, sharp and direct, like she's flipped some internal switch I didn't know existed. Every nerve fires. The man I was an hour ago doesn't exist anymore. There's only this. Her heat, slick and soft, pulls me in like she was made for me.

It's a feeling I didn't see coming—so complete it knocks the breath out of me. Like finding something I didn't know I'd lost. Like coming home to a place I've never been.

She says my name—barely a whisper—but it lands hard. Like a fault line splitting open inside me. Breaking the old. Rewriting the new.

Right here, right now, I'm not just Finn, the mountain guide.

I'm hers.

I stay buried deep inside her for a long moment, letting us both feel the simple, staggering intimacy of it. Her breath hitches, and her body instinctively lifts to meet mine. That small movement shatters the stillness. I pull back slowly, and then press forward again, beginning a rhythm that is a slow, deliberate worship. Her hips answer my slow thrusts, a perfect, unspoken communication. She is with me, in this, meeting me move for move. The scent of sex and woodsmoke fills the air, a heady, primal perfume. The only sounds are the crackle of the fire and our mingled breaths, the soft, wet slide of our bodies coming together.

Her pleasure hits me like a wave—tightening around me,

small pulses that make it harder to hold on. I feel it in the way she trembles, the way her body moves against mine.

I pick up the pace, going deeper, harder. Her moan—low and real—punches straight through me. She locks her legs around my waist, heels pressing into my lower back, pulling me in like she can't get close enough.

Her hands aren't soft anymore. They grip my shoulders, my back—nails dragging lines across my skin. I'm close to losing it, that last thread of control hanging by a breath.

I lift my head, needing to see her. Needing more than friction. I need *her*.

Our eyes lock, and I see a wild light in her eyes that mirrors the storm in my blood.

"Mags," I groan, the name torn from me, unbidden and raw. It's not Lena, the actress I see. It's Mags. *My Mags.* The woman of earth and fire currently coming apart beneath me.

Her eyes widen at the name—surprised at first, then something else. Something raw. It hits me hard, almost buckles me.

She arches beneath me, a sharp gasp escaping her as her whole body tightens, shaking. I brace myself with one hand against the cave floor, shoulder and back straining as I hold her through it—watching her fall apart, head tilted back, eyes slipping shut as the wave rolls through her.

The sight of her vulnerability, her unguarded response to a name only I have ever used for her, shatters the last of my control. The rhythm becomes frantic, each stroke taking me deeper, closer to the edge. My muscles tense, every nerve ending screaming. And then, the dam breaks. Pleasure explodes through me, a searing, all-consuming wave that whites out my vision. I hold her tight, burying my face in her neck as the tremors wrack my body, the world dissolving into pure, blinding sensation.

We're still tangled up, our bodies warm and spent. The aftershocks haven't fully settled, our breathing just starting to even out. It's quiet outside—the kind of quiet only mountain nights can hold—but in here, everything feels different.

Lena's fingers move across my chest in slow, lazy shapes. Light. Steady. Like she's memorizing me without saying a word.

"That was..."

"I know," I say, understanding what she can't put into words.

She props herself on an elbow to look at me, her blonde hair a gloriously messy halo around her. The firelight catches the gold in it. I get lost looking into her blue eyes—so different from the polished version she puts on for cameras.

"What happens now?" she asks. The question hangs between us, scarier than any cliff we've climbed.

I brush a strand of hair behind her ear. "Now we sleep. Tomorrow, we rejoin the others. And after that..." I can't finish the sentence. After that, she goes back to Hollywood, and I stay here trying to save Crystal Creek. Our worlds don't exactly overlap.

But she surprises me, like she has since day one. "After that, we figure it out," she says. "Together."

Together. The word hits me harder than it should. I've been on my own so long, the idea should scare the hell out of me. Instead, it feels ... right.

"Together," I agree, pulling her back down beside me. She settles against my good side, her head fitting perfectly on my shoulder. I pull the emergency blanket over us both.

As I start to drift off, I'm not thinking about tomorrow's problems. I'm thinking about the woman beside me at Crystal Creek. Not visiting—staying. Maybe the lodge could change without losing what makes it special.

"What are you thinking about?" she murmurs, half-asleep.

"The future."

"Mmm. Good thoughts?"

I hold her tighter, kissing her forehead. "Better than I expected, Mags."

She stirs, a small, sleepy smile touching her lips. "Mags," she repeats softly, tasting the name. "I like it." She burrows closer, a quiet confirmation that the name, like this moment, is something for us. Within minutes, her breathing evens out into the soft cadence of sleep.

I stay awake longer, listening to the mountain sounds and the steady rhythm of her breath. I've always rolled with whatever nature threw at me, but now, for the first time in a long time, I'm actually making plans. Real plans. And they all involve the woman in my arms.

Tomorrow will be complicated—the cameras, Elliott's questions, figuring out what this means when we're back in the real world. Big questions about whether my world and hers can actually work together.

But tonight, with the fire dying down and her warmth plastered against me, those worries feel a lifetime away. What matters is this—finding each other, finding pieces of ourselves we'd forgotten existed.

I kiss her forehead once more before letting sleep take me, making a silent promise to both of us. Whatever comes next, we'll handle it together. The mountain taught me that the things that last aren't the ones that never change—they're the ones that bend without breaking. Maybe Crystal Creek and I can learn that too. That growing doesn't mean giving up who you are. It means becoming something new. Something big enough for two.

Chapter Twenty

LENA

THE FIRST SENSATION is his nearness, a solid, comforting heat against my back. The scent of pine and wood smoke clings to his skin, now mingled with something that's all him. I lie still, a fragile peace settling over me. The memory of the night before pulses beneath my skin, a secret, vibrant hum. *Mags.* The low rumble of his voice from last night stirs in my memory. My lips curve. That name. It fits in a way "Lena" hasn't for years. It strips away the performance, the crushing weight of "Lena Kensington," leaving bare the woman I am only with him, the one I'm finally, tentatively, ready to discover. The one I want to be.

He moves, turning to face me. His eyes, hazel with flecks of gold catching the early light filtering into the cave, hold a tenderness I've seldom witnessed directed at Lena Kensington, actress and persona. A softness resides there, a quiet understanding that transcends the crafted charm and fleeting attention I'm accustomed to. My chest aches with something I can't name—a pull stronger than desire. It's like finding something I didn't know I'd lost. Belonging? Being seen? Maybe.

"Morning." His thumb traces the line of my jaw. The

calloused skin, roughened by the elements, rasps against me, a reminder of our different worlds. Yet in that touch, there's an unexpected intimacy, a grounding presence that steadies something. A tremor traces my spine, a phantom echo of the night's more intense sensations, a stirring of a newfound awareness of my body in his presence—a vulnerability that both excites and terrifies me.

"Morning," I say, my voice still thick with sleep, husky in a way that betrays the depth of last night—whispered confessions and shared breaths in the dark. The air in the cave is heavy, charged with things neither of us has said yet. I reach out, my fingers finding the strands of his hair, tangling in their surprising strength and softness. The gesture is small, but it carries weight. A quiet acknowledgment of this moment. Of him. *Of us.* A promise I'm not sure I know how to keep.

We lie there in silence, the world outside reduced to a distant hum. The last of the embers glow faintly, casting a soft light that blurs the hard lines of dawn and makes everything feel gentler than it should.

For now, this place is a sanctuary—temporary, but real. I study his face. The slight furrow between his brows hints at that quiet intensity I've come to recognize. And then, the faint smile when his eyes meet mine—something that hovers between amusement and understanding—makes my breath catch.

A shared secret we haven't dared to name. This man. So different from the polished charm of Hollywood's elite, from connections built on ambition and the spotlight. He's steady in a way that anchors me. Honest in a way that slips past every defense I've ever built. He doesn't see the curated version of Lena Kensington. Somehow, he recognizes Mags—the woman I'm only beginning to meet myself.

Stepping out of the cave an hour later is like waking from a dream into the blaze of reality. The mountain air is crisp, cutting, a reminder of the wildness out here. The world bursts into color—the deep green of the pines, the steely grey of the cliffs, the vast and indifferent sweep of pale blue sky. And with it, reality. Complications. Consequences. But also, something else I hadn't expected—clarity.

We need to make it back to camp without being seen emerging together from this hidden spot. My tent stands empty, evidence of my absence throughout the night. A complication we hadn't considered in our rush to solitude, nor in what happened between us after. The path requires careful navigation—both the physical trail down the rocky slope and the social terrain awaiting us. We'll need a story. A reason for my early morning absence, a plausible explanation for our separate returns.

"Go first," Finn says, his voice low, already slipping back into guide mode, though his eyes still hold the raw memory of the night. "Circle around the east side of the basin. Make it look as if you were scouting, checking the sunrise, whatever. I'll follow a different route, come in from the west fifteen minutes later. Act surprised to find me back already." *Act surprised. Right. Back to performing.* The thought lands with a familiar, dull thud in my chest, even as I understand the necessity.

I nod, accepting the need for subterfuge.

"Okay. But Finn..." I hesitate, needing to address the obvious. "Your arm. Your ribs. You're sure you're able to hike?"

He adjusts the bandage I made, his expression neutral. "Bruised ribs, sore arm. Nothing that'll stop me. I've hiked through worse." He avoids my eyes, pulling on his professional mask. "Go on. Before the others wake up."

I want to argue, to insist he let me check his injuries again, but the set of his jaw tells me it's useless. His pride is back in place. I give him one last brief look, memorizing the strong lines of his face in the morning light, then turn and pick my way down the slope, heading east as instructed.

The walk back to camp is a blur of conflicting emotions. Relief that Finn is alive and somewhat okay. Lingering warmth from the night spent in his arms. Anxiety about facing Elliott and the crew. Guilt over the deception. And a deep, unsettling worry about Finn pushing himself too hard, hiding the true extent of his injuries. Gram always said stubborn men were the quickest to meet their maker because they refused to admit when they needed rest.

I reach the edge of the camp as the first signs of stirring emerge from the tents. I take a deep breath, smooth my hair, and try to look like someone returning from a reflective morning walk, hoping the mud on my boots isn't too incriminating.

Carlos is the first one I encounter, kneeling by the cold fire pit. "Morning, Lena. You're up early."

"Couldn't sleep," I say, forcing a casual shrug. "Watched the sunrise from the ridge. It was incredible." I gesture eastward. "Any coffee started?"

"Not yet. Finn's not back, and Elliott's still..." Carlos trails off as Elliott's tent flap unzips with force.

"Alright, people, let's move!" Elliott booms, emerging with his clipboard. "We lost time yesterday. Need to make camp by nightfall. Where's Finn? He should have been back hours ago."

Right on cue, Finn strides into camp from the west, moving with a steady, ground-eating pace that masks the stiffness I know he must be feeling. His pack sits high on his shoulders, his expression calm, professional. Only I can detect the slight tension around his eyes, the careful way he holds his injured arm close to his body.

"Morning," Finn says, his voice even as he nods to the group. "Just got back."

Elliott turns, surprised. "Finn! At last. Any problems? We expected you sooner."

"Trail was slower than expected coming down," Finn replies, his voice smooth as he drops his pack near the fire pit without betraying any discomfort. "Dave's evacuation went fine. He's stable, getting treatment." His eyes shift to mine, offering a neutral acknowledgment. "See you made it back okay, Lena. Looks like you were out early too."

"It was stunning," I say, matching his tone and stepping into the lie. "You missed the best light." The words slide out smoothly, even as they knot something inside me.

Elliott studies us both for a beat, suspicion tightening his mouth, but he doesn't push. "Good, good," he says, already moving on. ""So, high camp today? We're back on track?"

"That's the plan," Finn confirms, moving to get the coffee started, his movements economical, hiding any sign of pain. "Weather looks clear. Trail should be manageable, mostly uphill from here. We'll reach high camp, then push to the filming location at Painted Peaks tomorrow."

Breakfast was tense, the usual camaraderie gone, replaced by a subtle strain. I watch Finn, seeing the subtle signs of discomfort he tries so hard to hide—the slight hesitation before bending, the way he favors his left side, the almost imperceptible tightening of his jaw when he lifts the heavy coffee pot. He catches me looking once and gives me a warning expression that practically screams *I'm fine, drop it.* But I can't. Worry, sharp and insistent, coils in my gut. A fall that left him bleeding and bruised, a night spent shivering in a cave before ... before. That's not 'nothing serious,' no matter how much he wants to pretend.

As the awkward silence stretches, Finn distracts everyone by emptying his pack onto a tarp near the fire. Protein bars, dried fruit, packets of nuts, and jerky tumble out in impressive quantities. "Brought extra rations," he explains, sorting through the pile. "Figured we could use them after the flood took some of ours. Help yourselves."

The mood instantly lightens. The crew gathers around, relief and interest replacing suspicion. Carlos grabs a packet of dried mango, Tom and Jake start comparing protein bar flavors, and even Elliott seems diverted for a moment, examining a package of smoked salmon jerky. It's a clever move, shifting the focus and reminding everyone of his role as the provider, the capable guide.

While the others are occupied with the unexpected bounty, Elliott outlines his filming plan for the day. "I want to focus on the final ascent. The struggle, the determination. Lena, we'll get shots of you using the compass, perhaps leading the way for a section. Show that transformation."

"As long as it doesn't slow us down," Finn says, his tone leaving no room for argument as he pours coffee. "High camp by nightfall is the priority."

As we break camp, I find a moment alone with Finn while the others are distracted by the food. "Seriously, Finn, how bad is it?" I whisper, indicating his arm with a nod. "You need to be honest. Pushing yourself could make it worse."

"It's handled, Mags," he says, his voice low and firm, using the name that feels like ours alone. The use of it softens the dismissal, but the message is clear ... *back off*. "I know my limits. We need to reach the Peaks."

"Your pride is going to get you hurt," I argue, my voice low. "You fell hard enough to be out all night."

"My experience is going to get us there safely," he counters, meeting my eyes. There's a stubbornness there I recognize from myself, but also a weariness he can't hide. "Trust me on this."

I want to push, but the rest of the crew is gathering, packs ready. Elliott is looking impatient. "Alright," I concede with reluctance. "But I'm watching you. One sign you're struggling, and I'm calling a halt, Elliott's schedule be damned."

A ghost of a faint smile touches his lips. "Wouldn't expect anything less."

We set out from the camp, the mood changed. The shared experience in the cave hangs between Finn and me, an unspoken current between us, while the need for secrecy creates a different tension. Elliott's suspicion adds another layer of complexity. The plan is clear: reach high camp by nightfall. But as we begin the climb, leaving the relative shelter of the basin behind, I can't shake the feeling that the most challenging part of this journey isn't the mountain ahead, but navigating what lies between us, and the secrets we now carry. And Finn, leading the way with his jaw set and his pain hidden, worries me more than any bear or storm we've faced so far.

Chapter Twenty-One

LENA

Waking up beside Finn feels normal now, a dangerous sort of normal. The first shock of sharing such close quarters has faded, replaced by a quiet intimacy that hums beneath the surface of every interaction. I lie still in the pre-dawn chill, his steady breathing grounding me against the silence of the mountains. The memory of that night in the cave—the way he called me Mags, the vulnerability in his eyes, the unspoken understanding that passed between us—settles within me.

I slip out of our shared sleeping bag arrangement with care, mindful of his injuries. He's awake, his eyes finding mine in the dim light filtering through the tent fabric. There's no awkwardness—only a quiet acknowledgment of our time together.

"Morning," I whisper.

"Morning," he says back, his voice still rough with sleep. He pushes himself up, and I see the wince he tries to hide as his ribs protest.

"Easy," I caution, instinctively putting a hand on his good shoulder. "Let me get the fire going first."

He doesn't argue, but nods, sinking back down with a sigh

that sounds like relief. That small concession, the willingness to accept even that minor bit of help, feels like a victory.

Outside, the air is crystalline, biting. The jagged peaks surrounding our meadow are painted rose-gold by the first rays of sun—an almost violent beauty. It's breathtaking, a stark, aggressive grandeur that seems to mirror the tension simmering within our small group, a tension that, right now, for me, is solely focused on the injured man I left in our tent.

I get the fire started, coaxing flames from the embers Finn banked last night, setting water to boil for coffee and oatmeal. The camp stirs, everyone moving with the stiffness of exhaustion and cold. Elliott is, predictably, the first one geared up, consulting his notes, his energy seemingly inexhaustible when it comes to the production. Behind me, I hear the zipper of our tent and turn to find Finn emerging, moving stiffly but purposefully toward the fire pit.

As I hand Finn a mug of steaming coffee, careful not to jostle his injured arm, Elliott strides over, clapping his hands together. "Alright team! The final push! Painted Peaks awaits! Scenery is epic, as promised. Let's pack up, I want to reach the main filming meadow by midday to catch the best light!"

Finn stiffens beside me, his jaw tightening, but he gives a curt nod. "Weather's clear. Trail's straightforward from here, mostly alpine meadow, gentle climb. We can make good time." He avoids my eyes, shifting back into guide mode, burying the pain I know is still there.

Breakfast is quick, fueled by anticipation and Elliott's relentless enthusiasm. I watch Finn as we break camp, noting the way he moves, the subtle bracing of his injured side when he lifts his pack. He looks at me and gives a small, almost imperceptible shake of his head. I bite back my concern, respecting his pride for now, though the worry stays curled tight in my stomach.

The hike from the base camp meadow toward the specific

filming location Elliott has chosen is, as Finn predicted, less strenuous than the previous day's climb. We traverse high alpine meadows carpeted with resilient wildflowers, navigate around small, jewel-like glacial lakes reflecting the towering peaks, and cross patches of lingering snow. The air is thin, demanding effort with each breath, but the landscape is awe-inspiring. Jagged granite summits pierce the impossibly blue sky, glaciers cling to shadowed slopes, and the silence is broken only by the wind and the crunch of our boots.

Elliott is in his element, directing Carlos and the other cameramen. "Get Lena walking toward that peak! Majestic! Frame her against the glacier! Show the solitude, the triumph!"

I play along, walking where he points, looking thought-fully at vistas, using Finn's compass now and then for effect. But my focus keeps drifting back to Finn. He walks point, setting a steady pace, his stride even, but I perceive the effort it costs him. I see the lines of pain etched around his eyes when he thinks no one is watching, the way his breathing is a frac-tion too shallow.

We reach the designated filming location—a spectacular high meadow nestled directly beneath the most dramatic cluster of peaks—before noon. It's undeniably perfect for filming. A small, clear stream meanders through it, wildflowers riot in patches of sun, and the backdrop is a breathtaking panorama of rock, snow, and sky. The crew lets out collective sighs of relief and awe.

"This is it," Elliott declares with triumph, dropping his pack. "Worth the climb. Okay, people, let's get base camp set up. We'll spend the next few days here, getting those key trans-formation shots for Lena, capturing the majesty, the solitude..."

I freeze, Elliott's casual words hitting like an icy wind. A few days? Up here? Like this?

My eyes snap to Finn, dread coiling low and sharp in my gut. He's pale beneath his tan, that muscle in his jaw ticking again. He looks spent—like he's running on nothing but grit and stubbornness. Staying isn't an option. Not if I want the man I ... the man I care about ... to make it off this mountain alive.

Before I can voice my protest, Finn grabs my arm, his grip surprisingly strong despite his injury. "Lena. A word. In private." His voice is low, urgent, stopping the angry response before it could leave my lips. He pulls me away from the group, behind a cluster of large boulders that offers minimal privacy but shields us from view, though I'm aware of Carlos's camera panning in our direction.

"What is it?" I ask, concern sharpening my tone as I see the desperation in his eyes.

"Don't fight him on this," Finn says, his voice barely a whisper, strained with pain and something else ... fear? "Don't argue about leaving."

"Are you kidding me?" I stare at him. "Finn, you're hurt! You need to get down, consult a doctor. Staying up here for 'a few days' is insane!"

"I know my body, Mags. I can manage." He grips my arms tighter, his eyes pleading. "But I need this job. I need the payment from this production."

"We talked about this," I begin, confused. "The lodge—"

"It's more than being behind," he interrupts, words tumbling out. "That damn contract ... if I don't finish this, if I'm the reason we cut it short ... they could take everything. The whole payment." His voice cracked. "Everything. I lose the lodge, Mags. Everything my mother..." He trails off, unable to finish, the raw vulnerability stark on his face.

The depth of his desperation hits me. It's not pride, it's raw fear—losing his home, his legacy. My heart aches for him. From where I stand, the fix seems so easy.

"Finn, listen to me," I say gently, covering his hand on my arm with mine. "The money doesn't matter. Forget the contract, forget Elliott. Your health is what's important. If it's about the lodge payments, I can help. I have money, more than enough. I can give you whatever you need to—"

He recoils as if I'd slapped him, pulling his arm away. The sudden absence of his touch feels like ice water in my veins. The warmth in his eyes vanishes, replaced by a glacial coldness that chills me to the bone. Hurt flashes across his face, masked by anger, and my stomach drops. What just happened?

"Give me?" he repeats, his voice dangerously low, laced with wounded pride. "You think this is about needing a handout from you? From Lena Kensington?"

The words hit like physical blows. Handout? That's not— I was trying to help. My chest tightens, breath catching. "No! That's not what I meant!" I stammer, panic rising as I realize how badly I've misstepped. "I meant—"

"I know what you meant," he cuts me off, his voice flat, devoid of the connection we shared over the last couple of days. Each word lands like a door slamming shut. "You think you can swoop in with your Hollywood money and fix everything. Solve my problems like I'm some charity case you picked up in the backcountry."

Charity case. The phrase slices through me, sharp and merciless. Is that what he thinks? That our night together meant nothing? That I'm some entitled actress playing savior? My throat burns with unshed tears, the ache spreading through my chest like cracks in ice.

"Finn, please, that's not fair—"

"Isn't it?" He takes a step back, putting physical distance between us, and the space feels like a chasm. "You think because we ... because the cave happened..." He spits the words out as if "cave happened' was an unfortunate accident, a regrettable lapse in judgment.

The dismissal hits me like a punch to the gut. When he called me Mags, when he looked at me like I was everything, when I felt more real than I have in years—reduced to nothing. My vision blurs, the mountain peaks swimming behind tears I refuse to let fall.

"...that gives you the right to treat me like I can't handle my life? Like I need rescuing?" The muscle in his jaw jumps again. "I won't take money from family, Mags, you think I'd take it from you? I handle my debts. I don't need your pity or your money."

Pity. The word fractures something inside me. All I wanted was to help him, to save what he loves most, and he's twisting it into pity. Making me the villain for caring. My hands shake, and I clench them into fists to stop the trembling.

"It's not pity!" My voice rises, frustration and hurt warring within me, threatening to spill over. "I care about you! I don't want to see you lose everything because of some stupid contract! I'm willing to risk my entire career telling Elliott we're leaving—"

"Risk your career?" Finn scoffs, the sound harsh and dismissive, missing the weight of my words entirely. The casual cruelty of it steals my breath. "What does that mean? You lose a role. You get another one. They make another movie. It's not real. Losing the lodge ... losing my home ... that's real. Don't compare your Hollywood drama to what's at stake here."

His words land like stones thrown at glass. My career, my world, everything I've fought for—dismissed as drama. Not real. The life I've built, the sacrifices I've made, the battles I've won and lost—none of it matters to him. I'm some actress playing dress-up in his real world. The pain is so sharp I can barely breathe.

He doesn't understand me at all. After everything, after

last night, I'm still Lena Kensington to him. A Hollywood fantasy. Not Mags. Never Mags.

"Then let me handle it my way," he says, his voice cold as he turns back to the immediate problem. "Stay out of it. Play your part for Elliott's cameras for a few more days. Let me earn the money I need to save my home. Don't make this harder than it is."

Play your part. The final hit. That's all I am to him—a performance. His words land like blows, each one driving deeper into the hollow space where my heart used to be. He's shutting me out, pushing me away, treating what happened between us like another problem to manage, a complication to his real worries. The vulnerability he's shown me has vanished, replaced by that impenetrable wall of pride and misunderstanding.

The hurt crystallizes into something harder, colder. If that's what he wants—if I'm a Hollywood problem to be managed—then fine.

"Fine," I say, my voice brittle, ice forming around the edges of the hurt, protecting what's left of me. "If that's what you want. Handle it yourself."

I turn away, blinking back sudden, furious tears, and walk toward the main camp. My steps stay measured, controlled. The spectacular beauty of Painted Peaks stretches in every direction—mocking, cold, indifferent. He threw my help back in my face. Chose his pride over trust. Over us. Over even trying to understand what I was offering.

The crew is setting up the tents in the meadow. I see the small, two-person tent Finn and I had been sharing. Ignoring it, I walk directly to where Carlos is laying out his gear near the tent he previously shared with Dave. *Fine.* He wants to handle it himself. He wants to pretend last night meant nothing more than shared body heat. Two can play at being cold and practical.

"Carlos," I say, my voice deliberately loud, carrying across the suddenly quiet meadow. Several heads snap our way.

"Yeah, Lena?" He raises his head, surprised.

"Finn will take Dave's spot in this tent tonight," I state, channeling every ice-queen role I've ever played to keep my expression unreadable, to remove the tremor from my voice. "Looks like you've got a roommate."

Carlos shifts uneasily, glancing toward Finn as he approaches, then back to the tent. "Uh, no problem," he says, studiously avoiding my face. He gestures toward the entrance. "Dave's space was on the left."

Finn nods curtly, drops his gear near the tent entrance, and walks away without a word.

"Good." I walk to the tent Finn and I had been sharing, duck inside, and emerge moments later carrying his sleeping bag and pack. I stride over to the tent Carlos will now share with Finn and drop Finn's gear near the flap.

A collective gasp ripples through the watching crew members, followed by dead silence. I turn to face Finn, who has stopped a few yards away, watching me, his expression unreadable but tight. The rest of the crew stares, silent and wide-eyed.

"There," I say, my voice clear and cold, projecting across the silence of the meadow. "You can handle things yourself. You won't need my *'medical monitoring'* tonight."

The words hang there—too specific, too revealing—and I realize, too late, that no one else knew.

But I don't stop to explain.

I turn on my heel and head for the tent originally assigned to us—my tent now. I duck inside and zip the flap closed with a rasp that feels final. Outside, the meadow is silent. Inside, the ache in my chest echoes loud enough to drown everything else.

Perhaps he was right. Perhaps our worlds are too different.

Chapter Twenty-Two

FINN

THE RASP of the zipper closing Lena's tent echoes across the silent meadow. It feels like a door slamming shut, not on the tent, but on ... something else. Something I hadn't realized I valued until the thought of losing it hit me, cold and hard. I stand there, rooted to the spot, watching as she disappears inside. She's dropped my gear at Carlos's feet like it's trash. *There. You can handle things yourself.* Her voice, brittle with ice I hadn't known she possessed, rings in my ears.

The crew gapes. Marco fiddles with his microphone. Even Elliott looks momentarily stunned, his mouth slightly open. Carlos blinks, clearly thrown, his attention shifting between me, the gear at his feet, and the tent Lena disappeared into.

"She's exaggerating," I say, voice low but firm. "Took a fall on the way back through the pass. Ribs are bruised. Cut my arm. Nothing major."

A few eyes shift away like they've been caught staring. I bend to grab the gear, ignoring the way it pulls at my side.

A collective gasp had rippled through them when she dropped my stuff—a sound that scraped raw against my frayed nerves. Humiliation burns hot at the back of my neck. She didn't only reject my decision, she publicly evicted me. In front of everyone. After everything ... after the cave...

My first instinct is pure, wounded pride. Anger flares, hot and quick. How dare she? After I pushed myself half-dead up Raven's Spine to get back to her? After I opened up about the lodge, about my fears? But the anger gutters as it flares, doused by a cold wave of realization. She's right. I pushed her away. I threw her offer back in her face, dismissing her. I let my fear and pride speak louder than sense, louder than the connection that had felt so real hours before. I told her to handle it herself, and now she is. Starting with me.

"Well," Elliott clears his throat, recovering first, ever the producer sensing drama. "Seems the sleeping arrangements are settled." He forces an expression that doesn't reach his eyes. "Adds another layer to the narrative, eh? Tension under the Peaks!"

I ignore him, walking over to Carlos's tent. "Sorry about this," I mutter to Carlos.

"Uh, no problem, Finn," Carlos says, looking anywhere but at me.

The rest of the afternoon crawls by in a haze of discomfort —both physical and otherwise. I busy myself with whatever tasks I can find, reinforcing the camp perimeter, double-checking the water source, rigging a better bear hang for what's left of our food. Anything to stay in motion. Anything to stop myself from thinking.

Mags stays near her tent, shoulders tense, her attention fixed anywhere but me. When our paths inevitably cross, she looks right through me—like I'm part of the scenery. Another rock in the meadow. I want to reach for her, to make her see me, to tell her I've been a damn fool. But the frost in her expression stops me cold. That chill cuts deeper than the bruises or the throb in my ribs.

Dinner is a quiet, miserable affair around the fire. Elliott talks too loudly, trying to inject life into a conversation that refuses to take shape. Mags sits off to the side, nursing tea, hardly speaking. I eat out of habit, the food dry in my mouth, my attention locked on the woman sitting ten feet away and somehow impossibly out of reach. The firelight dances in her hair. Her jaw is set in that familiar, stubborn line. And when she thinks no one's looking, there's still hurt in her eyes—a flicker of something raw and wounded. My fault. The thought settles low and heavy, duller than the pain in my side, but harder to ignore.

That night, sharing the tent with Carlos is ... awkward. He's a good kid, quiet and professional, but he's not Mags. The silence is heavy, punctuated only by the wind whistling outside and Carlos's occasional snore. Sleep evades me. My ribs throb. My arm aches. But worse is the hollowness in my chest, the replay of our argument behind the rocks. *I won't take money from family, Mags. You think I'd take it from you?* The words sound even harsher in memory. How could I have been so stupid? So blind? She was offering help and care, and I treated it like an insult. I'd let my fear of losing the lodge, my ingrained pride, make me cruel.

Morning brings no relief, only the prospect of another day pretending I'm fine while navigating the minefield of Elliott's filming demands and Mags's icy distance. Changing the bandage on my arm is a clumsy, painful process done hunched inside the tent. Carlos is already outside, probably giving me space after yesterday's public spectacle. The gash looks clean, her butterfly strips holding, but the surrounding skin is bruised and tender. My ribs feel like a moose has kicked them. Every deep breath is agony.

I force myself out, plastering on the stoic guide's face. Coffee helps. A little. I head toward the fire pit, bracing for the crew's reaction. Marco whistles a low, knowing tune under his breath as I pass. Yeah, the ribbing has started. Expected, but it doesn't make it easier.

Mags is up, talking with Carlos about camera angles for a sunrise shot. She gives me a brief, impersonal nod as I approach the fire, then turns back to Carlos. The easy camaraderie, the exchanged signals, the inside jokes—all gone. Replaced by a polite, professional wall I have no idea how to breach.

Elliott sidles up beside me as I pour myself a coffee. His voice pitches low. "Rough night, Hollister?" He smirks, enjoying the drama. "Must be tough getting kicked out by the leading lady. Anything juicy happen you'd like to share? Might be worth a little bonus for some exclusive insight into Ms. Kensington's 'transformation.'"

His offer, the slimy implication, turns my stomach. "Get lost, Elliott," I say, my voice flat and cold. "You want insight? Film the mountains. They're more honest than anything you're trying to create."

Elliott's smirk fades, replaced by a flicker of annoyance, but he backs off for now. He turns his attention back to Lena. "Okay, Lena! Let's get those contemplative wilderness moments! Walk along the stream! Gaze at the peaks! Look thoughtful! Look transformed!"

She does it flawlessly. Lena Kensington is back in control. She hits her marks, delivers the thoughtful expressions, and interacts with the landscape the way Elliott wants. She's giving him the performance that fits his story. The Mags who argued with me behind the rocks, who patched my arm with plants and fierce tenderness, is gone. Watching her slide back into that Hollywood persona hurts more than I expected. It's like watching her vanish.

I focus on the work—checking gear, monitoring the weather, keeping the camp secure. My interactions with Mags stay clipped and professional. Guide to client. Every polite exchange scrapes across something raw.

During a break, I spot her sitting alone by the stream, sketching in a small notebook she must have salvaged from her pack. It's the first time I've seen her do anything for herself on this trip. I walk over with a half-formed apology already on my lips, needing to ask about her drawing and somehow bridge this damn canyon between us. But she raises her head, her expression cool, guarded—the Lena Kensington mask locked down tight. Impenetrable. She doesn't want me near.

Message received.

I stop, the unspoken rejection a fresh twist in my gut. I turn away, the ache in my chest sharp enough to make me wince.

The next day follows the same pattern. Filming. Forced proximity. Polite distance. Elliott pushes for more shots of Lena "embracing the wild," having her identify plants—the ones she's sure of, avoiding any uncertainty—track animal prints Carlos points out, and build a small, perfect fire for a solo shot. She does it all with professional ease, revealing glimpses of the knowledge she possesses, fitting it into Elliott's revised "return to roots" narrative. She never asks about my arm or ribs. Never meets my eye for more than a fleeting second. The warmth we shared in the cave might as well be a dream—something that belonged to a different lifetime.

Physically, I'm going downhill. Constant hiking, thin air, no real rest—it's wearing me down. The pain in my ribs grinds on. Every morning, when I change the bandage, the skin around the gash looks angrier, more inflamed. It's not infected. Not yet. But it's not healing either. I need rest. Medical care. Things I turned down out of pride and fear. Things Mags tried to warn me about.

On the third afternoon at Painted Peaks, Elliott decides it's time for a new story arc. "The mentor and the student," he calls it. "The culmination of the journey. Mutual respect." He positions us near the cliff edge overlooking the mountains. "Finn, explain the geology. Lena, look impressed and ask insightful questions."

Standing next to her—close enough that I can sense her warmth, even in the stiff wind—is torture. I stumble through glacial carving and tectonic uplift, my voice stiff. Mags asks the right questions, cool and detached. No trace of the woman who kissed me, argued with me, fell asleep in my arms.

"Okay, good, good," Elliott says. "Now, a little closer. Perhaps Finn puts a hand on her shoulder? Guide her gaze to that far peak?"

I hesitate. Touching her now would be a violation. Like crossing a boundary I no longer have the right to approach.

"For the shot, Finn," Elliott says.

I raise my good hand and place it lightly on her shoulder. She flinches—barely, but enough. Enough to land like a punch to the chest. I pull away at once.

"Something wrong?" Elliott frowns.

"Wind shifted," I lie, turning from the camera. "Need to check the tents." I walk away, ignoring Elliott's sigh, ignoring the lens trained on my back, ignoring the sudden sting behind my eyes. That flinch said it all. I didn't bruise her pride—I broke something between us. Something fragile I hadn't realized we'd built until it splintered in my hands.

That night, huddled in the tent with Carlos's quiet breathing beside me, the weight of it all settles hard. Losing the lodge would gut me. It holds my past, my family, my sweat and sacrifice. But losing Mags ... losing the future we might've had—that's something worse.

I think about the expression in her eyes before I pulled her aside yesterday—that fierce determination. She was about to tell Elliott off, about to demand we leave, about to put my health before the filming, before her career. I recognized it, knew it. And I stopped her. Not to protect her from Elliott's threats, but to protect myself, to ensure I got paid. And how did I repay that fierce loyalty she was about to show? By mocking her world, rejecting her help, prioritizing my damn pride over her heart. Over us. The realization is a physical pain, sharper than what I feel in my ribs, deeper than the gash on my arm.

I look into the darkness, the silence of the tent amplifying the hollowness inside me. I need to fix this. But how? An apology won't be enough. Words sound hollow after the way I acted. I need to show her. Show her I understand. Show her she matters more than the lodge, more than the money, more than my stubborn fear. The first step, the hardest one, is admitting I was wrong. Admitting I need help. Not only financially, but also to help see past one's blind spots.

Tomorrow. Tomorrow, Elliott plans to wrap filming here. Then we start the hike down. On the way down, away from the pressure of the Peaks, I can find a way. Find the words. Find the courage to tear down my walls instead of hers. If she'll let me close enough to try.

Chapter Twenty-Three

LENA

I WAKE UP COLD. It's more than the biting chill of the high-altitude morning seeping through the tent walls. It's a deeper, hollow coldness that has settled in my chest, opposite to the memory of Finn's warmth when we were last together. Alone. Again. The small tent stretches around me, the silence amplifying the emptiness where his solid presence had once been. Last night, sleep was fitful, punctuated by the wind rattling the thin fabric and the constant, tight knot of hurt and anger in my chest.

I push myself out of my sleeping bag, the silence amplifying my solitude. No quiet breathing beside me, no shared warmth. Just me and the spectacular, indifferent beauty of Painted Peaks visible through the small tent flap. He chose his pride, his lodge, over us. Over the connection I thought we'd forged. He dismissed my world, my potential sacrifice, as if it were trivial. The memory stings, fresh and sharp.

Getting dressed is mechanical. Cold layers. Laced boots— sturdy ones Finn insisted I buy. Boots that carried me further than I ever thought I'd go, both physically and emotionally. Now, they're heavy.

Outside, the camp is stirring. The air is thin and clear, the sun beginning to touch the highest, snow-dusted peaks, turning them rose-gold. It's the epic vista Elliott dreams of, but today, it looks desolate. Finn is by the fire pit, talking in a low voice with Carlos, probably about the day's filming logistics. He moves with a pronounced stiffness, favoring his left side more than yesterday. He tries to hide it, straightening when he catches me watching, but the flash of pain in his eyes is unmistakable. He is hurting badly. And he's too proud to admit it, even after I practically begged him to let me help, even after … everything.

My worry wars with my anger. Part of me wants to march over there, check his bandage, demand he stop pretending. The other part, still smarting from his rejection, pulls on a layer of icy composure. *Handle it yourself*, I'd told him. Fine. Let him.

I pour myself coffee without acknowledging him, offering only a curt nod when he says, "Morning." No warmth, no shared glances. The easy rhythm we'd fallen into is gone— replaced by a brittle formality that presses in, tight and suffocating.

Marco suddenly finds his boots fascinating. Elliott watches us with open curiosity, calculating behind his coffee cup.

Let them look. Lena Kensington is back on set.

"Alright, Lena!" Elliott booms, clipboard in hand. "Last day of filming up here! Let's make it count! I want those final transformation shots. You, embracing the solitude. Finding peace in the wilderness. Connecting with your inner strength."

Inner strength. Right now, mine is a knotted mess of hurt, anger, and a confusing residue of tenderness for the man who won't meet my eyes. But I nod, summoning the actress. "Whatever you need, Elliott."

The day blurs into a string of curated moments. Walk here. Look contemplative there. Kneel by the stream and identify the patch of alpine arnica I pointed out yesterday—reciting its uses for bruises, courtesy of Finn, while ignoring the fresh one blooming behind my ribs. Build a tidy little fire. Stare thoughtfully into the flames.

I hit every mark. Offer every look Elliott wants. Quiet strength, gentle focus. Lena Kensington has worn the mask of resilience for years. But today, it slips. Because this isn't a performance. It feels like a betrayal—not of Finn, but of the woman he saw beneath the actress. The one I'd only begun to find again.

Finn stays mostly in the background, fulfilling his guide duties—checking the perimeter, monitoring the weather, ensuring the crew's safety—but keeping a physical distance from me unless Elliott forces an interaction. Elliott tries once, wanting a shot of Finn showing me how to read the clouds. "Mentor passing on his wisdom," Elliott directs. "Show that bond."

I listen, nodding, aware of the few inches separating us, the weight of everything unspoken pressing between us.

During a lunch break—more tasteless, dehydrated rations—I find a spot away from the others, near the edge of the meadow, and pull out my sketchbook. Drawing has always been my escape, a way to process things without words. I sketch the jagged peaks opposite us, focusing on the harsh lines, the unyielding granite, pouring my frustration onto the page.

"Mind if I join you?" Carlos stands there, holding his ration pack, looking hesitant.

"Sure," I say, closing the sketchbook. He sits down a comfortable distance away.

"Rough couple of days, huh?" he asks, his voice low.

"You could say that."

"Listen, Lena," he says, lowering his voice more. "About a few days ago ... Elliott filming your argument with Finn..." My head snaps up, and a sickening lurch goes through me.

"He filmed that?"

Carlos nods, looking miserable. "I tried to angle the camera away, but he insisted. Called it 'raw conflict.' He's probably uploaded it already via the satellite link."

A cold dread washes over me. Our private argument, Finn's vulnerability about the lodge, my disastrous offer of help, his prideful rejection—all captured, likely dissected by network executives seeking exploitable drama. The violation runs deep.

"He had no right," I whisper, clenching my fists.

"He never does," Carlos says grimly. "But he has the contract. I wanted you to know." He pauses. "Also ... Finn. He looks like hell. Are you sure he's okay to hike down tomorrow?"

"He insists he is," I say, bitterness sharpening my voice. "Says he can handle it himself."

Carlos nods, understanding more than he lets on.

The rest of the afternoon on camera is harder to stomach. Knowing Elliott has that footage—knowing he'll twist it into whatever version suits him—makes every scene feel hollow. By the time he calls wrap and announces we'll begin the descent *after* breaking camp in the morning, I'm wrung out—emotionally and physically.

As the crew starts prepping for tomorrow, packing cameras and sound equipment for the long hike down, I stand facing the sweeping, unforgiving beauty of the Painted Peaks. We made it. We reached the destination. But the victory feels hollow.

My fingers close around the small brass compass in my pocket—Finn's mother's. He gave it to me like a promise. A tether. Now it just feels like a weight, a reminder of the distance between us. The different worlds we come from.

He pushed me away. Chose his pride and his fear over trust—over *us*. Maybe he was right. Maybe I was foolish to think whatever this was between us could survive beyond this place.

Still ... a part of me wishes it could have.

Tomorrow, we start the hike down. Back toward the lodge, toward Port Promise, toward the life waiting for me back in Los Angeles. Part of me longs for the familiar comfort of my world, the predictability, the control. Another part aches with the loss of something I didn't know I was searching for until I found it here, with him.

As the crew gathers around the final campfire at Painted Peaks, sharing the last of the decent coffee and reminiscing about the expedition's highs and lows—the flood, the bear, Dave's bee stings—I keep my distance. I watch Finn across the flames. He's laughing at something Jake said, but the laughter doesn't reach his eyes. He shifts position, trying to find comfort for his ribs, and I see him press a hand to his side when he thinks no one is looking. My heart clenches. He's hurting. And tomorrow, we start the long hike down. He won't ask for help. And after yesterday, I don't know how to offer it.

I retreat to my tent, zipping the flap closed against the cold and the forced camaraderie outside. Lying alone in the darkness, I trace the outline of the compass through my pocket. The journey isn't over yet. We still have to get off this mountain. And I still don't know what happens when we do.

Chapter Twenty-Four

FINN

Leaving Painted Peaks feels like walking away from a battlefield. Not one littered with bullets and debris, but the quieter kind—where trust is the casualty. The meadow, sharp with morning light, feels altered now, its beauty undercut by the dull ache in my chest, one that has nothing to do with bruised ribs.

Packing up is all strained silence and averted looks. Mags moves with quiet precision, breaking down her tent—hers, not ours—methodically folding away what little we had. She doesn't spare me a glance. The crew follows her lead, careful and subdued. They all saw it happen. The shift. The fracture. Now they navigate around it like a fresh wound.

Even Elliott reins in his usual flair, offering only clipped directions. No jokes. No commentary. Only a shared, uncomfortable quiet that says everything.

Shouldering my pack is agony. I manage it with a grunt, shifting the weight to my left side. My arm throbs beneath the clean bandage I fumbled with last night, one-handed. My ribs burn with every breath. The days spent pretending I was fine —climbing, filming, holding it together—have taken their toll.

And now, contemplating the miles back to the lodge, it's like facing another mountain.

"Everyone ready?" I call out, forcing authority into my voice, pushing past the discomfort. "We stick together on the way down. The terrain is easier but stay alert. Loose rock, muddy patches from the storms."

Nods all around. Mags gives a curt acknowledgment without meeting my eyes. My damn fault. I told her to stay out of it, to let me handle it. And she is.

We start the descent, retracing our steps down from the high meadow. Going downhill should be easier, quicker. Gravity helps. But for me, each downward step jars my ribs, sending a fresh shock of pain through my torso. The impact travels up my spine, making my teeth clench. Using the trekking poles helps balance, as my right arm is mainly useless, but it doesn't ease the grinding ache. Mags walks ahead of me this time, behind Jake. She moves with a fluid grace that wasn't there on the way up, her body adapted to the rhythm of the trail, even with the weakness in her ankle. She points out things to Carlos now and then—a hawk, a patch of paintbrush —her voice calm and professional, fitting Elliott's "return to roots" narrative. She doesn't turn back. Why would she?

The miles pass. Elliott, sensing the lack of drama now that Mags and I avoid each other, focuses on scenic vistas and B-roll footage. He tries once to stage a shot of Mags helping me navigate a tricky section.

"Lena, perhaps give Finn a hand with that equipment?" he suggests, gesturing to Finn adjusting his pack straps. "Show that teamwork."

"Looks like he's got it," Mags replies, her voice perfectly level, devoid of the warmth from the cave, not even breaking stride. She leaves me to stumble through the loose shale alone. The rejection, quiet and public, lands like a kick to my already bruised ribs, harder because it comes from Mags, not the distant Lena Kensington. Confirmation of the line drawn between us.

We make better time on the descent, covering ground faster than we did climbing up, even with my slower pace. By late afternoon, we reach the valley floor near the stream. The air feels heavier here, warmer. As I scout for a campsite near the spring, I notice the crew is on edge—eyes scanning the slopes and dense thickets. Jake and Marco exchange low words, their attention fixed on a bend upstream, unease written in every stiff movement.

"What's going on?" I ask, lowering my pack. "Everyone looks spooked."

"Isn't this ... where we encountered it?" Jake asks, voice hushed, pointing to the bend with a nod.

"Encountered what?" I survey the area. The place looks normal. Valley floor, stream, trees.

"The bear, man!" Marco says, eyes wide. "The huge one! Came out of the trees over there."

A bear? While I was gone? "Big bear? What kind?"

"Golden," Carlos chimes in. "Massive. I read somewhere locals call him Grizzletoe? Said he's legendary."

Grizzletoe. I nod. "Yeah, that's him. Big old bear, unusual color. I ran into him once as a kid. He usually keeps to himself—rarely comes this close to the main trails." I study them more closely now, my voice tightening. "You saw Grizzletoe? Here?"

"Right here," Carlos confirms. "Stood up on his hind legs, checked us out. Scared Elliott."

"Lena faced him down," Jake adds, looking toward Mags with respect. "Talked to it, backed us all up until it wandered off."

I glance toward Mags, who's crouched beside the water filter, deliberately focused. She must sense my attention because she straightens and looks over, her expression unreadable. A shrug follows—cool, dismissive, a gesture meant to brush me off as much as the story she's downplaying.

"It wasn't a big deal. Remembered something about making noise."

Not a big deal? She stood her ground in front of Grizzletoe and kept this crew from unraveling. And yet here she is, shrinking the moment down to nothing. She's not underselling the story—she's drawing a line. I'm not inside the circle anymore. I'm not the person she turns to, not the one she trusts with the truth.

Jake snorts. "Not a big deal? The thing was the size of your Polaris, Finn. Perhaps bigger. Good thing he took one assessment of Lena and decided she was too much trouble." He winks, trying to lighten the mood, but the tension remains.

I process this. While I was dealing with Dave, Mags was here, handling a close encounter with Grizzletoe, keeping the crew safe, and downplaying it. Why hadn't she mentioned it? Part of keeping her distance? Or something else?

"Alright," I say, pushing questions aside. "Let's set up camp further downstream. Everyone keep alert tonight." The crew nods, the nervous energy returning as they unpack the gear.

I try to help, but my body protests. Even gathering firewood is an effort. Mags sees me struggling to lift a larger piece of deadfall. For a second, I think she hesitates, hand reaching out. Then she catches herself, turns away, and confers with Carlos about camera placement. That momentary lapse, the instinct overridden by the wall, hurts more than the physical pain.

Dinner is quiet. I force down some stew, needing fuel, but my appetite's gone. Mags sits with Carlos and Marco, laughing at something Marco says. The sound drifts across the campfire, a melody I'm no longer part of. It's like watching a scene from behind glass.

Later, as the others turn in—double-checking zippers, peering into the dark—I linger by the fire, looking into the flames, wrestling with regret and pain. How do I fix this? How do I bridge the distance? Words won't be enough. An apology feels too small.

She emerges from her tent, heading toward the stream for water. She pauses near the fire, her expression unreadable.

"Is your arm okay?" she asks, voice neutral. The first personal comment since our argument.

"It's fine," I say. "Bandage is holding." My mind is still grappling with the bear encounter she never mentioned. Facing down Grizzletoe, and she said nothing to me.

She nods. "Good." She hesitates, as if she wants to say more, then her expression closes off. "Get some rest, Finn. Long day tomorrow to get back to the lodge." Just like that, the guide assessing the other guide. No Mags in sight. Only Lena Kensington, professional and distant. She turns and walks toward the stream without looking back, leaving me alone by the dying fire.

It wasn't much. A brief check-in. Perhaps responsibility, not concern. But knowing what she faced ... it adds another layer to my regret. I stare into the embers, the physical discomfort forgotten, replaced by a different ache. An apology isn't enough. I need to show her. Show her I understand her—all of her. Show her I heard her. Show her I can change.

Tomorrow. On the hike down. I have to find a way to start if she'll let me.

Chapter Twenty-Five

LENA

THE METALLIC SCRAPE of tent poles collapsing jolts me from a restless sleep. Outside, the sounds of departure are underway—murmured voices, the clatter of cook gear being packed, the rustle of sleeping bags being stuffed into sacks. It's the last morning of this. The finality of it sits like a stone in my stomach, mixing with the hurt that's been eating at me for days—ever since Finn chose his pride, his damn lodge, over us. In my tent, listening to everyone else getting ready to leave together, I've never felt more alone.

Packing up is different today. There's a sense of an ending, though whether it's the end of the expedition or the end of something more fragile remains uncertain. The crew moves with a subdued efficiency, the usual banter replaced by quiet focus. We're all tired, worn down by the challenges, ready for the relative comfort of the lodge. Ready for hot showers and real beds.

I avoid looking at Finn as we eat a quick breakfast of luke-warm oatmeal. He stands apart, speaking in a low voice with Carlos about the route down, his face locked in the stoic mask he's worn like armor these past few days. He favors his left side, movements tight and deliberate, though he tries to hide it.

My eyes catch on the bandage peeking out beneath his rolled-up sleeve. Last night, sitting near the fire, he offered a clipped update—"Bandage is holding"—a statement more about pushing me away than keeping me informed. Not an invitation. Just a line drawn in the ash.

He made his choice. *Handle it yourself.*

We set out, leaving the basin behind, the sun climbing, promising warmth later in the day. The descent is easier than the climbs we've endured. The path, though still muddy in places and littered with debris from the flood, follows the stream's gradient downward.

Yet, the easier terrain does little to ease the tension coiling inside me. With every step taking us closer to the lodge, closer to reliable communication, closer to the life I left behind, the questions loom larger. What happens now? What happens when the wilderness is no longer forcing us together, when the demands of our separate realities replace the demands of survival?

Finn walks point, setting a brisk pace—eager to get back as much as the rest of us, though probably for different reasons. He moves with a relentless determination, pushing through pain I know is still there. I watch the steady set of his shoulders, the way he reads the trail with instinct, making subtle adjustments to account for his injuries. He's a force of nature in his own right—rugged, unyielding, and as impenetrable right now.

I fall in behind Jake and Marco, letting space grow between me and Finn. It's easier this way. Less temptation to close the distance. Less risk of being shut out again. I focus on the rhythm of hiking—the pressure of the trail beneath my boots; the forest sounds waking around us. Birdsong. The rush of the stream growing louder as we descend. The crunch of gravel underfoot. It's peaceful, but my mind refuses to follow.

Elliott, sensing the end is near—and perhaps aware the drama has cooled into silence—mostly leaves us alone, focusing his crew on B-roll: sunlight through trees, water tumbling over rocks, wide shots of the trail. Every so often, he directs me to look "thoughtfully reflective" or "wearily triumphant," and I oblige. The actress takes over, delivering on cue. Slipping into that familiar role is easy, almost comforting. But after the rawness of these past weeks, it doesn't fit the way it used to.

We cover miles. The air grows warmer, heavier with the scent of damp earth and pine resin, replacing the thin, sharp edge of the high alpine meadows. The trees rise taller now, crowding closer. The world presses in—less exposed, more intimate. Part of me welcomes the return to lower ground, the promise of comfort and safety. Another part mourns the loss of the vast, stark beauty of the peaks—the raw simplicity, the clarity that came when life was stripped down to the bare bones.

By mid-afternoon, a familiar landmark comes into view. It's the stand of old-growth spruce near the trail junction leading back to Crystal Creek Retreat. We're close. An hour, perhaps less. A wave of conflicting emotions crashes in—relief at the thought of an actual bed, exhaustion deep in my bones, apprehension about what comes next, and a quiet, unexpected pang of sadness. Sadness? For leaving this place that's been equal parts terror and ... something else? *Surprising.*

The final stretch is dreamlike. The trail flattens and smooths. Signs of human passage return—a faded trail marker, an old fire ring. Then, through the trees, it appears: the sprawling log structure of the main lodge, smoke curling from its stone chimney. *Home. For now.*

The crew lets out a collective whoop. Packs are dropped,

shoulders are slapped. Elliott beams, talking into his satellite phone, reporting our triumphant return to the network. I stand apart, taking it all in—the solid reality of the lodge, the manicured path leading to the door, the waiting Polaris parked nearby. It looks the same as when we left, what feels like a lifetime ago. But I'm different. Everything is.

Finn walks past me without a word, without so much as a glance in my direction, heading for the lodge entrance. His face is grim, his limp more pronounced now that the adrenaline of the hike has clearly worn off. He doesn't turn back. And just like that, it's over. Whatever 'it' was. Part of me, the stupid, hopeful part, wilts.

Nash comes out of the lodge, wiping his hands on a rag. A broad smile spreads across his face when he sees the crew, but when his eyes land on me, they soften with something like sympathy. "Welcome back, Hollywood. Heard you had quite the adventure."

"You could say that," I reply, managing a weak smile. He watches Finn disappear into the lodge, brow furrowing at the stiffness in his brother's stride. Then he looks back at me. "Is he moving okay? Looked like he was favoring that side pretty bad."

"He took a fall," I say, the words flat, stripped of the worry churning inside. "But he says he's fine. You're his brother—you know how stubborn he is."

Nash nods, something settling behind his eyes. "Sounds about right. That brand of idiocy runs in the family." He gestures toward Cabin Three. "Your cabin's ready. Figured you'd want some privacy after roughing it."

"Thanks, Nash." I shoulder my pack, desperate to be alone. To breathe. To process the chaos of the past few weeks.

Walking the familiar path to the cabin is like slipping through a doorway into another life. Inside, everything is as I left it. My suitcases rest against the wall, silent testaments to the woman who arrived here expecting a curated photo shoot, armed with designer clothes and overpriced skincare. I stare at the luggage. Several large suitcases, packed with outfits for every conceivable rustic chic scenario. Cashmere joggers I wore once. Silk blouses I never touched. Louboutin heels sacrificed to the dock. It all seems absurd now—relics from a different life, a different woman. Who was that person? What did she think she needed all this for? A hollow laugh escapes me. After days in the same two pairs of hiking pants and borrowed thermals, the sheer volume of stuff is almost obscene.

But first, a shower. The thought alone is heavenly. I turn the handle in the tiny bathroom, and the rush of steaming water hits like a miracle. I stand under the spray, letting the heat sink into sore muscles, scrubbing away layers of trail dirt, sweat, and campfire smoke. The grime runs off in streaks, revealing skin pale from lack of sun, dotted with scratches and bruises I don't remember earning. I wash my hair, savoring the scent of real shampoo, teasing out knots with generous handfuls of conditioner. Stepping onto the bathmat, wrapped in a towel that felt cheap and thin a week ago but seems like pure luxury now, is like shedding an entire version of myself. I'm lighter. Cleaner. But also exposed. The wilderness grime was a kind of armor.

Now, without it, I'm raw. Unfinished.

Back in the main room, I unzip one of the smaller suitcases, the one dedicated to skincare and makeup. Bottles, jars, tubes, and palettes gleam up at me—an arsenal designed to perfect, protect, and project the image of Lena Kensington. Hesitantly, then with growing autopilot familiarity, I begin the ritual. Double cleanse—first the oil to dissolve grime and sunscreen, then the foaming cleanser. Pat dry with a soft microfiber cloth reserved for my face. The toner, applied with a specific organic cotton pad. Essence patted into the skin. Then the serums—Vitamin C for brightness, hyaluronic acid for hydration, a peptide complex for firmness, each applied in a precise order, allowed moments to absorb. Eye cream tapped around the orbital bone with my ring finger. Finally, the moisturizer massaged in with upward strokes. It takes nearly twenty minutes. Twenty minutes of patting, smoothing, waiting. A ritual I've performed twice a day, for years. It used to feel crucial—a non-negotiable part of maintaining the brand. Now, standing back and looking at the array of expensive glass bottles cluttering the small cabin counter, it strikes me as excessive. Ridiculous.

I think of the past week. After losing my supplies in the flood, my entire skincare routine comprised whatever I could beg, borrow, or steal—lip balm when someone had it, and Finn's questionable hand lotion when my knuckles cracked from the cold. And yet ... my skin hadn't imploded. It had survived the wind, the sun, the dirt, and the stress. Checking my reflection in the mirror now, after the elaborate routine, do I look dramatically different from the way I did this morning? Perhaps less tired, marginally more 'glowy,' but was it worth the hundreds, the thousands, sitting here? Worth the hours? My God, how much had I poured into this chase for flawless perfection? This serum alone cost more than a month's groceries. Was it truly for 'skin health,' or was it fuel for the Hollywood machine, a desperate attempt to stay eternally camera-ready, always younger, smoother?

The simplicity of the wilderness—using what was necessary, letting the rest go—feels more appealing than this bag full of expensive promises. The face in the mirror resembles Lena more, yes, but the thought leaves a bitter taste.

Feeling restless, displaced, I wander into the bedroom, towel-drying my hair. My eyes land on the bedside table. My cell phone lies there, plugged into the wall where I left it over a week ago. Picking it up, I see the screen light up—two bars of service, flickering now that I'm back near the main lodge. And messages. A cascade of missed texts and voicemail notifications that must have trickled in whenever the signal momentarily connected. Most are junk or updates from friends I haven't had the headspace to think about. However, one notification stands out, marked as urgent, and time stamped several days ago.

It's a text from David. *Lena, urgent. Call me ASAP. Big news.*

David. My agent. Big news usually means one thing: a role. A project. A lifeline thrown from the world I thought I might be ready to leave behind. My stomach clenches. The timing lands like a cruel joke, arriving moments after I started questioning the very world this call represents.

I peer out the cabin window. Across the clearing, near the main lodge, I spot Finn and Nash by the Polaris. Nash claps his brother on the shoulder, says something that makes Finn shake his head, then they both turn and go inside. He didn't come over. Didn't ask how I was after the hike. Retreated into his world, his pain, his pride. The ache in my chest isn't sharp —it's the slow, hollow kind.

I look down at the glowing screen in my hand, David's message demanding attention. Hollywood is calling. Opportunity, fame, the life I fought for—it's all waiting for me.

But first ... the compass. I get dressed and slip it into my pocket, where it sits heavy—a tangible link to Finn, to the trust he placed in me, however briefly. I need to return it. Close the loop. It's the right thing to do, a necessary ending to a story he already walked away from.

Steeling myself, I grab my phone and head for the lodge. Afterward, I'll go to the east deck—the one place I know gets a strong enough signal—and make the call that might pull me back to my old life for good.

I reach the wide porch of the main lodge. The door is closed. Taking a deep breath, I raise my hand to knock, the compass cool against my palm. Before my knuckles connect with the wood, I hear Finn's voice from inside, low and strained, talking to Nash. Curiosity, stronger than my resolve to keep my distance, prompts me to pause and listen.

"...don't know, Nash," Finn is saying, his voice tight with frustration I recognize. "The bank ... and this whole production. If I don't complete the full contract, if I don't get that final payment..."

My heart sinks. He's still worried about the money, about the lodge. I should knock. Interrupt. Give him back the compass and walk away. But then Nash speaks, his voice carrying through the door.

"Forget the money for a second, Finn. What about her? Are you gonna let her walk away after everything?"

A long pause. Then Finn's voice, rougher now, laced with something that sounds like regret. "What choice do I have? She's Hollywood. I'm ... this." The words, muffled through the door, land like a physical blow, stealing the air from my lungs. *No, Finn, you're wrong. That's not ... that's not all I am. Not anymore.* But he believes it. Believes we're too different, that I'll inevitably leave, that what happened between us— what felt so intensely, terrifyingly real to me—was circumstantial for him. A wilderness fling. Is that all it was? Is that all I am to him? Perhaps he's right. Falling for someone this quickly, under these circumstances, is reckless. The stuff of fairytales, or the movies I star in. Who does that work out for in real life?

The hurt from our argument hits again, sharp and raw. It twists in my gut, settles into something cold and cynical. Returning the compass can wait. So can clearing the air. He's made up his mind. It may be time for me to make up mine.

Clutching the compass tight in my hand, I turn away from the lodge door. David's message burns in my pocket. The east deck has the best reception. *Okay, David. Let's hear your big news.*

I walk around the side of the lodge, finding the wide wooden deck that overlooks the creek and the mountains beyond. The signal bars on my phone jump from three to four. Solid. Taking another deep breath, steeling myself against the emotions warring inside, I dial David's number. It rings once, twice...

"Lena! Finally! Thank God, I was thinking a bear actually ate you. Listen, you are not going to believe this..."

The sun dips lower, painting the sky in bruised purples and oranges.

Chapter Twenty-Six

FINN

I STAND LOOKING out the lodge kitchen window after explaining my perspective to Nash, the scent of coffee and wood smoke flat and stale. His words echo in the quiet. *What about her? Are you gonna let her walk away after everything?*

The question hits harder than the fall on Raven's Spine. *Walk away?* I shoved her out the door with my ego and hesitation. *She's Hollywood. I'm... this.* Saying it out loud makes the stupidity of it click into place. Since when do I give up without a fight? When did I let fear steer the wheel?

My ribs ache, a dull fire under my shirt. My arm throbs. But none of it compares to the weight in my gut—that grinding regret. I picture her face again when I threw her offer back at her. How the light drained from her eyes. How she rebuilt the shield of Lena Kensington in front of me—the woman I made her become again.

"So that's it?" Nash asks, still leaning against the counter, arms crossed, eyes sharp and unrelenting. He never left. Waited for my silence to answer the question for me. "You screw up, push away the first woman who actually sees you past the grumpy-loner thing, and now you ... quit?"

"It's complicated, Nash," I say, turning from the window —away from the mountains that usually bring me peace but now stand there, watching, like they know better. "More complicated than deciding to fight."

"Is it?" Nash pushes off the counter. "You messed up. You were scared—scared of losing this place." He gestures around the kitchen. "Scared of perhaps not being enough for someone like her. I guess you did what you always do, you put up a wall." Every word is a punch, accurate and bruising. He's not wrong.

"She offered me money, Nash," I say, the justification sounding weak even to my ears. "Like I was some charity case."

"So? Her world runs on money, Finn. Perhaps that's how she shows she cares. Did you stop to think about that? Or did your pride register the insult?" He steps closer. "She faced down Grizzletoe, Finn. *Grizzletoe.* According to Carlos, she didn't blink. That woman isn't afraid of much, except perhaps getting her heart stomped on by a stubborn ass who doesn't know a good thing when it lands on his doorstep."

His words hit their mark. She had faced the bear. She had offered help, regardless of how clumsily it came out in her world's currency. She had regarded me, in the cave, as if I were someone worth recognizing.

"What am I supposed to do now?" The question feels ripped from my throat, raw and unfamiliar. Asking for help, even from my brother, goes against every instinct.

"You go find her," Nash says, his voice softening but losing none of its force. "You apologize. Not some half-assed 'sorry if I hurt your feelings' crap, but a sincere apology. It might require some groveling, brother, the kind you're terrible at. Tell her you were wrong. That you were scared. Tell her how you feel, for once in your damn life." He claps a hand on my good shoulder. "Then you let her decide. But don't you dare let her walk away thinking you didn't fight for her because you were too proud or too afraid to try."

No. I can't let it end like this. I owe her more than that. An apology, yes, but more. An explanation. The truth. Maybe it's too late, perhaps she's decided I'm not worth the trouble, but I have to try. Nash is right. I can't let her walk away without fighting. For Mags. For what we had. Can't lose that.

Decision made, heart pounding a wild rhythm against my sore ribs, I push open the kitchen door and head out into the clearing. The crew is milling around, packing personal items, probably getting ready for dinner soon. Elliott is talking on the satellite phone near the porch, his voice loud. No sign of Mags.

Her cabin. She needed solitude after the hike, Nash said. I walk the path to Cabin Three, my boots crunching on the gravel, each step jarring but fueled by a new urgency. I need to talk to her now, before the wall between us sets in, before she disappears fully into the Hollywood life I know is pulling at her.

I reach her door, hesitate, then knock. Once, twice. No answer. Nothing from inside. Maybe she's in the shower. Or maybe ... she doesn't want to see me. The thought lands like a cold fist in my chest.

I turn from the building, scanning the clearing. Where would she go?

I spot Marco coiling cables near the lodge porch.

"Seen Lena?" I ask.

Marco jerks a thumb toward the east side of the lodge. "Saw her heading out to the deck a few minutes ago."

That's all I need.

I head that way, faster now, rounding the main lodge until the wide wooden deck comes into view.

And there she is.

Standing at the railing, phone pressed to her ear, back

mostly to me. Her posture is straight, poised—the way she carries herself when the cameras are on.

Lena Kensington.

I stop, hidden by the corner of the building, my intention to apologize choked by a wave of dread as I catch the tone of her voice. I should turn around, give her privacy. But I can't move. Her voice carries on the breeze, snippets of conversation drifting toward me. It's crisp, professional—the voice of the polished actress. t's jarring—so far from the softer tones of Mags I heard in the cave. The contrast hits hard, a gut-wrenching realization.

I love her. All of her—the woman who faced down a bear and the one who commands attention on screen. But hearing this voice now, the one that sounds like she's choosing that other life, feels like listening to the part of her I connect with most disappear.

"Yes, David, the connection's stable... No, no bear encounters today..." A quick laugh, devoid of actual humor. "Unbelievable, I know... When? Next week? That's ... fast."

Next week? My gut tightens.

"An A-list director? Seriously? Wow. Okay." She pauses, listening, her fingers tapping on the wooden railing. "Yes, the timing is sudden, but after everything here ... perhaps it's what I need." She means an excuse to leave. Figures. The words hit hard, stealing my breath. Confirmation. She's ready to leave. This place, this experience, us—it was a detour, an unpleasant necessity before returning to her real life.

"Okay. Yes. Tell them yes," she says, her voice firming with decision. "...Arrange the pickup? Hank the pilot? Tomorrow at the dock? Got it... Yes, I'll be ready... Thanks, David. Talk soon."

She lowers the phone, looking out at the mountains for a long moment, her shoulders slumped. Then she takes a deep breath, straightens, and turns. Her eyes widen when she sees me standing there at the corner of the deck, surprise quickly hidden behind that cool, guarded look she'd perfected. She knows I overheard.

Wordlessly, she walks toward me. She stops a few feet away, the space between us charged with everything unsaid. She reaches into her pocket and pulls out the small brass compass —my mother's compass. She holds it out to me.

"Here," she says, her voice flat, neutral. "Thanks for letting me use it."

I look at the compass lying in her outstretched palm. The worn brass gleams in the late afternoon light. A guide. A promise. Entrusted to her. I want to tell her to keep it. Tell her to use it to find her way back. Back here. Back to me. But the words stick in my throat. What's the point? *Tell them yes. Pickup tomorrow. Next week. A-list director.* Her words, her decision, played over in my head—an inevitable answer. The gap between her world and mine isn't wide—it's real. I made it that way. She's Hollywood. I'm … this. I told Nash that. And now it sounds less like fact and more like a choice I made.

My hand is heavy as I reach for the compass. Our fingers brush—barely. One flicker of something real. Then it's gone, buried under everything we didn't say.

"Right," I manage, my voice sounding rough, unfamiliar. I close my fist around it, the metal warm against my skin. "Glad it was useful."

She nods once, eyes shifting past me to some distant point beyond my shoulder. The silence stretches, thick and suffocating. There's nothing left to say. I ruined it. A woman like Lena never looks back.

She doesn't say a word. Just turns and walks past me— back to her cabin, her packed bags, her real life waiting far from Crystal Creek.

I stay on the deck, the compass heavy in my hand, watching her go.

The mountains loom in the distance, dark against the dusk. The air's cold, but not as cold as the hollow settling in my chest.

I did this. No one else.

I don't know how long I stand there, the compass digging into my palm. The sun dips lower, turning the sky red over the peaks. The crew's voices fade as they head toward the main lodge for the dinner Nash made. Eventually, the cold seeps too deep for me. Turning from the mountains, from the path Lena took, I walk back toward the lodge, feeling hollowed out.

Nash is in the great room, stoking the fire in the massive stone hearth. He raises his head as I enter, takes one look at my face, and his expression turns grim.

"Didn't go well, huh?" he asks, his voice low.

I shake my head, sinking onto the worn leather couch near the fire. I open my hand, looking at the compass. "She's leaving. Tomorrow. Flying out from the dock."

Nash comes over, sits beside me. "What happened?"

I tell him. Everything. Overhearing the call. The job offer. The A-list director. Her saying yes. Her returning the compass. The finality of it all.

"So, you ... took it back?" Nash sounds incredulous. "You didn't say anything? Didn't fight?"

"What was there to fight, Nash?" I look at him, then away. "She came here to breathe life back into a career everyone had buried. She was blacklisted—written off. And somehow, freezing nights, natural disasters, and a camera crew in the middle of nowhere gave her what she needed. They recognize her now. The producers, the headlines. They understand what she's capable of." I drag a hand over my jaw. "She's getting everything she came here for. A second chance. A fresh start. How could I ruin that for her by asking her to stay? She's going back to her world. The world she wanted. I heard her excitement."

"You heard part of a phone call, Finn," Nash says, leaning forward. "You don't know what she was thinking. You don't know what that job means to her—or what this means, between you two." He gestures vaguely. "Maybe she said yes because she thought she had no other choice."

The thought is another twist of the knife. Could that be true?

"Doesn't matter now," I mutter. "She's leaving."

"Only if you let her." Nash stands, pacing in front of the fireplace. "Dammit, Finn! Are you going to sit here feeling sorry for yourself while she flies away? Go talk to her! Tell her she's wrong! Tell her you're an idiot! Tell her whatever the hell's in that stubborn heart of yours!"

"And say what? 'Don't go back to your million-dollar career—stay in the woods with a broke lodge owner who might lose everything?'" Bitterness coats every word.

"So what if that's the truth?" Nash throws his hands up. "You think she doesn't know that already? You think she doesn't care about the guy who knows seventeen ways to cook tree bark and looks at her like she hung the damn moon? You won't know unless you try!"

His words hang there. The fire crackles, spitting embers onto the hearth. Outside, the wind rises, rattling the lodge windows. *Try.* Simple word. Brutal ask. Especially after she handed back the compass. After she walked away.

"I need ... I need to think," I mutter, pushing up from the couch. Pain lances through my ribs and shoulder.

"Don't think too long," Nash warns. "Hank's plane leaves at nine."

Chapter Twenty-Seven

LENA

THE FINALITY of zipping up the last suitcase lands like sealing a coffin. Maybe my own. Mags—the woman who surfaced in the Alaskan wilderness—was never built for the real world. Not with pride in the way. Not with two lives pulling in opposite directions.

I look around Cabin Three. It had become a sanctuary before the expedition. Now, it's a room. Impersonal. Empty. My hiking boots, scuffed and muddy, sit by the door. Out of place next to the sleek designer luggage, lined up for departure. Those boots carried me through terrain I never thought I'd survive, pushed me past limits I didn't know existed. Now they're relics. Souvenirs from an expedition that cracked me open and left me raw.

I run a hand over the smooth wood of the small table, remembering the spot where Finn's mother's compass sat yesterday before I returned it to him. That final, cold exchange on the deck replays in my mind—his flat acceptance, my brittle pride masking the shattering hurt. She's Hollywood. I'm ... this. His words to Nash, overheard through the lodge door, echo. He'd decided for both of us.

A honk outside signals Nash's arrival with the Polaris and the small trailer for my luggage. Time to go. Time to leave Crystal Creek, Finn, and the confusing tangle of emotions Alaska has unearthed. Time to step back into the role waiting for me, the one David's excited voice described yesterday—A-list director, guaranteed distribution, filming starts next week. A career resurrection, practically gift-wrapped. Everything I thought I wanted.

Dragging the suitcases outside is like hauling anchors. Nash helps me load them into the ATV's trailer, his usual easy-going charm muted by the concern in his eyes. He doesn't pry. Doesn't ask. Secures the bags with efficient movements that remind me so much of Finn it makes my chest ache. *Stop it, Lena. It's done.*

"All set?" he asks, wiping his hands on his jeans.

"Ready as I'll ever be," I say, forcing a lightness I can't reach.

I climb into the back seat of the Polaris, the engine rumbling to life beneath me. As we pull away from the cabin, heading toward Port Promise, I look back once at the main lodge. No sign of Finn. Of course not. Why would he come out? I'm another guest leaving. One less complication in a life stretched thin.

The ride is bumpy, jostling both body and heart. The landscape blurs—towering pines, dense undergrowth, flashes of the creek catching sunlight between branches. The same wilderness that felt wild and unforgiving when I arrived now feels known. Almost as if it belongs to me. The thought hits hard.

"Heard you faced down Grizzletoe while Finn was gone," Nash yells over the engine's roar.

I shrug, trying to downplay it. "Made some noise. He seemed more curious than aggressive."

Nash chuckles. "Curious grizzlies are still grizzlies, Hollywood. Takes nerve to stand your ground like that. Finn was impressed when Carlos showed him the footage."

Finn viewed the footage? And he was impressed? The information comes as a strange and confusing counterpoint to his cold dismissal of me. Why wouldn't he say something? But then, why would he? We weren't talking.

"Speaking of Finn..." I begin, hesitant, needing to know, even though the answer will probably hurt. "Is he ... did you see him this morning?"

Nash keeps his eyes on the road ahead. "Nope. I haven't seen him since he left yesterday. Headed toward town, looking like he was carrying the whole damn world." He turns toward me. "He takes things hard, Lena. Especially when he thinks he's messed up. Which, trust me, he knows he did with you."

"He made his choice clear," I say, bitterness coating the words. "His lodge comes first. Always."

"The lodge is important, yeah," Nash concedes. "It's tied up with Mom, with his pride in building something himself. But don't mistake that for meaning you aren't important." He navigates a rough patch. "Sometimes my brother's so afraid of failing the people he cares about, he pushes them away first. Stupid, I know. Runs in the family."

His words offer a sliver of understanding, but they don't erase the hurt. Finn's fear might explain his actions, but it doesn't excuse the way he dismissed me, my offer, my world.

We lapse back into silence, the roar of the ATV filling the space between us. As we near Port Promise, the collection of old buildings coming into view around the harbor, a sudden, impulsive idea strikes me.

"Nash," I say, leaning forward. "Is May's diner open? I've been craving those sourdough pancakes since the first time I tasted them."

Nash turns back, surprised. "Should be. The plane's not

due for another hour. Want to stop in for breakfast? Those pancakes are worth the detour."

"I'd love to." Anything to delay the inevitable departure, to grasp one last piece of this place. "Besides," I add, trying for a joke, "once I get back to LA, it'll be nothing but kale smoothies and personal trainers judging my carb intake. Gotta fuel up while I can."

Nash laughs, the sound genuine this time. "May's pancakes will fill you up. Might need a nap on the plane."

He pulls the Polaris up outside the familiar, crooked building with the "May's Café" sign. Inside, the diner is warm and smells heavenly—coffee, frying bacon, and that distinct tangy scent of sourdough. May raises her head from behind the counter, her face breaking into a wide smile when she sees me.

"Well!" she says, wiping her hands on her apron. "Thought you'd be halfway to Anchorage by now, Lena."

"Couldn't leave without another plate of your legendary pancakes," I say, sliding into a worn vinyl booth. Nash follows, grabbing menus.

"Good choice," May approves. "Short stack or tall?"

"Tall," I say without hesitation. "And coffee. Lots of coffee."

"Same for me, May," Nash adds.

"Coming right up." She disappears into the kitchen, humming.

"So," he says, his expression turning serious. "Big movie role waiting for you back home?"

I nod, picking at a loose thread on the vinyl seat. "Apparently. A-list director, starts next week. The kind of opportunity David says could erase the whole Martinez mess." It sounds like the perfect solution on paper. The answer to my career prayers. So why does it feel so hollow?

"Is that what you want?" Nash asks, his voice low, his

expression steady—too perceptive. Too much like his brother's.

The question hangs in the air. Do I want it? The career resurrection, the return to the spotlight, the familiar rhythm of scripts and sets and red carpets? A few weeks ago, I wouldn't have hesitated to say yes. Now...

"It's what I came here for, isn't it?" I deflect, unable to voice the uncertainty churning inside. "To fix my image, get back on track."

"Yeah, but is it what you want?" Nash presses. "After everything?"

Before I can answer, May arrives with two steaming mugs of coffee and sets them down. "Nash Hollister," she says, fixing him with a stern look. "Didn't I ask you to move that fifty-pound bag of flour onto the top shelf in the pantry? My back's not getting any younger. I need a private word with Lena before she flies off."

Nash smiles, recognizing the dismissal. "Yes, ma'am." He slides out of the booth. "Hold those pancakes for me, May, I'll be back." He pauses by the table. "And Lena?" His expression is earnest. "Think about it. What you want." He gives me a quick nod and heads toward a back door in the diner.

May slides into the seat Nash left, her shrewd eyes examining my face. "He's right, you know. You look like a woman running away from something, not toward something."

"I'm running toward my career," I protest.

"Are you?" May sips her coffee. "Remember what I told you when you first got here? About Alaska changing people?" I nod, remembering her words in the community center after the wedding fiasco. "This place gets under your skin," May continues. "Strips away the nonsense, shows you what's real. Question is, what did it show you?"

What did it show me? It showed me I was stronger than I thought, more capable. It showed me the hollowness of the life

I'd built. It showed me Magdalena, the girl I'd buried. It showed me Finn ... and the sharp, unexpected joy and pain of a connection that felt more real than anything I'd ever known.

"It showed me ... things are complicated," I hedge.

May chuckles. "Life usually is, honey. Especially when hearts get tangled up in stubborn pride." She leans in. "Finn Hollister's a good man. Solid. Like these mountains. But he's got a blind spot the size of Denali when it comes to letting people in—especially when he thinks he's failing. He pushes hardest when he needs help the most."

Easy for her to say, I think, a flash of my earlier anger returning. *She didn't hear what he said, how he said it.*

"He made it clear he doesn't want my help," I say. "He has a problem, and I thought I could throw money at it. That didn't go over well."

"Money?" May raises an eyebrow, her expression sharp but kind. "Honey, that man's trouble goes deeper than any check can cover—though I'm sure he could use that too. But offering cash to a man like Finn, especially when he's cornered? That's like handing a steak to a drowning moose. Useless, and more likely to insult than help." She shakes her head, holding my eyes with quiet certainty. "What he needs is support. Belief. Someone who sees past the pride and sticks around anyway. He doesn't need saving. He needs a partner." She pats my hand. "And maybe you needed someone who could recognize the woman underneath the actress."

Her words hit their mark, piercing my defenses. *A partner.* Not a savior, not a fixer. Someone to stand beside him. Someone who understands him, flaws and all. Someone like ... Mags.

"Think on that," May says, sliding out of the booth. "I'll go get those pancakes started." She heads toward the kitchen, leaving me alone with her words and the smell of brewing coffee.

He needs a partner. Could I be that? Could I bridge the gap between Lena Kensington's world and Finn Hollister's? Did I want to? The questions swirl, unanswered.

A few minutes later, May returns, balancing a plate piled high with three huge, golden discs steaming, served with whipped butter and real maple syrup. She sets it in front of me. They smell divine. I take a bite, and the tangy, complex flavor explodes on my tongue. It's the best thing I've ever tasted.

May sits back down, sipping her coffee while I eat. The diner is quiet except for the clink of my fork and the hiss of the coffee machine.

"You know," May says, watching me eat, "I saw something spark between you two the minute you walked into that wedding reception. Like flint striking steel."

I almost choke on my pancake. "Are you kidding? We're like oil and water. Fire and gasoline."

May gives a knowing look. "Sometimes fire and gasoline make for one hell of a bonfire, honey. Warms you right down to the bones, if you're brave enough not to run from the heat."

My heart gives a painful lurch. Brave enough? Was I brave enough? Or was I running back to the safety of smoke and mirrors?

Nash returns as I'm finishing the last bite. "The plane is fueled up. Hank's ready when you are." Panic flutters in my chest. Time's up. Decision made. Plane waiting.

I slide out of the booth, feeling numb. I reach into my purse for my wallet, pulling out a few bills. "Thanks for breakfast, May. It was ... everything I hoped for."

May waves my money away. "On the house today, honey. Consider the advice free too." She gives my arm a squeeze. "Remember what I said. Sometimes home isn't where you started, it's where you belong. Don't let fear cheat you out of finding it."

I walk out into the bright Alaskan morning, Nash beside me. The float plane bobs at the end of the dock, Hank waving from the cockpit. *This is it. The escape hatch. The return to normalcy.*

Nash unloads my suitcases from the trailer, stowing the larger ones in the plane's designated cargo hold while Hank observes. I climb into the small plane, settling into the co-pilot seat. Nash tosses my carry-on bag in behind me.

"Safe travels, Lena," he says, his expression holding a question he doesn't voice.

"Thanks, Nash. For everything." He closes the door and steps back onto the dock.

Hank starts the engine, the propeller sputtering to life, then catching with a roar that vibrates through the small cabin. We taxi away from the dock, turning toward the open water. The plane lifts off, climbing higher, Port Promise shrinking below us.

I look out the window, the landscape that has become familiar unfolding beneath me like a map. The winding creeks, the dense forests, the jagged, snow-capped peaks in the distance, where we were. It's beautiful. Wild. Untamed. Like what Finn stirred up in me. Like the woman I was becoming —before I let hurt and fear push me back toward the safety of what I knew.

We fly in silence for what feels like an age, though the shoreline of Port Promise remains visible behind us. Hank is humming beside me, focused on his controls. My mind replays May's words, Nash's question, Finn's face in the cave, his rejection behind the rocks, his overheard confession to Nash. She's Hollywood. I'm ... this. He believes it. But do I?

"Funny thing about this place," Hank says, his voice startling me from my thoughts. He gestures out the window with his chin. "People come here thinkin' they're escaping somethin'. More often than not, they find themselves face to face with whatever they were runnin' from. Can't hide from yourself up here."

His simple words, delivered in that straightforward Alaskan drawl, hit me with the force of revelation. I've been hiding for years—first behind Lena Kensington, now behind hurt and resignation. Running back to Hollywood isn't about choosing my career. It's choosing the mask. Choosing safety over the terrifying, exhilarating possibility of being truly seen, truly known. Choosing Lena over Mags.

My breath catches. My heart pounds, a frantic drumbeat. *What am I doing?*

"Hank," I say, my voice trembling. "Hank, turn the plane around."

He turns his head, surprised. "Ma'am?"

"Turn it around," I repeat, firmer this time, conviction solidifying within me, chasing away the cold hollowness. "Take me back to Port Promise. Now."

Chapter Twenty-Eight

FINN

MY HEAD FEELS like someone split it open with an axe, then filled the crack with sand and cheap whiskey. A low groan escapes my lips as I try to shift position, but my ribs scream in protest. *Where the hell am I?* The gentle rocking motion beneath me isn't the solid ground of the lodge or even the less-than-solid floor of Carlos's tent. It's the rhythmic sway of water. Salt and diesel fumes assault my nostrils, mixed with the faint, familiar scent of fish. Kane's boat, *Seas the Day*.

Memory returns in jagged fragments. Driving the Polaris down from the lodge last night, the compass heavy as lead in my pocket, Nash's frustrated words echoing in my ears. Reaching Port Promise well after dark. Stopping by the darkened General Store, banging until Rhys unlocked it, buying a bottle of the cheapest whiskey he had. Heading for the docks after that, needing the cold bite of the salt air, the solitude of the harbor. Kane's boat was tied up empty, and I climbed aboard with my bottle half gone already. I remember settling into the wheelhouse, drinking alone, talking to myself—maybe yelling, cursing—about Hollywood actresses and bank notices and stubborn pride and the gut-deep knowing that I'd thrown away the best thing that ever happened to me. Then nothing. Blackness. Must have passed out here on the bench seat.

A roar splits the morning quiet—the unmistakable sound of a float plane engine sputtering to life, then catching. Hank's plane. *Lena's plane.* Panic, cold and sharp, cuts through the hangover haze, jerking me upright despite the protest from my ribs. What time is it?

I scramble up, ignoring the agony in my head, stumbling out of the wheelhouse onto the deck. The sun is well above the horizon, glinting off the water. Across the harbor, the plane is leaving the dock, its propeller churning spray as it taxis toward open water. Nine AM. Nash warned me. *Hank's plane leaves at nine.* She's leaving.

"No!" The word rips from my throat, raw and desperate. "Wait!" I leap from the deck of *Seas the Day* onto the dock. Adrenaline surges, fueled by pure panic. I sprint down the planks, waving. "Lena! Mags! Wait!"

The plane doesn't stop. It turns, aligning itself with the open channel, the engine noise swelling to a deafening roar. Too far away. She can't hear me. Can't see me. I keep running, stumbling, shouting her name until my voice cracks, until my lungs burn with the effort and the cold morning air. The plane lifts off the water, climbing, banking as it gains altitude, heading south. Toward Anchorage. Toward LA. Toward the life she chose.

I skid to a halt at the end of the dock, watching the plane become smaller and smaller against the vast Alaskan sky until it disappears. *Gone. She's gone.* Defeat hits me—cold, final— extinguishing the last of the adrenaline, leaving only pain and a gaping emptiness in my chest. I stand there gasping, leaning on the railing, the compass in my pocket dragging at me like dead weight. Too late. Too damn late. Too proud. Too scared. Too stupid.

"Well, hell," Nash's voice comes from behind me. "Looks like you missed the boat. Or the plane, in this case."

I turn. He's standing there, leaning against a piling, holding two steaming mugs. He must have arrived from the diner, probably witnessed the whole pathetic display. His expression is sympathetic, but there's an underlying 'I told you so' in his eyes.

"She's gone, Nash," I say, the words tasting like defeat.

"Yep. Saw her take off." He holds out one mug. "May sent coffee. And probably some judgment, knowing her."

I take the mug, the warmth seeping into my cold hands. "May's always right."

"Usually." Nash takes a sip from his mug. "So. What now?"

"What do you mean, what now?" I look out at the empty sky where the plane disappeared. "It's done. Over. She's gone back where she belongs."

"Where she belongs? Or where you decided she belongs?" Nash raises an eyebrow, and his quiet challenge cuts deeper than I expect. "Are you gonna stand there feeling sorry for yourself, or are you gonna figure out what you want?"

I flinch, turning away from the sharp edge in his eyes. "Doesn't matter what I want. I heard her on the phone. She took the job. She left."

"Maybe this one would have stayed," Nash says, his voice low. "If you'd given her a reason to." He sighs, shaking his head. "You know, for a guy who knows these mountains like the back of his hand, you're pretty damn lost when it comes to women, brother."

"Tell me something I don't know." I drain half the coffee in one gulp, the hot liquid burning my throat.

"Alright, I will." Nash leans closer. "You love her." It's not a question.

I stare at him, the blunt truth of it hitting me like an

avalanche. *Love her?* Mags? Lena? The woman who infuriated me, challenged me, saw through my bullshit, patched up my arm, faced down a grizzly, and somehow found her way past all my damn walls? *Yeah. Damn it, yeah.* "Yeah," I admit, the word rough, torn from somewhere deep inside. "Yeah, I do."

"Then what the hell are you still doing here?" Nash demands, gesturing toward the empty sky. "Go after her!"

"Go after her? Where? How?" The absurdity of it hits me. "She's on a plane to Anchorage, then probably hopping a private jet back to LA to star in some movie with a sought-after director! I'm stuck here with a failing lodge and cracked ribs!"

"So fix it!" Nash slams his mug down on the railing. "Sell the damn lodge if you have to! Ask Dad for help! Ask me for help! Figure it out, Finn! Is this place," he gestures back toward the mountains, "more important than her?"

Is it? The question hangs there, stark and unavoidable. The lodge is my mother's memory, my pride, my anchor. But Mags ... Mags felt like coming home in a way I hadn't known was possible.

"No," I say, the answer solidifying with sudden clarity. "No, it's not."

A slow smile spreads across Nash's face. "Well, alright then."

"But she's gone," I repeat, the despair returning. "How do I find her? What do I say?"

"You start by figuring out how to get to LA," Nash says practically. "Then you show up on her doorstep. And you grovel. Like I told you. Flowers might help. Or maybe one of those fancy coffees she likes. Whatever it takes."

LA. Hollywood. A world away from everything I know. *Could I do that? Leave Crystal Creek, even for a time?* The thought is terrifying. But the thought of never seeing Mags again ... that's worse. Unbearable.

Okay. I can do this. I'll call Hank, ask if he can fly me to Anchorage later today. I'll figure out a flight to LA. I'll find her agent's number somehow. I'll show up. I'll apologize. I'll tell her I love her—all of her, Lena and Mags. That I was an idiot, scared and proud, but I know now what matters. I'll sell the lodge, move to LA, whatever it takes, if she'll give us a chance. It's a crazy, half-formed plan. But it's a plan. It's fighting.

As the resolve solidifies, a familiar sound breaks the morning quiet. A low drone, growing louder. Both Nash and I look up, squinting against the sun. It's a float plane. Banking low over the harbor. Heading toward the dock. Hank's plane.

My heart stops, then slams against my ribs with painful force. Is it ... could it be?

"No way," Nash breathes beside me, his eyes wide.

The plane touches down on the water, taxiing toward us, engine sputtering as Hank cuts the power near the dock. The side door pushes open. And Lena climbs out.

She looks unsteady for a moment, gripping the strut for balance, her eyes scanning the dock. Then she sees me. Her expression is impossible to read—relief, uncertainty, maybe lingering hurt. She takes a hesitant step onto the dock, then another, walking toward me. I can't move. Can't breathe. *Is this real? Did she come back?*

She stops a few feet away, the same distance as yesterday on the deck, but the space feels different now, charged with possibility instead of finality.

"Did you forget something?" I manage, my voice hoarse.

A shaky smile touches her lips. It melts away the last of Lena Kensington, revealing the Mags I fell for.

"Yes," she says softly, her eyes locking with mine, clear and blue and holding everything I thought I'd lost. "Everything important."

And then she's closing the distance, rushing toward me, her arms wrapping around my neck, her face burying against my chest. I react instinctively, pulling her tight against me, my arms locking around her waist, ignoring the protest of my ribs, breathing in the scent of her hair, the faint trace of expensive soap mixed with something wild—something purely Mags. In this moment, holding her, nothing else matters—not the pain, not the lodge, nothing but her."

"I'm sorry," she whispers against my shirt. "I almost ran. I almost let fear win."

"No, I'm sorry," I say, my voice thick, pulling back enough to look down at her face. "Mags, I was an idiot. Scared. Proud. I pushed you away when all I wanted was to pull you closer. I heard you on the phone, and I assumed the worst. I didn't trust you. Didn't trust ... this." I gesture between us.

"I said yes to the job," she admits, tears welling in her eyes. "Because you hurt me. Because I thought ... I thought you were right, that our worlds were too different. That I didn't belong here."

"You belong wherever you want to belong," I tell her fiercely, cupping her face with my good hand. "And I want you to belong here. With me. If you'll have me."

"But the lodge ... the money..."

"Forget the lodge," I say, meaning it with everything I've got. The truth hits me, sudden and clear. "It's wood and stone. It's not worth losing you. I'll sell it. I'll follow you to Hollywood. I'll learn to drink those kale smoothies. Whatever it takes, Mags. Because losing you ... that's the only failure I can't face."

Tears spill over, tracking paths down her cheeks, but she's smiling now, a watery, brilliant expression that lights up her entire face. "You'd do that?"

"In a heartbeat."

"You don't have to sell the lodge, Finn." She reaches up, her hand covering mine on her cheek. "May explained things. About partnership. About pride. About Hollywood solutions versus Alaskan problems." Her thumb brushes my cheekbone. "I don't want you to give up your home for me. I want to be part of your home. If ... if you'll still have me."

"Still have you?" I laugh, the sound rough with emotion. "Mags, I love you. All of you. Lena, Mags, the woman who knows plants and faces down bears and somehow worries about moisturizer. I love every complicated, surprising, terrifying part of you."

"Oh, Finn," she breathes, her eyes shining. "I love you too."

And then I'm kissing her, right there on the dock in the bright morning sun, pouring every ounce of regret and hope and love into it. She meets me with equal fervor, her arms tightening around my neck, her body pressing against mine. It's not like the desperate, exploratory kisses in the cave. This is a kiss of arrival, of recognition, of choosing each other despite the odds, despite the different worlds. It seals a promise, feels like a new beginning.

We break apart, breathless, foreheads resting together. The world comes back into focus—the lapping water, the cry of a gull, the faint sound of Nash clearing his throat from somewhere behind us. Hank leans out his window, gives a thumbs-up, then starts unloading Lena's mountain of luggage onto the dock before preparing for takeoff again.

Nash walks over, grinning. "Guess Hank figured he wasn't needed for the return flight after all." He nods toward the pile of expensive-looking suitcases now sitting on the dock. "You planning on setting up shop here permanently, Hollywood?"

I look down at Mags, seeing her, maybe for the first time, without fear clouding my vision. Her expression is wide, full of a future I thought was lost.

"So," I say, my smile spreading across my face, the ache in my ribs momentarily forgotten. "Does this mean you're staying?"

She laughs, the sound of pure joy echoing over the water as Hank's plane engine roars back to life. "Try and make me leave."

I pull her close again, my heart full. "Right, then," I say against her hair, watching Hank's plane taxi away empty. "Let's get your things and go home."

Chapter Twenty-Nine

LENA

THE FIRE SIGHS in the stone hearth—it sighs, like it's bored with sitting there burning—casting long, dancing shadows across the log walls of the great room. Log walls. Sometimes it hits me that I live inside what resembles a Lincoln Log masterpiece. It's the only sound besides the wind moaning around the eaves, doing its best ghost impression from a low-budget horror flick. It speaks of the deep Alaskan fall settling in, stripping the aspens bare and whispering promises of snow. Promises I'm not sure I'm ready for.

Three months. It's been a lifetime—long enough for the LA gossip cycle to spin through three scandals and forget my name, thank God—and also the blink of an eye since Hank's float plane lifted off without me. Left me standing on the Port Promise dock with Finn, hearts wide open, futures uncertain, and me wondering if I'd packed enough warm socks. Spoiler alert, I hadn't.

I trace the rim of my wineglass, admiring how the firelight makes the Cabernet look even more expensive and brooding. Finn sits beside me on the worn leather sofa—a piece of furniture that looks as if it wrestled a bear and lost but is surprisingly comfortable. His shoulder is pressed against mine, a solid, reassuring weight. He's reading—an actual book, pages and everything, not scrolling doom on a tiny screen. It's one of his quirks I find endearing, right up there with his ability to chop wood like a lumberjack superhero and his quiet wariness of anything involving kale. His reading glasses are perched on his nose. They're the ones that still make me do a double-take sometimes because really—him, being all Clark Kent! The tension that seemed permanently etched around his eyes when I first met him has mostly dissolved, replaced by a quiet contentment that suits him.

Life had found its rhythm here, a beat marked by deer sightings and debates over the best way to stack firewood. The frantic energy, questionable catering, and existential dread of the film crew are a distant, bizarre memory. Elliott, bless his narrative-obsessed heart, spun the whole ordeal into a "Hollywood star finds her roots" masterpiece, milking my dubious "wilderness competence"—which meant Finn told me what to do and I didn't die—for all it was worth before vanishing back to LA.

The show aired two months ago, and Elliott's version of events actually worked. Bookings started trickling in—people wanting the "true wilderness experience" they'd seen on television. Finn's payment from the production covered the immediate bank crisis, buying us breathing room. But the lodge needed more than breathing room. It needed a future. Real investment in infrastructure, cabin upgrades, equipment that wouldn't break down every other Tuesday. That's where I came in—Finn finally agreeing to a partnership after I explained that "angel investor" wasn't code for "hostile takeover."

It's still a hustle, but the panic has receded, replaced by the more manageable stress of "Will the generator start?" and "Do we have enough coffee for the winter?"

He closes his book, marking his page with what looks like a folded napkin, and turns to me, his arm sliding around my shoulders. The casual intimacy still sends a little thrill through me. "Lost in thought, Mags?"

"Thinking," I say, leaning into his warmth, which smells of wood smoke and competence. "About how different everything is." And how okay I am with it.

"Different good? Or different 'Dear God, what have I done, I miss room service?'" His expression is steady, searching. Even after three months, he sometimes looks at me as if I might spontaneously combust into a cloud of Chanel No. 5 and demand a non-fat latte.

"Different good," I assure him, meeting his eyes. "Mostly." I give him a small smile. "Though I wouldn't kick room service out of bed."

We sit in silence for a moment, the fire crackling—probably judging my life choices. The bear rug beneath our feet, once a terrifying reminder of nature's indifference, now feels ... fluffy. Soft. Surprisingly comforting.

"Do you ever regret it?" Finn asks, his voice low, almost hesitant. The familiar guard is back in his eyes for a moment, that fear of not being enough, and it makes my heart squeeze. He's still worried I'll bolt.

"Regret what? Agreeing to try your questionable 'mystery meat' stew last week? Slightly. Leaving my conditioner behind on the last supply run? Deeply."

He squeezes my shoulder. "Turning down that movie. The A-list director. David called it a career-making opportunity." He looks down at our joined hands resting on my knee. "You gave up a lot to stay here, Mags."

Ah, that regret. The memory of that phone call still makes my stomach clench. David had sounded personally offended. "It was a tremendous opportunity," I acknowledge honestly. "The kind Lena Kensington spent years chasing. Mostly for the awards season wardrobe budget, if I'm being honest." I glance toward the man beside me, sturdy and real in his perpetually worn Henley. "And the director? Let's say his reputation preceded him, and not in a good way."

"But?" he asks.

"But..." I sigh, trying to articulate the tangle of feelings. "It felt like choosing the costume—probably something uncomfortable involving Spanx—over the actual person. Like agreeing to keep playing a role when I'd found out the character underneath was way more interesting, albeit less likely to get good table service." I look around the fire-lit room, at the worn wood, the slightly askew painting of a moose, the man beside me who still occasionally forgets where he put his keys. "Staying here ... felt like choosing something real. Messy and complicated and sometimes involving actual bears, but real." I poke his arm. "You're part of the 'real,' by the way."

"So no more Hollywood?" Finn asks gently.

"Not right now. Maybe not ever. I'm taking a break from being Lena Kensington—could be temporary, could be the end of that chapter entirely. I'll know when I know."

Finn lifts my hand, pressing a kiss to my knuckles that's far too charming for a man who owns this much flannel. His eyes hold mine, unwavering. "I never expected you to stay, you know. After our argument ... after I was such a prize-winning idiot..."

"You were impressively stubborn," I agree, tracing the faint scar above his eyebrow with my fingertip. "Reached new heights of stoic grumpiness. It was almost admirable," I add with amusement. "But I recall being fairly headstrong myself. Something about demanding answers and refusing to be intimidated by bears or bank managers?"

"Maybe," he concedes, a small, reluctant smile touching his lips. That expression still gets me every time. "But Mags, I need you to know, if you had gotten back on that plane ... if you'd decided that movie, that life, was what you needed ... I wouldn't have stood here moping."

My breath catches. *Okay, shift in tone.* "What do you mean?"

He turns toward me, cupping my face with his hands—hands that can fix a generator or be infinitely gentle. His expression is serious. No trace of grumpy now. "I meant what I said on the dock. Losing you isn't an option. I would have figured it out." He takes a breath. "Sold the lodge, rented it out, learned to navigate LA freeways—which frankly sounds more terrifying than any fjord—followed you, become a pool boy if I had to. Whatever it took. I wouldn't have let pride, or fear, or this pile of admittedly beautiful logs keep us apart. Not again."

Okay. Wow. His words—the raw conviction simmering beneath them—knock the air right out of me. That's ... more than any grand gesture I've witnessed in my last five rom-coms combined. This vulnerability, this willingness to uproot his whole life for us ... it crashes through all my usual defenses and lands straight in my chest. Tears prick at the corners of my eyes. *Damn it.*

"Oh, Finn," I whisper, covering his hand on my cheek, feeling the rough, steady warmth of his skin.

He leans in, his forehead resting against mine. Close enough to see the creases at the corners of his eyes.

"I know," I say, my voice thick with unexpected emotion. And I do. It's in the way he looks at me when he thinks I'm not paying attention, the way he automatically makes me coffee first thing, the way he grudgingly agreed to let me attempt decorating the guest cabins. Phase One—Operation Banish Beige is pending.

He pulls back, his eyes searching mine, the intensity softening. "So, no regrets? Not even about the distinct lack of decent Thai food within a 500-mile radius?"

I laugh, wiping away a stray tear. "None," I confirm, my voice soft but firm. "Not a single one. Though I reserve the right to complain about the Thai food situation. Loudly."

The air between us crackles again, but this time, it's pure electricity. The confession, the shared vulnerability, has cranked up the heat more effectively than tossing another log on the fire. He leans closer, his lips finding mine in a kiss that speaks volumes—shared history, inside jokes, quiet battles won, and the thrilling uncertainty of what comes next. It's slow, deep, familiar, yet still sends a jolt right to my toes. His hand slides to my waist, pulling me closer on the sofa that has known better days. My fingers tangle in his hair—still soft for a rugged mountain man. The kiss deepens, urgency simmering, fueled by the confession, the isolation, the simple, overwhelming miracle of this. He groans against my mouth, a low rumble that vibrates straight through me.

He breaks the kiss, his breathing ragged, eyes dark with a desire that mirrors my own. "This sofa"—he glances down at the long-suffering leather—"is not ideal for ... vigorous activities."

I raise an eyebrow. "Are you blaming the furniture for what's about to happen? Bold move, Finn. Or are you suggesting a change of venue?" My breath hitches as his hand slides beneath my sweater, his calloused palm warm against the bare skin of my back. Goosebumps erupt.

"Thinking the floor might be more ... accommodating." His eyes drop to the thick bear rug spread before the hearth. The one I swore I'd never get near.

A thrill shoots through me, sharp and immediate. Finally, putting those tracking skills to good use. "Leading the way, wilderness man?"

His answering smile is pure, unrestrained Finn—all rugged charm and wicked intent. He stands, pulling me up with him, then draws me down onto the soft fur of the rug.

Apparently, Mr. Bear had excellent taste in conditioner. The firelight is warm on our skin as clothes seem like a terrible, unnecessary invention. Shedding them becomes a shared project, efficient and perhaps a little frantic, punctuated by kisses and muttered appreciations. Skin against skin, firelight flickering, shadows dancing like exhibitionists on the walls. The only sounds are the crackling flames putting on their show, the jealous-sounding sigh of the wind outside, and our ragged breaths.

His hands rediscover familiar territory, yet somehow it feels brand new, igniting sparks with every touch. My hands map the solid geography of him, emboldened by the raw desire hardening his eyes. This isn't the desperate, terrified coupling in the cave. This is slow-burn turned wildfire, deliberate and deep, grounded in three months of shared mornings, arguments over who finished the coffee, and the quiet miracle of building a life together. It's knowing and being known, flaws and flannel included. It's choosing this, choosing each other, with emphasis.

He enters me with a sigh that tangles with my own, a perfect, breathtaking fit. A coming home. The rhythm builds, slow and deep, then faster, more urgent, a frantic dance mirroring the pulse hammering beneath our skin. Firelight paints us gold, shadows merging and writhing. We move together, lost, found, until the world narrows to pure sensation, pure connection, cresting together in a shattering release that leaves us sprawled, breathless, tangled like poorly stored Christmas lights on the comfortable bear rug.

Later, wrapped together under the soft cashmere throw I definitely didn't order online during a moment of weakness, his arm is a warm, grounding weight around me. My head rests on his chest, where the steady drumbeat of his heart anchors me more than anything ever has. Peace settles over me —quiet, deep, and complete. LA might as well be a different galaxy. A noisy, glittering planet I visited once. This—the man currently breathing contentedly into my hair, the wild beauty outside these windows, the unexpected woman I'm becoming —this is what's real. What fits. Even the rug burn, I think drowsily, is probably worth it.

"Mags?" Finn says, his voice sleepy, muffled by my hair.

"Hmm?"

"You're smiling. What's so funny?"

"Am I?" I snuggle closer, pressing a kiss to his warm chest. "Must be the excellent company." I pause. "And the fact that I think the bear rug winked at me."

He chuckles, a sleepy rumble, tightening his hold. "Yeah," he sighs with contentment. "Must be."

The fire burns low, casting a final, soft glow. Outside, the vast Alaskan night holds its breath. And here, tangled up with my grumpy mountain man on a possibly enchanted bear rug, I know without any doubt I've found where I belong.

Epilogue

FINN

JANUARY'S GOT Crystal Creek locked down tight under snow. Inside the lodge, the fire's cranking, fighting off the cold that wants to creep through every crack. Mags sits by the hearth sketching something, drinking coffee from that fancy espresso machine I got her for Christmas. Six months since she turned that plane around, and she's still here. It still feels like I got lucky.

The partnership's working—both the business side and the personal side. We've found our rhythm. It's good.

Reid's snow machine whines up the track from Port Promise, cutting through the quiet afternoon. I glance out the window, watching his headlight bounce as he climbs toward the lodge.

"The researcher?" Mags asks without looking up.

"Should be." The university booked winter transport and support months ago. Specifically wanted access to Black Creek basin in January. Not many outfits will take that on, but Nash has the equipment and the money was decent.

Reid pulls up near the porch and kills the engine. A bundled figure climbs off the back, hauling gear that looks expensive and scientific. Reid starts unloading equipment cases while his passenger shoulders a heavy pack.

Reid comes in first, stomping snow off his boots. "Brought your scientist," he announces. "Dr. Thorne. Float plane was only a few minutes late."

Dr. Aris Thorne follows him in, pushing back her parka hood. Younger than I expected, maybe mid-thirties, with sharp green eyes that immediately start cataloging the room. Her face is red from the cold, but she moves like someone who doesn't let weather slow her down.

"Thank you for the ride," she tells Reid, then turns to us. "I'm Dr. Aris Thorne, University of Alaska. I arranged logistics support with Nash Hollister?"

"Welcome to Crystal Creek," I say, standing up. "I'm Finn, Nash's brother. This is Mags. Nash is out checking equipment, but he'll be back soon. Coffee while you wait?"

She heads straight for the fire, holding her gloved hands to the flames. "Yes, coffee. Black."

Mags sets down her pencil. "Cold flight up from Anchorage. You're here about caribou?"

"Winter migration patterns," Dr. Thorne says, taking the mug I hand her. "Six-week study in Black Creek basin. The university arranged comprehensive support."

"That's remote country in winter," I tell her. "Nash is your best bet for getting equipment in there safely. He's got the vehicles and knows the terrain."

Dr. Thorne's eyes move around the room—the mounted moose head, hunting photos on the walls, the general look of a place built by hunters. Something changes in her expression.

"The university called this a 'wilderness logistics company,'" she says carefully. "What exactly do you do?"

I glance at Mags. There's something in the doctor's tone I don't like.

"Transport, equipment hauling, route planning," I

explain. "Nash gets people and gear to places they couldn't reach otherwise, especially in winter."

"And?"

She's looking at one of Nash's hunting photos now—him and a client with a big bull moose. Her mouth gets tight.

"I see," she says quietly.

The room feels colder despite the fire. Mags clears her throat.

"We could show you to your cabin while you wait," Mags offers. "Get you settled and warmed up properly."

Dr. Thorne barely glances toward the cabin. "I'd rather discuss protocols with Mr. Hollister first."

The sound of Nash's ATV grows louder, then cuts off as he parks. A few minutes later he comes through the door, stomping snow and pulling off gloves.

"Equipment's all set, weather's holding," he tells me, then notices our guest. His easy smile appears. "Dr. Thorne, I'm guessing?"

She turns to face him. "Mr. Hollister."

"Nash," he says, offering his hand. "Hope the flight wasn't too rough."

"It was fine, thank you." She shakes his hand briefly.

Nash heads for the coffee pot, clearly in a good mood. "Great. Been looking forward to this. Don't often get to support real research in the basin. Most of our winter clients are trophy hunters."

The words hang in the air like a lit fuse.

Dr. Thorne goes still. "Trophy hunters?"

Nash pours coffee, missing the warning signs. "That's right. We run one of the best hunting guide services in the region. Moose, caribou, bear. We have high success rates and access to remote territory." He turns back with professional pride. "We also do photography trips, research support, whatever people need to access the backcountry."

"I see." Her voice has gone flat. "The university booked me with a hunting operation."

Now Nash picks up on the tension. His confidence wavers as he looks between Dr. Thorne's rigid posture and my neutral expression.

"Problem?" he asks.

Dr. Thorne sets her coffee down like she's handling explosives. "Mr. Hollister, I study wildlife conservation and human impact on caribou migration. The university told me you provided 'wilderness logistics.' They didn't mention your main business is killing the animals I'm trying to protect."

Nash's jaw tightens. His easy manner disappears. "My business is legal and ethical, Doctor. We follow all regulations and fund conservation through license fees. We also provide the only winter access to places like Black Creek basin."

"Access for what? Researchers or hunters looking for trophies?"

"Both," Nash says coolly, leaning against the mantel. "Like it or not, hunting is part of wildlife management in Alaska. And my operation pays for the vehicles and equipment you need to get your research done."

Mags squeezes my hand. She's enjoying this more than she should. I have to admit, watching Nash and this scientist square off is entertaining.

Dr. Thorne looks trapped but angry. Winter doesn't offer many options for remote research access, and she knows it.

"My research requires minimal ecosystem disturbance," she says stiffly. "Your hunting activities won't interfere?"

"My activities follow legal seasons and permitted areas," Nash replies. "They also pay for the vehicle sitting outside, ready to haul your equipment through ten miles of snow in subzero weather. Want to discuss payload capacity?"

Long pause. Dr. Thorne stares at Nash, clearly fighting with herself. Nash stares back, his reputation on the line.

Finally, she nods curtly. "Fine. Let's plan this expedition, Mr. Hollister. Daylight's limited."

"Excellent," Nash says, though his smile has an edge. "Let's talk logistics."

They head back outside into the cold, already sounding more like they're negotiating a ceasefire than planning a research trip.

Mags picks up her pencil. "She seems friendly."

I pull her closer, kissing her temple. "Friendly as a cornered wolverine with opinions about everything."

Mags laughs. "Think Nash met his match?"

"Maybe." I watch them through the window, examining Nash's equipment while clearly still arguing. "Nash told me something else. She's not after just any caribou. She's specifically tracking one bull the university calls 'Waldo.'"

Mags looks up. "Waldo?"

"Apparently, he's famous for giving researchers the slip. Been doing it for years, always in the worst possible terrain. Reid says Dr. Thorne's been trying to collar him for three years."

Mags raises her eyebrows. "Three years?"

"Smart caribou. Makes a game of leading scientists on wild chases through impossible country, then vanishing when they think they've got him cornered."

A smile spreads across Mags's face. "So she's not only doing research. This is personal."

"Exactly. Nash thinks he's signed up for standard wildlife support." I shake my head, watching my brother and the determined scientist load equipment while still clearly negotiating terms. "Poor bastard's about to get caught between a woman on a mission and one very clever caribou."

Outside, wind picks up, swirling snow around the two figures bent over maps and gear lists. Whatever happens with this expedition, it won't be boring.

"Poor Nash," Mags says, though she sounds more amused than sympathetic.

"Poor Nash," I agree. "And poor Waldo. He's got no idea what's coming for him."

———

Need more Port Promise?
Nash and Aris are next in *Misty Meadows*.

Other Books by Kelly Collins

A Port Promise Series

Timber Ridge

Crystal Creek

Misty Meadows

An Aspen Cove Romance Series

One Hundred Reasons

One Hundred Heartbeats

One Hundred Wishes

One Hundred Promises

One Hundred Excuses

About the Author

International bestselling author of over 50 novels, Kelly Collins crafts stories that keep love alive. With a heart full of romance and a vivid imagination, she blends real-life events into captivating tales that contemporary romance, new adult, and romantic suspense fans will fall for over and over again.

For More Information
www.authorkellycollins.com
kelly@authorkellycollins.com

Printed in Dunstable, United Kingdom